GW00643717

IRISH GHOST STORIES

IRISH GHOST STORIES

Edited by
David Marcus

BLOOMSBURY

First published 1999

Introduction copyright © 1999 by David Marcus

This compilation © 1999 by Bloomsbury Publishing Plc

The copyright of the individual contributors remains with the respective authors

The moral right of the authors has been asserted

Bloomsbury Publishing Plc, 38 Soho Square,
London W1V 5DF

A CIP catalogue record for this book is available from the British Library

ISBN 07475 4468 9

10 9 8 7 6 5 4 3 2 1

Typeset by Hewer Text Ltd, Edinburgh
Printed by Clays Ltd, St Ives plc

Contents

CONTENTS

Introduction

S omeone once said, or wrote, that only the rich can afford ghosts and only the mad believe in them. A manifestly refutable assertion on both counts. How do I know? Because although I've never actually seen a ghost, I've had one. In fact I still have him – and I'm neither rich nor mad.

It's no big deal really; there's not even a tale hanging on it. Not a tale, just another assertion – this one by James Stephens, the man who wrote 'The Crock of Gold', a very wise man who knew. He said, 'Women mature at sixteen, men at sixty. When you turn sixty yourself, you'll see I'm right,' and his big, sad eyes slowly closed like window blinds descending at dusk. We were sitting in a Lyons corner-house in London, long before I was within spitting distance of turning sixty.

I'd have to spit backwards now to turn sixty, and he *was* right. For when I reached that watershed age, I began to ask myself if I was mature. Crazily, hilariously, the question put me in mind of cheese. But then, anything but hilariously, what I thought of was that if a cheese isn't consumed when it's mature, the next stage is that it goes off. That brought me to my senses, matured me, filled my inner ear with the train of thought hurtling towards the tunnel, screaming, 'You can't take it with you.' Well, I didn't particularly want to take anything with me. What began to concern me was what I would leave, the me I would leave behind. And that's the ghost I've had since.

Not a very traditional ghost, is it, and the ghosts in this anthology are also all very different from their head-tucked-underneath-his-arm ancestors. A thief, a thigh bone, seafarers, items of apparel, hurlers, soldiers, a composer, and other strange emanations, including a trio who might almost be modern Irish spirit-cousins of Pirandello's six characters in search of an author translated from stage to page. None of the people they haunt could be said to be rich, and certainly none of the distinguished Irish writers who introduced them to me were, or are, mad. Come in and meet them. They're well worth knowing. I think you'll like them.

DAVID MARCUS

BRYAN MacMAHON

The Revenants

I t could be argued that in an age of silicone chips, micro-
wave ovens and genetic engineering witches do not exist.
However, they do. Without a witch or two it would be a lack-
lustre world. If a society for the preservation of witches is to be
established, it will not be before its time.

For all the world it happened to be the Feast of the Dear
Departed. Just before midnight Old Maag was trudging her way
home from a cottage on the edge of the town where there had
been a turkey gamble – a rural diversion in which the winner of
a series of card games of Forty-five receives a scrawny turkey as
first prize. Old Maag was in foul humour for she had won only a
single game in a long evening of gambling.

Those playing with Maag never made bold on the old
beldame, for she had the reputation of enquiring by improper
means after things lost, hidden or to come. Rumour also
credited her with having spilled the hot blood of a cockerel on

1

the ace of hearts and of having held up the card at the Consecration of the Mass so as to procure luck of the wrong kind.

Maag never praised the living: she invariably praised the dead. At times she scolded or upbraided the dear departed or spoke to them with amiable irritation, just as she would address a kettle reluctant to boil or a door that would insist on blowing open without apparent cause.

Conflicting thoughts contending in her brainpan, Old Maag staggered alone in the darkness. There was a fitful wind but an erratic moon. Of a sudden she stopped at the graveyard gate on the edge of the town. She glanced sidelong at the ranked crosses faintly showing in the meagre light. Black Harry, her Lord and Master, pricked her. She stood irresolute for a while, then pushing her head between the bars of the gate she began to intone:

> Gentle ghosts gone like foam
> Some of you sadly, wanting at home.

As the words left her lips, a coconut rosary beads hanging from a spike of the gate began to melt into dripping chocolate.

There was an echo of hypocrisy to the complaint. The cry of a widow at the edge of her husband's grave as her eyes secretly sieved the mourners in search of a new man. A husband bemoaning a dead wife while inwardly cheering for conjugal liberty. There was a further echo in the hag's chanting – one tinged with malice and a desire to upset the normal condition of affairs.

The Good Provider also heard the incantation as He hears the chirp of every sparrow in the ivied eaves of creation, the rusty whinge of every peacock in the gardens of the Eastern World, the minor modal song of each black-backed whale under each island cliff in the Northern Hemisphere and that unbelievable medley of minor sounds with which the air is replete, though largely unheard by pure humans.

The Provider left off His whimsical painting of new varieties of butterflies and parrots. As He listened to the reiterated call of the Old Lady, a smile framed his pearly teeth in the recesses of his curling beard. To Himself He said softly, 'I'm a little tired of cant. I'm tempted to teach someone or other a lesson.'

'Just the very night to do so,' He added.

Maag tried to withdraw her head from between the bars of the gate. Her head was a prisoner. So was the rest of her old body. At first she refused to panic. She told herself that she was among her own. Above her was a heaven of scudding moon-light.

As midnight chimed rustily from the steeple of an old church in the town, the clay on the surface of a grave a short distance from the gate began to heave, crack and part. It did so utterly without sound. Faintly at first, but gradually growing clearer by the second, there hung and whirled a little mist of ectoplasm, that viscous substance, if substance it can be named, which exudes, seeps, or emanates from the body of a spiritualist medium during trance and which now through the whim of the Provider was percolating through the cracks of the grave. Gradually, as Maag watched it with intensity, the spinning shape became edged with prismatic hues, the whole writhing and wriggling as if balanced on a tail not unlike that of a huge tadpole or the play-top of a giant child.

This primal shape became still larger: it then almost

imperceptibly divided into three parts which wove back and forth, in and out, up and down, until, not unlike a pupa or chrysalis, they changed into rather human shapes. These shapes assumed the forms of an elderly man with an aureole of silver hair, a buxom woman in her late prime and a girl who had obviously just emerged from puberty into young womanhood.

Maag watched this, the whites of her ancient eyes showing at intervals faint blue in the fitful light of the sky.

There was nothing even vaguely eerie about the three personages now standing on the pathway. They could have been late family mourners come to pay respects to a common grave. Their clothing, if clothing it could be called, seemed to be a kind of institutional grey. The elderly man was seen to be carrying a black walking cane on which silver mountings glinted at intervals.

The trio drifted towards the gateway where the eyes of the imprisoned Maag recognised Old Malcolm Dunn whose nickname was Sagacity, his daughter Lizzie Grigg, née Dunn and his grand-niece, Mary Josephine Lavelle. The girl, a first year University student of biology, had drowned in the quarry pool having fallen in while picking whitethorn blossoms in early May, an undertaking which everybody in the country-side knew was most unlucky.

At the squeeze-belly stile, although the gesture was completely superfluous, the elderly sage stood aside to allow the two females to precede him. Lizzie Grigg, who went first, paused to offer Old Maag a hostile stare as if to indicate the measure of her resentment at the disturbance of their eternal rest. The old witch closed her eyes and turned her head away.

The revenants then drifted off towards the town leaving

behind them the serried crosses and headstones, the squat spotted tombs, the sprinkling of marble angels with bird droppings on their heads; presently they reached the poor radiance of the first of the street lamps and later still moved along the pavement of the main street of the country town.

There was no one abroad: from the recessed doorway of the town bank a cigarette tip glowed and faded; at the same time a button or two on the young Garda's tunic took and lost the gleam. The Garda poked out his head, swivelled it to glance up and down the street – it was obvious that he was less concerned about seeing than being seen. To the Garda the fluent passage of the triform on the opposite pavement could have been a drift of fog or turf smoke. The younger woman kept looking about her. Dreamily, as if sleepwalking, she tagged a little behind her companions.

A brindled cat scurried out of an archway; stopping short before the shapes it made a horseshoe of its back and spat-hissed upwards in their direction. An old stray sheepdog sleeping on a bakery grating on the pavement roused himself with a deep growl and made a semi-circle on the roadway to allow them passage. An inevitable owl from the ivied castle tower rustled its wings above them as it crossed in the upper air of the street.

The revenants turned off the Main Street and entered a narrow row of tall houses of faded red brickwork, their fronts flush with the line of the street. Outside one of these houses Sagacity, who was leading the way, stopped and turned to his companions.

'Things have changed,' he said in a deep minatory voice. His daughter Lizzie Grigg nodded grimly. Mary Josephine looked up at the house with an anticipatory smile.

'Discretion is called for,' Old Malcolm said severely. 'Also tact and control. Daughter,' he added, addressing Lizzie. 'Bear in mind that you are merely wife of the First Part.'

Lizzie pursed her already tightened mouth. As her father raised his hand to lift the heavy knocker, he paused to look up at a first-storey window over which dark blinds were drawn. Turning again; 'A wife of the Second Part now shares what was once your conjugal couch,' he said. With a glance at Mary Josephine he added, 'There is also the new wife's nephew named Andrew Soople. A young man of twenty-three. An electrician.'

Mary Josephine's lips came easily apart. 'I danced with Andrew once,' she breathed.

Sagacity knocked on the door.

All three waited. There was no response.

'Louder!' said Lizzie Grigg.

'Please,' from the grand-niece.

Old Malcolm knocked a little more loudly than before.

In the first-storey bedroom above their heads, Judy Grigg née Soople, second wife of Billy Grigg, her pneumatic form squashed against her husband's back, raised her head from the pillow. As the knocking again re-echoed through the house her fingernails clutched her husband's breast.

'That our door?' she gasped.

'Dineen's,' Billy growled through half sleep.

The knocking came again. It sounded like thunder. 'Someone is dead,' Judy gasped. 'Go down Billy Grigg and see who it is.'

Billy cursed under his breath. He swung slowly out on to the floor. Too sleepy to recall that the window was paint-bound he tried in vain for a moment to raise the sash.

6

Dragging on a long brown cardigan and cursing still more vehemently he shuffled downstairs in old carpet slippers. Reaching the front door he bent his head.

'Who's out?' he muttered.

'Open, you fool!' Lizzie shouted from outside.

Billy's first reaction was to growl, 'Where's your bloody key, woman?'

On the sudden realisation of the true state of affairs he drew back from the door and made the sign of the cross on himself. Cautiously indeed, the while reassuring himself that he was still half asleep, he drew the bolt, twisted the knob of the lock and opening the door on its safety chain, peeped out. 'Whassit?' he asked.

Like three cold draughts of air the shapes brushed past him in the little space allowed. Then as they stood in the hallway, Billy Grigg managed to gasp as if in confirmation of his wildest conjecture. 'Holy Christ, it's Lizzie, Ould Sagacity and Mary Josephine herself out of the Quarry Hole.' Again he blessed himself feverishly.

Lizzie drifted into the kitchen followed by her father and the young woman. As wife of the First Part she groped on the dark wall just inside the kitchen door. 'Where's the light switch?' she asked peremptorily. 'It's to the right of the door now,' her former husband answered, a bullfrog of bewilderment in his throat.

Lizzie switched on the dim light. Looked around her imperiously and proprietorially. Peered at the Consecration Certificate above its now quenched votive lamp. A new certificate indicated that the house had been re-dedicated to the Sacred Heart in the framed oleograph above. No mention now of herself or her two fine sons in Wyndmoor, Philadelphia. Lizzie, folding her arms across her breasts as if in preparation for a battle, took a seat adjacent to the fireplace. Mary Josephine was already seated.

Billy stood framed in the doorway. His face was chalk white; after an appropriate silence, 'What brought ye?' he asked hoarsely.

'Wanting at home,' sniffed Sagacity.

'Remains to be seen,' Lizzie commented.

The girl made a pleasant humming, purring sound in her nose.

'We buried you decent,' Billy was addressing his first wife.

'You could hardly leave me overground,' the woman countered.

'What way are you, Malcolm?' Billy asked his ex-father-in-law.

'Perpendicular,' the old man said.

Mary Josephine continued to smile vaguely. Her head was held a little to one side. She appeared to be listening to sounds coming from upstairs.

'Herself will get a shock,' Billy ventured.

'That she might for fear she mightn't!' Lizzie sneered.

'Is there someone upstairs besides Judy?' from Mary Josephine.

'Andy Soople, Billy's nephew. An electrician.'

'A cuckoo,' Lizzie sniffed.

'I danced with him in Ballybay,' the young woman said.

'Judy gave up her widow's pension when she married me,' Billy said.

'Or was it her Old Age Pension?' from Lizzie.

'What age is Andy now?' Mary Josephine asked meekly.

'Twenty-three,' from Billy.

'Married?'

'No!'

'I was twenty when I tumbled in,' the girl said, not without pride. 'I'm still that age.'

Billy became alert to footsteps on the stairs. He hurried out into the hallway. Feverish whispering was heard outside. Cuff-huffling and a sense of consternation. Voices. 'Dead?' 'Alive.' 'Come in and see.' Peering and peeping. Advancing and retreating. Urgency and mystification. Then, 'Are you out of your mind?' and 'For God's sake call Andy.' The faces that peered were coloured red from the red bulb above them in the hallway. And from natural or supernatural agitation. After considerable tugging, Billy led in his wife Judy. She resembled nothing more than a nanny-goat on a halter. She groped just inside the kitchen door, gripped a chair and sat on its edge. She wore an out-at-elbows cerise dressing-gown. She spread her fingers across her mouth and gawked. She made no attempt to greet the visitants. 'You, Divine Lord,' she kept repeating as she blubbered. The dribbled spittle leaked through her fingers and ran down the back of her hand. 'Mine,' Lizzie said, addressing her father and indicating the cerise dressing-gown. She looked up at the mantelpiece. 'Where's my blue vase?' she demanded.

'The cat,' Billy gulped.

'A cat with butter-fingers maybe,' Lizzie said. She looked up at the walls of the kitchen. 'Such a daub,' she added with a grimace. Her stare settled on a paler rectangle on the wall. 'Your stickyback is gone, Dad,' she said.

'In the attic,' Billy put in.

The First Wife glowered at the range.

'My Rayburn is gone too,' she commented.

'This one heats four radiators,' Billy said.

9

Judy had come to some kind of terms with herself. With a superhuman effort she asked with all the sweetness she could muster, 'Will I wet a pot of tea?'

'Are you able?' Lizzie said.

'That's enough,' her father chimed in.

'She can't keep it bottled up,' Mary Josephine ventured.

'Strong or weak?' asked the wife of the Second Part.

'Strong,' said Sagacity crisply.

Billy grabbed the chance to escape. 'I'll plug in the kettle,' he said. In the scullery he filled the kettle and looked at himself in a mirror hanging over the sink.

'What dimension am I in now?' he asked his reflection. 'What did I have for supper? With God's help, it's only a nightmare. If it's for real, I'll roll with the punch. I'm not to blame. All I did was marry a widow when my prime wife had gone over. Now she's back, the prime wife that is. I mean to say, I mean to say, I mean to say this doesn't make me an extra-marital canoodler does it? I mean to say, am I bigamist or eejit? Eh? It's twenty past one o'clock in the morning in a small sane Irish town and here are three come-backers looking for tay. One of them died of a superfluity of wisdom, another died of enmity and another died of romancity – the last a girl who tumbled down through the blackthorns and choked on green scum and frogspawn. I mean to say, a man's brain should not be subjected to such enormities. My moral stance was sound,' he assured his reflection.

The kettle had begun to sing. Billy clattered ware onto a large tray. 'Imagine,' he continued in a mumble, 'after where she has been and seen, what bothers her now is the colour of the kitchen wall. Is it Nile Green or Woodland Verdure? Eh? They're bloody well not going to sleep here tonight. I mean to say, if this got out, look how it would affect my standing in this town. If Judy doesn't scoot 'em, I'll find some way of doing so. If only people kept hens in their back gardens nowadays like they did long ago, the cockcrow might call 'em home. By golly, but that gives me a bloody good idea. Hurry up kettle and boil!'

Click went the control of the electric kettle. Billy continued to sing in a low voice at the point where the kettle left off.

Still muttering to himself Billy, bearing the tray laden with tea things, returned to the kitchen. 'I should have put a stronger bulb in the kitchen – the light might put the skids under 'em. "Wanting at home" my royal Irish arse. Have I everything, tea, milk, sugar, biscuits? Myself is the crackers. Maag had a hand in this I'd swear. That's what I get for refusing to buy her pishoguey home butter. Get up Tom Coffey and drink your tay.'

The three revenants looked down morosely at the tea tray. Billy began to fill the cups. 'Shamrock tay,' Lizzie said. 'Three leaves only.' As Judy made to bridle up, Andy Soople appeared in the doorway! All fell silent. He wore a vivid silk dressing-gown.

Mary Josephine put up a ghostly hand and patted her ghostly hair. Lizzie looked from the girl to Andy. Billy flashed a look at Judy. Sagacity closed what was formerly the aperture of his mouth.

All the others saw that Mary Josephine had eyes only for Andy. Andy had electric eyes only for Mary Josephine. Billy made some unheard mumbles of introduction. No one offered to shake hands.

The group was frozen to tableau for an appreciable period of silence.

'Can you bake meal bread?' Lizzie stabbed at Judy.

11

'With caraway seeds, yes.'

'Not if you soak them first.'

'My scones were famous.'

'Someone told me they were like birdlime.'

'Once you have a good oven you can bake anything.'

'Can't beat oven and radiators together.'

Sagacity made a sound like the warning cough of a mortal. Billy gestured to the untouched fare on the tray. 'I daresay you'll have to go back before long,' he said.

'We were thinking,' Sagacity said solemnly, 'of staying around for a few nights.'

'I'd love that,' said Mary Josephine, her eyes on the flowered dressing-gown.

'And where would you stay?' Billy asked.

'After all the ullagoning you had,' said Lizzie with severity – she was addressing Billy, 'the least you might do is put us up for a few nights.'

'Can't stay here,' from Judy. 'All the rooms taken up.'

'Might stay with real old friends, then.'

'As you please.'

Sagacity turned to Billy, 'Do you still keep pigs?' he asked in an effort to raise the conversation to a more placid plane.

'There's a by-law now against keeping pigs. At a pinch we might put up Mary Josephine,' he then added.

'All or nothing,' from Lizzie.

'Three musketeers,' the sage said.

'My coffin wasn't up to the mark,' Lizzie said, glaring at Billy. 'And I always told you I detested a brown habit.'

'We searched the house for your Child o' Mary cloak and veil.' Billy countered. 'Couldn't find it.'

'Pawned perhaps,' from Judy.

'Water under the bridge,' Sagacity said dismissively.

'Would any of you like to go to the toilet,' Judy was addressing the revenants.

'Toilet?' all three said together. Lizzie put their common scorn into words. 'Do we look like people who go to a toilet?'

Since it seemed that no one was interested in having tea, Billy took up the tray. He went out to the scullery and stole open the door leading to the small back garden. Nothing there but shadows, high stars and stillness. A small upper window of the living-room was open so he could hear the conversation in progress inside.

'I got Andy to install a new bathroom suite in pale rose,' Judy was saying.

'Chamberpot to match?' from Lizzie.

'The Master room is en suite,' Judy countered.

'I built up this place,' Lizzie said. Indicating Billy, 'When he comes across he'll be buried beside me.'

'No guarantee,' from Judy.

Out in the meagre garden Billy plucked a blade of grass. He licked the insides of his thumbs and closed them about the grass blade. Placing his lips against the slit he blew a cock-a-doodle-doo. Malcolm alone seemed to heed the bugle call of eternity implicit in the mock cockcrow. The others took little notice. The wives were at it hot and heavy. Mary Josephine's eyes dreamed on. Then lights flickered in the eyes of the young electrician. Billy crowed again. The call now seemed to be making some impression.

Malcolm indicated that it was time to return to their proper home. Mary Josephine drew close to Andy. 'Do you ride a motorcycle?' she breathed. 'A little,' he murmured.

Lizzie played her final card. Outfacing Judy she said,

'You've small claim to a man if you haven't a child by him; without a child all you have are words and paper. My sons in Philadelphia won't see me wronged.'

The cock crew the third time. 'We'll be off now,' Sagacity said. His two fellow revenants indicated assent. The older man cleared his throat with a measure of finality. All prepared to listen. Billy stood in the doorway of the kitchen.

'Our visit here has been a wound of eternal law, a lesion of time and space,' Malcolm began – 'the result of a whim rarely indulged in by the Provider. Why He chose us as exemplars I cannot explain except perhaps that we are ordinary folk and thus are typical. If I hold aloft the flame of a ha'penny dip I cannot illuminate the summit of Mount Fuller. The common head louse, *Pediculus capitis*, cannot be expected to solve a quadratic equation nor a rhinoceros to do crochet. The Provider, the Prime Instigator, obviously has a keen sense of humour, how else could He endow humans with the ability to appreciate and reconcile the more bizarre elements of human life consequent upon which recognition the zygomatic muscle of the upper lip responds in a series of nervous spasms – a minor epileptic fit in fact – a phenomenon which mortals, limited in the matter of precise terminology, call laughter. Superficial observers marvel at man's exploration of space but express little wonder at the fact that the common elver, equipped with only natural radar no bigger than a pinhead, can crawl 5,000 miles of slime on the ocean floor to find its way to a pool in the stream below the town.'

'You never lost it,' Billy said in admiration.

'Hitachi and Mitsubishi make powerful machines,' the girl whispered in the young man's ear. 'There's also the Moto Guzzi.'

The young electrician had closed his eyes, tightened his fists on imaginary handlebar grips, and was shuddering in imaginary speed.

Sagacity glared at the whispering girl and the shuddering electrician. ' "Wanting at home" is a misnomer,' Sagacity went on. 'We are intruders,' he said including the other revenants in the declaration. 'Once the game of a person's life is over a new hand of cards is dealt. In this game we have no further part. If the greatest loss to family or nation or mankind were to return in response to the plaint of a hag or the love ache of an adolescent, the revenant would cause an upset. I go further,' he said with severity. 'We are dirt! Inasmuch as dirt has been defined as displaced matter, a piano in a cornfield is dirt and a cowpat in a drawing-room equally so. A whore in a convent, a virgin in a brothel – dirt! But if piano and cowpat, whore and virgin exchanged places, *pari passu* as it were, the result is harmony. Let us be on our way.'

The trio of revenants drifted towards the door. Mary Josephine moved last; as she passed the young man she whispered in his ear, 'Faster, my love. Myself on the pillion behind you. Like Oisín and Niamh riding to the land of the Ever Young.'

When the revenants reached the churchyard gate they found the old gossip still enstocked between the bars. Her face was white and drawn; her eyes shone like those of a snared hare. Her rump stuck out behind as if somehow she had managed to achieve a position of repose.

Sagacity poked at the old woman's buttocks with his walking cane. Although the ferruled end passed through her flesh without causing pain, the old woman winced, squealed and twisted. As with an odd laugh, Old Malcolm poked again, the crone turned her neck so awkwardly and indeed so fortunately as to release her head from the bars of the gate. The old woman tottered backward, dragged her trailing shawl over her shoulder and staggered away through the mid-road darkness.

Sagacity led the way through the stile. Mary Josephine lingered; 'Safety last,' she whispered with a final look backward at the dim cut-out of the town skyline. Following the others, she extended her arms and then drew them close to her breasts as if hugging them about a young man's waist. She shuddered as if in response to the shuddering of a machine.

Reaching the grave the three forms stopped. A cloud covered the moonface. 'Ready, steady, go,' the Sage intoned. Three swirls of paint colour gathered momentum, grew larger, then tapered to the shape of large spinning tadpoles. Then all three forms merged into a single unit and slowly screwed down into the grave. The final glint, indicating that they had been there at all, could have come from the silver mounting of a walking cane or the ray of the moonlight tweaking a gleam from the broken glass of a wreath on an adjoining grave.

This episode which townspeople are wont to describe rather quaintly as a 'caper' was observed by the Provider who was watching out of one of His myriad eye-corners. There He was peering down over the ambo of the universe and taking it all in.

'I still have the old touch,' He mused. 'This reconciliation of opposites constitutes a form of relaxation I should indulge in more often. I possess splendid resources. What with spheres and stallions, volcanoes and vesicles, redwoods, rooks and ravioll, puffins, plasticine and politicians, asparagus, anatomy and algebra, the litany of material to hand is truly endless. To blazes with stasis – I favour kinesis,' He said with a rare burst of emphasis.

Then, thoughtfully, 'I'll have to keep a closer eye on what's afoot on PE. Fission and fusion in the nuclear sense indicate the pride of my creatures. Knowledge yes, but sagacity to use it also. I mean to say, I mean to say, all this genetic manipulation, clones of a basic nature, in vitro experiments, the uterus as a hostess, embryo banks, untimely rippings, chromosomatic aberrations not to mention human–beast hybrids as prefigured in mythology by the centaur Leda and the Swan – all this might merit a little attention from my Good Self.'

The Provider paused. 'I'll have to keep a more watchful eye on my matchstick subjects,' He said. Then with an omnipotent smile, 'I might even steal their thunder by cross-fertilising there with here as on a Superb Occasion I did in the long ago of what they call time.'

The Supreme Personage mused in silence for a while. Then aloud, with no one to hear Him in the vast echo-chamber of space, 'Young couples keep reminding me of what has proved trustworthy over the centuries. Yes, yes, yes, but nowadays they appear to be sliding off the gold standard of Old Love . . . I must scribble the letters OL on the back of my hand to remind me that that mystical, almost metaphysical attribute is currently under siege and that I must do something, something . . . about it.'

'Drastic? – No! Dramatic? – No! Punitive? – not quite!' Then, 'Corrective.' He added with a smile, – 'that's the word I was looking for.'

CONALL CEARNACH

The Homing Bone

P rofessor David Gillespie was a distinguished anatomist. It is scarcely necessary to add that he was a Scotsman; for has not a wise Providence ordained that the principal products of Caledonia shall be marine engineers, metaphysicians, and anatomists? Equally brilliant on what are technically known as the 'hard' and 'soft' parts of the human frame, he was particularly strong on the subject of the skeleton; and to hear him lecture on the petrous portion of the temporal bone was a revelation to the unsophisticated first-year student of medicine. In the lecture theatre he would stand at the rostrum, of a morning, and taking a bone for his text, he would hold forth for a full hour. Common 'grinders' could point out foramina and muscle-insertions well enough for examination purposes; but their instruction was dry and uninteresting. In Gillespie's hands a bone became a thing of beauty. His lecture was not a lecture; it was not a sermon; it was an oration. He would wax eloquent as he went along, and his enthusiasm was infectious.

Not infrequently, when his peroration closed with some apposite quotation from the poets, a spontaneous burst of applause went up from the crowded benches; and students, as they wended their way to pastures new, would remark to one another: 'Man, but Gillespie's just great!'

Professor Gillespie came of Highland Gaelic stock; a stock which is far from materialistic; and his grandmother was reputed to have possessed the gift of 'second sight'. Many a time young Davy had shuddered as he listened, by the fire of the crofter's cottage, where he first saw the light, to the weird, uncanny tales of the Highlands; but five years' hard work at the Edinburgh School of Medicine had knocked the nonsense out of him in more ways than one. Now, at the age of fifty-four, one of the leading anatomists of Europe, he could afford to bestow an indulgent smile on the narrator of tales pertaining to the supernatural. A man who, for twenty years, has spent most of his waking hours in the atmosphere of the Dissecting-room, is almost as much at home with the dead as with the living. His stock-in-trade, so to speak, being corpses, the creepiest story about 'corpse-candles' naturally leaves him unmoved. Yet the fear of the supernatural is so deeply ingrained in human beings, and the stories, heard in boyhood days, sink so deeply into the subliminal self, that the acquired scepticism of later years is, after all, the merest veneer, which may vanish in a moment if only circumstances arise in which a sufficiently strong appeal is made to those hereditary instincts and pre-historic beliefs that slumber beneath the surface.

So much, by way of preface to the secret history of the curious happenings which led to Gillespie's resignation of his Chair of Anatomy, and his retirement into private life; a step which astonished all who heard of it, for he was regarded as being but at the zenith of his powers. I now tell the tale as it was told to me by Cochrane, who heard it from the lips of Gillespie himself.

When the British Medical Association held its annual conference in Dublin, Gillespie was invited to preside over the Anatomical Section; and his address at the opening meeting of the section was as brilliant as might have been expected from one of his reputation. The conference over, Gillespie devoted his time to sight-seeing. He spent a day visiting the Cathedrals, and, in the afternoon, he prowled about the quays and back streets of the city. Half an hour was given up to viewing the vaults of St Michan's, with its celebrated mummies, and crossing over the Metal Bridge he wended his way through Cook Street, that home of undertakers, where every shop resounds to the stroke of the coffin-maker's hammer.

Having passed through this gruesome quarter, he wandered further afield, until he came upon the old church of St Walburgh's. The ground about the church had long been closed to burials, and he found some workmen engaged in levelling the churchyard. The tombstones had been removed and arranged along the churchyard wall; for, since the inscriptions they bore were no longer legible, they had served their purpose, and were mere cumberers of the ground. During the levelling process some relics of mortality had become uncovered, and in one corner there lay a jumble of odd assortments of skulls and some large bones.

Gillespie's professional eye detected, amid the heap, a splendid specimen in a perfect state of preservation. It was a thigh-bone, or as an anatomist would more accurately describe it, a left femur; that of an adult man, for, by the trained eye, the sterner sex can be distinguished even in the bony structures. The Professor coveted the bone, and foresaw in it the material for an interesting and instructive paper. He had no qualms of conscience about securing it; only, in deference to any susceptibilities on the part of the Irish workmen, he did so quite unostentatiously, and walked away with the coveted femur concealed beneath his overcoat.

Arrived at his lodgings, he stowed it in his bedroom until after dinner; when he proceeded to brush away the adherent earth from the bone with a clothes-brush, and settled down to gloat over his treasure. From the great length of the femur, and the powerfully developed trochanters, he deduced the fact that the man who had owned it must have been an exceptionally tall and muscular individual; and the professor fell to wondering whether the said individual had been an Irishman, or one of the old Norse stock whose descendants among the Dubliners retain somewhat of the Viking characteristics. He sat in his dressing-gown until eleven o'clock, and strove to visualise the appearance which the owner of the bone must have presented in life; then he yawned sleepily, and dropping the femur into his portmanteau, lest he might forget it in his hurry to catch the morning boat, he tumbled into bed and fell fast asleep.

His sleep had not lasted for long when he was visited by a horribly vivid dream. In his dream he seemed to be awakened by a sound of knocking at his bedroom door. Before he had time to say 'Come in!' the door opened, and four skeletons entered, carrying a coffin on their bony shoulders. They deposited their burden on two chairs beside his bed, and stood like waiting mutes. Suddenly the lid of the coffin flew open, and its occupant, a tall skeleton, sat up and pointed first at the professor, and then to its own lower limbs. Following

21

the gesture, Gillespie looked and saw that the left femur was missing. Still sitting up in the coffin, the tall skeleton leaned forward towards the bed and clutched the professor by the throat with a vice-like grip of its bony fingers.

Gillespie gasped for breath, gave a strangled scream, and woke up in a fright. It took some little time for him to realise his surroundings. He sat up in bed to find his heart palpitating violently, his brow wet with perspiration, and about his scalp a curious sensation associated in the lay mind with the phenomenon known as 'the hair standing on end'. It was decidedly a novel experience for the professor, for he boasted that he never dreamed dreams, or that if he did, they were so unimportant that his waking moments contained no recollection of them.

The explanation was perfectly simple, he told himself. During the conference his meals had been more irregular than they would have been at home. Some of the dinners, too, were more elaborate than those to which he was normally accustomed. Why, he wondered, could not a party of grave and learned scientists foregather without over-eating and over-drinking like a lot of schoolboys at a picnic? Then the material of his dream had been supplied by his afternoon saunter through that extraordinary street of coffin-shops, and the bone purloined from the churchyard completed the tale.

Yet, in that dark room, in the small hours of the morning there were stirrings of the hereditary fears – the fear of the dark and the fear of the dead; and he fell to moralising over the fact that Providence had for some reason or other seen fit to endow the human scalp with a set of '*erector pili*' or hair-raising muscles, and the further curious fact that that particular set of muscles could only be called into play by supernatural (or

22

superstitious) terrors. Did not the pious Aeneas' hair stand on end at the apparition of his beloved dead wife, Creusa? But the professor's classics were decidedly rusty, and while attempting in vain to complete the line 'Obstupui, steteruntque comae' – he fell asleep once more.

However, he was not destined to enjoy his resumed slumber for long. The ill dream was repeated with variations. Once more the door opened, the four skeletons entered, bearing a coffin which they placed on chairs by the bedside; but this time the lid did not fly open. Instead, the professor found his gaze directed by the bony forefingers of the skeletons to the name-plate on the coffin-lid; and, to his horror, he saw the name of the deceased was set forth as DAVID GILLESPIE.

While he still gazed in horror-stricken silence, a troupe of skeletons came crowding into the room, and circled round his bed in a dance of death, their bones rattling like castanets, and their grinning jaws gnashing as though chanting a hymn of hate. Closer and closer they circled, until one gigantic skeleton halted, and raising an enormous thighbone, aimed a stunning blow straight at the professor's head. Gillespie instinctively put up one arm to ward off the impending blow, and the effort awoke him.

This time he was indignant. He had refused several offers of hospitality from Dublin hosts, preferring to select quiet lodgings for himself. That was one of his idiosyncrasies; for he strongly objected to sitting up into the small hours, smoking and talking 'shop'; and experience of many Medical Congresses had proved such dissipation to be the normal sequel to accepting the hospitality of professional colleagues. And now here he was faring no better, or rather worse. Confound it all!

His digestion must be completely upset. If only he had strolled into the country, instead of through those unhealthy back streets adjoining the Liffey. His head felt decidedly queer, too, and he reflected that it was probably that queer feeling which had coloured the finale of his second nightmare. Could it be something more serious than indigestion?

Gillespie had read somewhere that Chinese physicians attached great importance to the prognostic interpretation of their patients' dreams. Did the curious variant by which he distinctly saw his own name inscribed on the coffin-lid portend a dangerous illness? Such gruesome visions reminded him of the creepy tales heard in his childhood days. His grandmother, who was popularly credited with 'second sight', used to tell of how she had seen a coffin, with her husband's name on it, carried past in the moonlight, three days before he died.

One story recalled another. There were stirrings in the subliminal mind. As a boy he firmly believed in ghosts. Why exactly had he lost that belief? Like the Missionary, in one of Robert Louis Stevenson's fables, he began to think that after all there might be something in it. The French called ghosts 'revenants', folk who came back. Came back for what? If he told his dream to any of the old wives in his native village they would roundly assert that the dead Irishman, or Dane, as the case might be, had come back for the femur that had been stolen from the churchyard. This introduced another train of thought; consecrated earth. Yes, the bones which had served him for purposes of lecturing for the past twenty years were bones that had been taken from the Dissecting-room, macerated and bleached. They had never been interred; had never lain in consecrated earth. Should he, in deference to sentiment, restore the femur to the churchyard, after first making a neat sketch and recording the exact measurements?

Needless to say, Gillespie in his normal waking mood, and in broad daylight, would never have soliloquised in this strain; but, as I have already hinted, the dark brings back forgotten fears and scruples, and the professor was by no means in a normal mood. His thoughts were running on this long unused track for some minutes, when he dozed asleep again. But did he? For that is a question which no man living can answer – not even the intelligent reader. Gillespie stoutly denied that he did. Cochrane declared that he only dreamt that he did not; that, in point of fact, what followed was part of the same dream, and that it was a part of the dream to dream that he was awake.

Be that as it may, let us abide by Gillespie's version for the present. He was (let us premise) still awake, and following out this line of thought, when he heard a dull knocking sound in the room. It was a muffled tapping, repeated at regular intervals, and appeared to proceed from the closed portmanteau which lay on the floor close to the dressing-table. Although the room was quite dark, Gillespie instinctively glanced in the direction from which the sound proceeded, and as he did so he became aware of a faint, hazy luminosity of rectangular form. The luminosity increased in brilliance, until it became quite evidently the outline of the portmanteau, with a distinct view of its interior, as though it had been placed against a fluorescent screen, under the action of exceptionally powerful Röntgen Rays; and the object which stood out most clearly, as in an actual skiagraph, was the purloined femur. So sharply was it defined that it appeared to impress a photograph of itself on Gillespie's brain; and then the fluorescence died away, and the room was plunged in darkness again.

By this time, the professor was (so he asserted to Cochrane) as wide awake as ever he had been in his life; his every sense strung to the highest pitch of expectation; but thenceforward he was obliged to depend solely upon his sense of hearing for information as to subsequent events. He distinctly heard, he alleged, a noise as of someone fumbling with the catch of the portmanteau; the click with which it opened; and a dull, thudding sound, as of someone walking in the room with a wooden leg or crutch. Next, his bedroom door swung ajar, and the someone or something stumped slowly down stairs and along the matting of the hall. The front door opened slightly – enough to send a current of air sweeping up the stairs and into the bedroom – and closed again noiselessly.

All this time, Gillespie was mentally alert, and experienced no abnormal sensations, except for a tense feeling about the head, and a curious inability, or even unwillingness, to move or speak. Then came a blank in consciousness, and he remembered no more until he awoke to find it broad daylight.

A knock at his bedroom door heralded the arrival of no more supernatural a visitant than the maid-of-all-work with his boots and shaving-water. He rose with something of an effort, and the act of stooping for his boots and hot water caused his head to throb violently; while the singing in his ears almost deafened him. But, like Macbeth, the terrors of the night being gone, he felt himself a man again; and he was in a humour to explain his present, as well as past experience in terms of materialistic philosophy. Dyspepsia; that was the explanation in a nutshell. Dyspepsia, coupled with a restless night.

Shaved and dressed, he hastened to complete his packing, and opened his portmanteau to stow away his shaving tackle and toilet brushes. As he opened it, he recollected with a smile how he had debated with himself in the watches of the night the advisability of returning the stolen bone to the church-yard; but he decided that such an action would be a concession to a temporary aberration of superstitious weakness; better keep it as a memento of his visit to Dublin.

Now if Professor Gillespie had been an untidy, unmetho-dical man, this story would not have been told; but the fact remains that nothing would do him but to empty the contents of the portmanteau on the floor, in order to pack away all his belongings neatly. And then it was that he made the discovery that caused him to abandon the idea of catching that day's boat, and sent him instead to consult Cochrane in Merrion Square. He discovered that the bone was missing!

It was only when he had thoroughly satisfied himself that it really was missing, by replacing the contents of the portman-teau, article by article, repeating the process several times, and making a thorough inventory of the objects in the room, that he decided that there was something wrong. Had he at his time of life begun to indulge in day-dreams, or was he the victim of hallucinations? He would have sworn in any court of law that he had conveyed the bone to his room the night before, brushed it clean, and placed it in his portmanteau. Was that waking experience on a par with the visions of the night? Was he taking leave of his senses?

He toyed with his breakfast, and informing his landlady that he had changed his mind, and intended to leave by the evening boat instead, he made a last desperate effort to regain his normal bearings. Mid-day found him once more standing in the churchyard of St. Walburgh's. The workmen were still engaged in levelling the surface, but one of their number was re-interring the heap of bones which had been laid aside in the corner. Only one portion of skull and a few long bones were left uncovered; and among the latter, in precisely the identical position which it occupied when Gillespie's eyes first lighted upon it, was the great left femur!

There was no mistaking it; for, apart from the size and abnormal development, it was as free from churchyard mould as though it had been freshly washed and dusted. Instead of throwing light on the subject, this only complicated matters still further. What was the meaning of it all? His head sang and throbbed so much that it was with difficulty that he made his way as far as his lodging.

In the afternoon he went to Cochrane's, and sent in his card. It had the opposite effect to that which he intended; for, instead of seeing him immediately, Cochrane kept him waiting until he had seen the last of his patients, hoping to settle down to a long chat on subjects arising out of the Conference.

When Gillespie's turn did eventually come, and he had finished relating his strange experiences, both in dreaming and waking states, Cochrane put to him a few questions, and set about a thorough examination. Every medical consultant has his own particular fad; and Cochrane's fad was blood-pressure. Once he adjusted the sphygmomanometer, and found that the professor's blood-pressure stood at 210, he cared nothing about reflexes or pupil-reaction. Blood-pressure explained everything, and in Cochrane's opinion the whole matter was simple.

Gillespie, like most anatomists and other specialists, had forgotten all he ever knew about the ordinary practice of medicine. He thought that, so long as he was oblivious to the flight of time, his arteries were in a similar state. As a matter of fact, they were prematurely senile and sclerosed from the routine of his life and the mental pre-occupation which had caused him to neglect precautions suitable for a man of middle age. It was highly probable that the bursting of a small arteriole in the brain had given rise to the sensation of a 'stroke', metamorphosed into a blow aimed at his head by the skeleton of his dream fancy.

The upshot of the consultation was that Gillespie was prevailed upon, under stress of warnings as to the serious consequences of disobedience, to resign his Chair of Anatomy and retire from public life. He took a quiet bungalow in his native air, and persevered in the gentle exercise treatment prescribed by Cochrane; but rest had come too late, for he was carried off by a severe stroke within seven months of his resignation; so that Cochrane's diagnosis was not very far wrong after all.

I first heard Cochrane tell this story at a clinical lecture on arterio-sclerosis; but at the time he mentioned no names. It was since I qualified that I wormed the whole tale out of him, with full particulars, as well as he could remember them. Still, blood-pressure will not explain everything; and I firmly believe that Gillespie did remove the femur from the church-yard, and stow it in his portmanteau. To my mind, the only question that remains unanswered is this: 'How did it find its way back again?'

JOSEPH HONE

The Captain in the Pipes

T he Mossops had a problem: they were unhappy.
    Henry Mossop had seen the Aer Lingus Fly-Drive
advertisement in the *Telegraph* Colour Magazine and thought
the unusual holiday offered might form a cure to their dumb
distress. For that, as he saw it, was their problem: they had
ceased to communicate. So he had gone into the travel agent in
Plymouth that same day and booked two passages to Ireland
forthwith.

The Mossops had never been to Ireland. But Henry, in the
course of his career, had known a number of Irish people.
They were a lively, talkative race. And this, together with the
other friendly attributes of the country generally, he saw as an
ideal tonic for their own awkward condition.

There was the change of life to consider, too, Henry
thought: or rather, the fact that life hadn't changed. He
was nearly forty – and Chief Communications Officer on a
Type 42 Guided Missile Destroyer, *H.M.S. Trent*. But his long-

expected promotion to the same position on the carrier *Ark Royal* had not materialised and a sense of failure had begun to nibble at the edges of his soul. Their son Giles had been put down in a prep school near Tiverton; he had two weeks' leave coming up in October . . . Fresh fields, pastures new, Henry Mossop thought, as he left the travel agency.

Sheila Mossop wore fashionable, hexagonal-shaped spectacles but always squeezed the toothpaste from the very bottom of the tube. She too was nearly forty, with thin brown hair, cut short, coming in wisps over her ears – rather a small and decided person, yet not a mousy woman, though latterly she had come to see herself as such. In fact she was bright and forthcoming by nature. But these qualities were largely dormant in her now.

Her problem was not one of communication with her husband. She sometimes thought he talked too much, in fact. She had simply wanted a larger family – something to extend and occupy herself with during her husband's many absences: she had wanted a *proper* family, she had always told herself, a bunch of children growing up like flowers all round her. But Henry, she had long ago realised, lacked adventure in that direction. He had been parsimonious in bed to begin with, afterwards miserly – and finally his love-making had become quite bankrupt. She had tried several times to resuscitate the currency with him but without success, for she was shy and inexperienced in such matters. And though she forgot this failure now in her day-to-day affairs, she nursed the hurt obscurely deep inside her.

Henry, on the other hand, viewed the problem differently: he believed that his wife had become frigid. Though he was sensible enough, as he saw it, to regard this as a natural misfortune and not a fault of either of theirs. It was a disability concomitant with the approach of middle age and a flaw in English women generally, he felt.

An old friend and former shipmate of his, who served aboard the QE2, whom he had consulted about the problem some months previously, had tactfully intimated that he should force himself upon his wife. 'It's the only way – in the circumstances,' he had said, before buying another round of gin and tonics at the local golf club – large ones this time.

Henry found himself thinking about this advice as they drove down from Dublin in their hired car – delayed by a large herd of cows just outside a town called Naas on the main road to Cork. The animals wobbled their udders and jostled their big brown backsides against the side of the car, squeezing past the bumpers. No, Henry thought with disgust – I cannot rape her. His friend's advice, he decided – though possibly suited to some of the passengers aboard the QE2 – was not a course of action open to an officer in Her Majesty's Senior Service.

They drove on, in silence, across the long rolling countryside, on an almost empty main road, the sun beginning to dip from a cloudless blue sky. The weather, Henry thought, was unseemly for the country and the time of year. It had been a very hot day.

The hotel, a small four-square early Victorian building which had once been a rectory, lay a mile outside Kinsale – on a hill above the small fishing port where black and white terraced cottages ran down to the quay with several smart hotels along it, for the place was a busy and popular tourist resort during the summer season. But now, in mid-October, it had reverted to its ancient ways: a few elderly figures walked the quiet back streets up the hill; a trawler made ready for sea; a family packed up their car in front of the hotel, down from Cork for the day.

The view from the hotel was calm and beautiful in the last of the sunlight. The Mossops, having unpacked and dressed for dinner, sat next to the big bow window in the drawing room sipping Tio Pepe. It was a pleasant room, like that of a private house, with deep chintz armchairs, hunting prints, together with a restrained Russell Flint reproduction over the mantelpiece entitled 'Persian Market'. They looked out at the long, grey-blue swell of the Atlantic beyond the headland to their right. Calm as a millpond, Henry thought contentedly. He sipped his sherry again and put the glass down carefully. The little round table between them was antique, done in highly polished rosewood.

There was no bar in the hotel. But drinks were readily available to residents, Mrs Jackson, the proprietress, had told Henry on arrival. Meanwhile, the sherry came with the compliments of the house, she had added sweetly.

Henry remembered her smile. It had been a strange thing – warm and full, yet somehow set like a transparency over a sad face. Sixtyish, he thought – genteel Irish with a soft southern burr in her voice and an abundant flow of hair, so healthy-looking that he had been surprised at its complete whiteness, an unnatural white, like a powdered eighteenth-century wig. There was something sensuous and attractive about her, Henry decided. But he couldn't exactly identify it. Perhaps it was the way she walked – very lightly, delicately, like a young woman tip-toeing to bed. And she had deep blue eyes, unclouded still – like a girl's, too – which she looked directly at you with, as if issuing a slightly risqué invitation. He mentioned this fact to Sheila.

'Yes,' she replied. 'She speaks with her eyes – and listens with them as well. But why Jackson? That's not an Irish name is it?' They sipped their sherry in silence, pondering this fact.

Shortly afterwards they heard brisk footsteps outside on the gravel and saw an elderly, rather angry-looking man stomping past the bow window. He was dressed in a heavy blue windcheater and stout hiker's boots with plus-fours – though neither the weather nor the ground underfoot merited such accessories. He disappeared from view and they heard the hall door open sharply, the draught flap grating abrasively across the floor.

They were surprised when this brusque entry was not followed by any sound of movement in the hall, nor by the door closing again. The Mossops looked at each other and then out of the window. But the view was empty.

They were startled when they turned back to see the man standing behind them in his stockinged feet, holding his boots in one hand.

He was very small, they noticed now – hardly more than five feet in his socks – his face badly weather-beaten, the skin shrunk against the bones, dark and leathery as the Tollund Man. A large pair of old naval binoculars hung from his neck. His ears were too big for his head and the lobes drooped noticeably: his sparse hair was parted on the left and combed severely sideways in the old fashion. He breathed heavily, his little ferret blue eyes gleaming at them in outraged curiosity. Despite his diminutive size he exuded dominance. It was as if two large men had just come into the room and not one small one.

'Good evening,' he said, coming towards them. 'You'll be the Mossops.' He held his one free hand out. 'Captain Jackson.'

Henry stood up automatically, as if back on board ship.

'Good evening, sir. Henry Mossop. And this is my wife Sheila.'

The Captain took her hand, held it for some long seconds, looking at her appraisingly. 'Very nice indeed,' he said at last. 'Let me join you for a drink as soon as I'm out of these togs.' He looked at the sunset through the bow window, the shadows settling gently over the sea and the village below them. 'Well below the yardarm,' he remarked. Then he turned back to Mrs Mossop. 'Going to be a change though. Glass is falling.' He looked back out over the bay. 'Can't see the Old Head. Always means a change.' Then he turned to Henry. 'Good trip? From Plymouth – saw from your booking. Needn't ask, need I? – saw it at once. Navy man, eh?'

'Yes, sir. The *Trent*. Communications officer—'

But the Captain had turned away. 'Won't be a moment.'

Then he turned back. 'The *Trent*? Guided Missile Destroyer?'

'Yes, sir.'

'Well done. Was with the *Prince of Wales* myself.' The Captain left the room.

'The *Prince of Wales*?' Sheila asked.

'Yes. Battle cruiser. The last war. Went down with half her crew off Singapore in 1942.'

'How strange.'

'Yes. Don't suppose it was his fault.'

'No. I meant – him, being married to Mrs Jackson.'

'Yes.'

They sipped their sherry once more and pondered this fact.

*   *   *

The tapping started that night.

The Mossops' room gave out directly southwards, looking over the rim of the headland straight down to the Atlantic. They had gone to bed early, leaving their bedroom window slightly open, for it had been a warm day and the room still retained a lot of the heat. It was this which puzzled Henry when he woke, some time after midnight – the fact that the central heating had suddenly come on in the middle of the night, in warm weather, for the tapping came from the radiator just beneath the window.

He lay there, half asleep, listening to the confused medley of taps and groans – the water coursing through the system, warming the boards and metal and making them creak, just as his own central heating behaved in Plymouth when it was started up from cold. He drifted off to sleep again.

The tapping noise was louder and more regular when he woke a second time. And since he was warm enough already he decided to turn the radiator off, thus getting rid of the noise at the same time.

He got out of bed and touched the metal ribbing. It was stone cold. And the tap at the bottom was already firmly turned off. Looking out of the window he noticed that a wind was starting to blow strongly from the south-west, rustling the curtains. He could hear the distant thud of waves now, the huge Atlantic breakers falling on the headland in the dark night. The Captain's forecast had been correct: the weather was brewing up. He shut the window and went back to bed.

Just as he lay down he realised something was wrong. His long experience in naval communications alerted him, some sixth sense warning him before he could identify the source of his unease.

Then he recognised it – the tapping coming strongly from the radiator now: three taps, then three with longer intervals; three more short ones. A pause, before the sequence was repeated.

Henry sat up in bed. There was no doubt about it. An S O S signal was coming through the pipes in morse. A Mayday call.

His first thought was that the Captain might be playing some elaborate joke on him – tapping the central heating pipes somewhere downstairs. Henry thought he recognised the sort of man: a retired naval hearty, gone to seed in the wilds of Ireland, up to some prank with an imagined fellow spirit. But as he listened to the continuous cry for help rattling through the pipes Henry began to doubt this. The joke was too elaborate – and too serious. Henry's morse was a little rusty but he soon picked up the drift of the message.

'S-O-S S-S I-N-V-E-R-N-E-S-S L-A-T-5-1.3-4-N L-O-N-8.3-2-W B-O-I-L-E-R-G-O-N-E R-E-A-R-H-O-L-D F-I-L-L . . .'

Henry jumped out of bed and turned his side light on. Sheila woke in the next bed and began to mumble something. But by then Henry was scrabbling about in his jacket looking for paper and something to write with.

'What's happened?' Sheila asked, calmly, in a way that Henry had come to hate.

'Wait – quiet!' Henry got a chair and sat next to the radiator where he started to take down the message. The tapping had become less coherent now, more hurried.

'A-B-O-U-T T-O A-B-A-N-D-O-N S-H-I- L-A-T-5-1.3-4-N . . .'

'Are you mad?' Sheila went on, sitting up in bed.

'Shshsh,' he said. But the tapping stopped just then.

Without thinking, so drawn was he by the urgency of the

event, Henry began to tap a message back, using his pen as a morse key on top of the radiator.

'R-E-C-E-I-V-I-N-G Y-O-U A-T K-I-N-S-A-L-E R-E-P-E-A-T P-O-S-I-T-I-O-N A-R-E Y-O-U R-E-C-E-I-V-I-N-G M-E . . .'

But there was silence then. The noises had quite stopped.

'Henry, do get back to bed. What's wrong? What is it?'

'It's a message, don't you see.' He turned to her, amazed at her lack of concern. 'The ship is sinking.'

'Nonsense. It's just the radiator.'

Just then it started to go again, but faintly now.

'S-O-S A-B-A-N-D-O-N-I-N-G S-H-I-P L-A-S-T P-O-S L-A-T-5- 1.3-4-N L-O-N-8.3-2-W S-O-S . . .' The tapping suddenly stopped.

'Do come back to *bed*,' Sheila said rather petulantly. Henry looked at her, his lips quivering with excitement and enmity.

'Just some quirk in the central heating,' Sheila said to him next morning at breakfast. 'Some bizarre electrical disturbance. The storm last night perhaps – a ship somewhere out there.'

'We listened to the Irish news this morning. And the BBC. There was nothing – no reports of any ship sinking. And how can it have been a quirk in the central heating? The heating wasn't on.' Henry ate another sausage. He felt nervous, elated – for the first time in years: a feeling he'd last remembered properly when he had read about Gagool the Witchfinder in *King Solomon's Mines* as a child. Henry felt childish suddenly. For of course, on the surface, the whole thing did seem ridiculous and impossible. On the surface. Yet on the other hand he had heard the message, had written it down . . . Henry sipped his coffee silently, thinking. He looked up. Sheila was saying something. He hadn't heard her.

'Do wake up, Henry.'

'I'm sorry.'

'I said, "I like it here. It's a lovely place." ' She looked at him with tenderness, for the first time in months. But he didn't notice it.

After breakfast, while Sheila was upstairs getting ready to go out for a walk with him, Henry wandered into the hall. Above a big blue glazed porcelain umbrella stand and next to a large barometer, he found himself gazing at a framed Marine chart, covering south-west Ireland. His eye caught the latitude line of 51 north – and then the longitude 8 west. Allowing for the extra degrees on each line which he had received in the messages the previous night, he made a rough visual transfix on the chart, running one index finger north, the other westwards. The lines bisected each other on a spot about five or ten miles out to sea, directly south of the Old Head of Kinsale. Henry felt the skin around his shoulders prickle. At the same moment he became aware of someone standing behind him. He turned.

The Captain was looking over his shoulder – or trying to, for he was in his stockinged feet again, holding his boots in one hand.

'Morning,' he said breezily. 'In for a spell of bad weather. Glass's still dropping. Quite a rough stretch of coast, this, when it blows. Don't suppose you know it. Navy doesn't come to these parts any more. Though they used to, of course. We had a base in Cobh before the war. Queenstown it was then. Lot of Admiralty dependants still live around here. *Lusitania* went down off the Old Head in 1915. Brought the Yanks in. Lot of wrecks . . .'

'Yes.' Henry turned. He decided not to tell the Captain

about the tapping in the radiator. It might seem stupid. On the other hand it would do no harm to ask him about the ship itself. The Captain, after all, had given him a natural opening.

'Yes.' Henry went on, 'I seem to remember a ship – the *Inverness*, wasn't it? – went down near here.'

There was silence. The Captain licked his dry lips.

'The *Inverness*? Hadn't heard of it. Not in my time. There was the *Loch Tay* in '37. And a German coaster, the *Bremerhaven*, the same year. And during the war, of course quite a few others. But not the *Inverness*, as far as I know. Why do you ask?'

'Oh, I heard about it – an Irishman on the *Trent*. He had a relation . . .' Henry let the words die away, embarrassed at his lie.

The Captain made a dry, cackling noise, the sound rising from deep within his throat. Henry thought he was laughing. But he was simply trying to coax some phlegm up. The Captain humphed vigorously several times before moving away.

The sky was fairly clear but it was very windy when they went out, with white horses scudding all over the angry grey sea beyond the fishing port. Henry had brought his own binoculars with him and together they walked through the village and up the far side of the valley and along the grassy promontory towards the Old Head. From here, beyond the ruins of what looked like an old army barracks on the cliff, Henry gazed out to sea, swinging his glasses widely over the whole stormy vision. A small trawler was making heavy progress, running against the tide for shelter, riding the waves like a car on a roller coaster, sometimes barely moving at all against the huge swell.

Sheila was cold. 'What are you looking at? Let's go back.'

'That ship — it must have been like this. Out there.'

'Damn that ship. Aren't we having a holiday — away from all that?'

'Yes. I'm sorry.' They turned back.

But the mystery of the S.S. *Inverness* continued to hang in Henry's mind like the sword of Damocles all morning. He felt he had behaved unprofessionally about it. Shouldn't he at least have told someone about the messages? Then he reminded himself again that the whole thing was impossible: no ship could communicate through a central heating system; no one would have believed him.

None the less, the incident continued to agitate him. So that, when they stopped for coffee at the Trident Hotel on the quay on their way back, Henry decided to telephone a friend of his, a fellow officer on the *Trent*, whom he knew to be currently on shore leave in Plymouth. He gave the man details of the message and asked him to check with Lloyds Shipping Register in London and call him back at his own hotel that evening if he came up with anything. Sheila looked at him with sour incomprehension when he returned from the telephone booth.

Before lunch, upstairs in the bedroom of their own hotel, Henry saw the Captain standing at the end of the small rose garden, looking over the last of the wind-blown petals, gazing out to sea with his glasses. Getting his own binoculars out again, while Sheila was in the bathroom, Henry followed the Captain's line of vision. But there was nothing out to sea except the tossed spume rising in white drifts from the violent water.

* * *

The Captain didn't join them for a drink that evening. He had a fluey cold, Mrs Jackson said, and was trying to kill it quickly upstairs in bed with whiskey and lemon. Mrs Jackson looked tired, her attitude preoccupied, even unhappy. Apart from the few other guests, she had her hands full with the Captain as well, she seemed to imply, hurrying about between the reception desk, the kitchen behind, and their bedroom upstairs.

At seven o'clock Henry's friend in Plymouth telephoned. Henry took the call in a little cabin at the end of the hall, closing the door firmly behind him. His friend had most of the details to hand. He read them out, the line crackling with static, and Henry jotted the information down on a pad supplied by a firm of bottlers in Cork.

'. . . the S.S. *Inverness*, a 3,000-ton cargo steamer, launched at Clydeside in 1912, originally owned by the North British Transport and Trading Company in Edinburgh, sold to the Irish Shipping Lines in 1930 – had sunk with the loss of half her crew on the night of October 9, 1932, five miles off the Old Head of Kinsale, on a voyage with mixed cargo from Cardiff to Galway. Reports from the few survivors confirmed the Mayday messages received at the time: the ship's boiler had sprung a leak in heavy weather and had subsequently exploded. The boat had sunk shortly afterwards, going down stern first, the rear section badly holed beneath the waterline. The Master of the ship, who had not survived, was a Captain Patrick Hennessy of Irish Shipping Lines . . .'

When Henry returned to the drawing room Sheila wasn't there. He found her upstairs crying in their bedroom.

'I'm sorry,' he said, sitting down beside her and trying to console her. 'I won't go on with it all. But I had to find out about it. Can't you see? I had to.'

'Damn that ship,' Sheila gasped through her tears. 'Damn all your ships.' She stood up to get a handkerchief. Then, in the silence the moment before she blew her nose, they both turned in horror to the window. The radiator had started to tap again. Henry went over to it.

'It's all right,' he said, smiling at her with relief. 'This time it really is the heating. It's on. The maid must have done it when she came to turn down our beds. Don't worry. It's not another message.'

But Henry lied. Though the radiator had indeed been turned on, the tapping was another message. He heard the first of it: '. . . T-A-I-N H-E-N-N-E-S-S-Y A-R-E Y-O-U R-E-C-E-I-V-I-N-G . . .' But by then Henry had shepherded his wife quickly out of the room and down to dinner.

They shared a bottle of light Beaujolais with their steak and afterwards Sheila slept more soundly than usual. But Henry found sleep impossible. The radiator had remained quite silent. But he was sure it would start up again. And when it didn't he felt disappointed.

Some time before midnight, however – the wind getting up outside and the sea booming strongly again in the distance – he heard a slow drip of water coming from the window. When he got up to investigate he found the tap at the bottom of the radiator was leaking slightly. He put his fingers round it, staunching the drops, and at once the morse started again. It came in spurts but faded right away whenever Henry took his hand off the pipe, so that he had to bind the tap with a handkerchief before he could make any sense of the message. What he heard made his shoulder-blades prickle.

'. . . he was at Cobh, you see – Jackson, with the Admiralty, in 1931 – just after I took over the Inverness. Mary and I were living in Cork then . . .' The message began to fade. Henry pressed his fingers hard against the handkerchief and it came back again. '. . . met her at a naval reception – and when she was shopping – came round to see us – he had something . . .' The morse here became confused, almost frantic, and Henry could no longer follow it. Gradually it cleared again. '. . . when I took over the Cardiff – Galway run I knew he was with her – that was the end of . . .' The message became incoherent again, slowly fading. Then, after about half a minute, the original Mayday message came back very strongly: 'S-O-S . . . S-O-S . . .' Then there was silence.

Henry took his hand off the pipe. Rain beat on the window above him, the storm gathering strength from the south-west. A window or a door slammed somewhere outside as he crouched in the darkness of the bedroom as if shielding himself from the weather. Jackson, he thought, with the Admiralty in Cobh in 1931: and Captain Jackson with his Irish wife – or rather, as it appeared, with Captain Hennessy's wife – retired in Kinsale forty-five years later. Was that how it was? And if so, how could he help? What help was there for an infidelity so old and a long-drowned sailor complaining in the night? Henry found himself disbelieving the whole thing for a minute – until he remembered his conversation with the Captain in the hall about the Inverness. That was real enough, as had been the Captain's denial that he knew anything about the ship. If the Captain in the pipes was right, Henry thought,

Jackson must see him now as some live ghost come to haunt him all the way from Plymouth.

A plumber came from the village next morning to repair the leaking radiator. While the man was in his bedroom Henry – mentioning his qualifications and anxious to look over the system for himself – offered to help him check the central heating installation downstairs: perhaps something was wrong with the electrical circuits in the time switch, for he had explained to the plumber the uneven performance of this mechanism.

The boiler was housed down some wooden steps in a small basement beneath the kitchen. The room smelt of burnt oil and oily tools, like the engine room of a ship Henry thought. There was a neat row of spanners and other engineering equipment above a work bench to one side and some old cabin trunks piled up in one corner. Henry suddenly noticed the white lettering on one of them: 'Lt. A. P. C. Jackson, Admiralty Buildings, Section 17/F, Queenstown, Co. Cork, IRELAND.'

Together they looked over the time switch above the boiler. Then they unscrewed the cowling next to the chimney and tested the hot water thermostat beneath; finally they removed the igniter and tested it. Everything seemed in perfect order. The plumber went upstairs to check the electric pump in the main hot press, while Henry remained below to activate the time switch, thus giving the whole system a complete test. On a signal from above he threw the switch and the boiler came to life with a soft roar. It had not been in operation for more than a minute when Henry noticed a small leak in the cold water input pipe. It wasn't much, just a dribble beneath the control tap. But the colour was strange, a red colour. Rust, Henry thought, as he wiped his hands, hearing the plumber coming down the steps again. But it wasn't the plumber. It was Captain Jackson.

'Spot of trouble?' he asked from the stairway, dressed in an old paisley dressing-gown and slippers.

'Not really. Just a small leak in the cold pipe from upstairs. I thought maybe I could help over the electrics – thought the circuits might be out. But they're okay.'

'Kind of you to lend a hand.' The Captain took a large spanner from above the work bench and came towards Henry, who stepped back involuntarily. The boiler was roaring now and the temperature was beginning to rise in the confined space. The Captain brandished the spanner, enhancing his grip on it. Henry readied himself. But the little man moved away from him at the last moment and bent down to one side of the boiler where he started to tighten – or loosen – the large nut on the input valve.

'Gets clogged up after the summer, not being used,' he said. But he failed to make much headway in his work. As he bent down, however, the collar of his dressing-gown pulled back, and Henry noticed a series of neat little red indentations running across his neck. Teeth marks – love bites? Henry wondered.

The Captain stood up. 'There. That'll do it.'

But he had not done it. The drip continued undiminished.

'Full steam ahead, eh?' The Captain's eyes twinkled in the gloomy light and he looked at Henry mischievously.

Just then, before Henry could make any suitable response, a loud tapping noise came from the input pipe, from the valve which the Captain had been tending. It was morse again,

Henry realised at once. 'B-A-S-T-A-R . . .' But he lost the rest
of it, for the Captain immediately picked up the spanner again
and gave the pipe a resounding clout with it. 'Bloody pipes,'
he said, putting the spanner back carefully in its allotted pouch
above the work bench. The noise stopped abruptly. But the
leak didn't.

It was Sheila's bath late that night which brought things to a
head: her scream half way through washing. She was looking
at the taps when Henry arrived from the bedroom, sitting bolt
upright in the water, rubbing her hands, her face creased with
fear and pain.
  'What happened?'
  'The tap . . .'
Henry moved to put his hand on it. 'Don't!' she shrieked.
'It's live. It's electric. I just touched it.'
  'Nonsense, Sheila.'
  'It *is* you fool. It's live.'
  'All right. Don't shout. Just get out of the water – *carefully*.'
Sheila got out, wrapping a towel prudishly around her.
Henry got one of his pipe cleaners from the next room. Then,
exposing the metal core at one end and pushing the other into
the rubber heel of his shoe, he brushed the tap lightly with the
metal. A jagged blue spark sizzled between the two extremi-
ties.
  'My God,' Henry said. 'I'll get the Captain. This is crazy.'
  Turning to leave the bathroom, he heard the cistern above
the lavatory warbling gently and the noise of water trickling
fast down the sides of the bowl. Then he noticed that, instead
of draining away, the level of water in the pan beneath was
slowly rising. Sheila followed his glance. She came to him,

fearful – the towel dropping away from her, holding to him, embracing him almost.

'Let's get away from here, darling. Right away. There's something wrong. Please!'

He held her for a moment before shepherding her gently into the bedroom. 'How can we? It's the middle of the night. We'll get another room.'

He didn't push her away. Instead she fell from his arms in disappointment, collapsing on her bed. The moment's reconciliation had been lost.

'I'll get the Captain,' Henry said. The weather was blowing up once more outside, another night storm running in from the Atlantic. 'Stay here. Don't move. Don't touch anything,' he said, before going out on to the landing, closing the bedroom door carefully behind him.

The passage-way was dark. The hotel slept. But he thought he knew where the Jacksons' private rooms were – up a small stairway at the end of the landing. He knocked quite loudly on an un-numbered door.

'What is it?' a voice said petulantly after some moments.

'It's Mossop. Can I see you? It's urgent – I'm sorry to—'

The door opened abruptly. Captain Jackson glowered at him, a minute and angry figure in his paisley dressing-gown and stockinged feet. Henry explained. The Captain humphed. 'We'll take a look downstairs then. Shut off the electrics. Can you give me a hand? Your line of country.'

Henry didn't want to go with him but the Captain was already herding him down the passage-way. In the kitchen he picked up a big torch. The wind was buffeting the windows furiously now, shaking the whole house. But the roar from the boiler immediately beneath them seemed louder still, unnaturally loud. The Captain opened the door to the basement and they moved down the steps. The heat was intense. The metal cowling above the boiler shimmered and there was a large pool of water beneath the main input pipe. The valve was leaking badly now. Henry went forward.

'You'll have to turn everything off,' he shouted. 'Have you got some candles for upstairs?' He turned. The Captain had disappeared.

The door at the head of the steps was just closing. Henry heard the key turning in the lock as he rushed up towards it. He hammered on it furiously. Then he heard the Captain's voice – vigorous, brutal.

'Two can play at this game, Mossop. Getting me up in the middle of the night with your bloody tricks, are you now? Oh, don't think I don't know what you're up to! Come to plague me about the *Inverness*, tapping out morse on the central heating pipes every evening. And you were down here this morning tampering with the system. Well, now you've messed the whole thing up – you can just stay there with it and cool your heels.'

Henry heard him move away. He went back down the steps. The cowling round the bottom of the boiler, where the oil-feed was, had begun to glow and the leak in the input pipe was really running now, the blood-red water seeping across the floor towards him. Henry grabbed the big spanner before running back up the stairs and attacking the stout door viciously with it.

Mary Jackson had woken with the knocking ten minutes before and now she felt cold – the wind and rain whipping at the windows, the full angry force of an Atlantic gale storming the house. She leant over to the side of her high bed and turned her electric blanket on.

A moment after her hand had moved the switch, she arched herself in a fearful spasm, as though the mattress had become a bed of nails. Her head knocked violently against the bed-head as the voltage struck her, coursing through her limbs, making her whole body tremble for a moment, as if at the apex of some great pleasure. Then she lay back, quite still, taking to death like the little death of love.

As the Captain came up the stairs he saw that one of the central heating pipes that ran along the landing skirting board had sprung a leak, the water spraying out in an arc above him, the edges of it spattering his face. He held on to the banisters for a moment, undecided. The house thudded and banged and seemed to move in the big wind, to list and dive in the storm. Then, ducking through the spray, shielding his face, he went purposefully forward.

When he opened their bedroom door he saw his wife looking at him, her head twisted sideways on the pillow, lips slightly open. He thought she was about to say something to him – something angry, for from a distance her expression seemed annoyed. But when he came closer he saw that she had been gazing straight through him with a frozen expression of awful pain.

He thought she might still be alive and could be resuscitated with the kiss of life. He forgot his damp hands and face and didn't notice his wife's arm still lying across the electric cord, so that when he bent over her and put his lips to hers, his whole body shuddered and convulsed, as hers had done, in a brief but violent agony. He fell across her on the bed, joining her inseparably in a last embrace.

In the Mossops' bedroom the lavatory bowl had overflowed and the water by now had risen half an inch over the bathroom floor and begun to trickle out into the bedroom, swamping the fitted carpet. Sheila Mossop sat with her feet up on the bed, as if it were a raft, and watched the water soak across the room, forming a moat between her and the door. She was afraid to move – afraid to step in the water, or to touch the metal door handle and escape out on to the landing. She sat there listening to the fearful wind and, when the lights in the bedroom suddenly went out and some moments after one of the windows blew open in a ferocious gust, she screamed. She stayed where she was for some moments, the wind and rain streaming across the room and the curtains flapping like pistol shots. No one heeded her screams and since there was no water on that side of the bed she put her feet down gingerly and went over to try and close the window.

Walking towards it, pressing against the wind, she put her hand out into the darkness, searching for the window clasp. Instead she touched something damp and soft. The next moment the curtain had wrapped itself round her shoulders, the material slapping viciously about her breasts. She tried to disentangle herself from it. But, before she could do so, the storm grasped her and pushed her backwards into the room – so violently that the curtain was torn from its runners and she fell, hitting her head on the floor.

She lay there stunned for a minute and when her mind cleared she gazed up into the blackness with relief. Henry had come back. She couldn't see him in the darkness but she could hear footsteps. He was walking over by the window, trying to close it, she thought. She propped herself up on one arm, rubbing the back of her head.

'Henry? Thank God. I'm here – by the bed. I fell . . .'

There was no reply. She heard the squeak of some kind of abrasive clothing – a mackintosh or oil-skin – as the footsteps left the window without closing it and approached her.

'Henry?'

Now she was terrified but she could no longer scream. Instead she fought, blindly, as the elements of wind and rain seemed to burst above her now, falling on her, pinning her to the floor. Her nightdress whipped up her legs as she struggled – yet vainly struggled, for what she felt above her, pressing down on her, had no body, no substance – was simply a weightless force which she could not touch, nor rid herself of, yet which possessed her fully and with pain. Her arms and thighs ached with it – and with the struggle she made to escape, turning first one way and then the other. Finally she ceased the fight and gave herself to the strange agony.

When Henry found her she was lying half naked on the floor, the beam of Captain Jackson's big torch spotlighting her like the victim of some hit and run accident, the curtain pulled harshly round her neck and down her midriff. He put the torch on the bed and lifted her up, a bundle of damp flesh, her head lolling back over his arm. He thought her dead. But when he laid her flat and rubbed her body and started to resuscitate her mouth-to-mouth, she regained consciousness rapidly and began to struggle with him violently, pushing him away.

'Get dressed, then,' he said rather abruptly. 'Quickly. We're getting out.' They could hear the few other guests outside on the landing now, moving down the stairs, evacuating the building. Henry managed to get her into her dressing-gown. Then, grabbing a few of their things and shoving them in a suitcase, he helped her across the swamped carpet and out on to the landing. Here it was wetter still and they moved down the stairs after the others through a rainfall of water. It sprayed from pipes above the skirting boards, streamed from radiators, leaked from ceilings, and when they got down to the hall they had to paddle through the water, several inches deep by the reception desk.

'What about the Captain and his wife?' someone shouted from the darkness outside as Henry and Sheila hurried forward, the last to leave as they thought. Henry turned and shone the torch back as they got to the hall door. The water was flowing down the stairs and for an instant Henry saw the Captain standing on the half-landing, an exultant figure in a naval cap and oilskins, holding firmly on to the banisters as though on to a swaying bridge, like a mad man happily sinking with his ship. He was just about to go back for him when the explosion rocked him forward, pushing them both out into the night. The boiler had gone up.

Outside, stumbling on to the gravel drive, they saw the back of the building, where the kitchens were, spurt with flame as the fire caught on, feeding on the oil supply. Soon all that part of the hotel was ablaze, rafters and slates falling to the ground, while the front of the house smouldered damply against the flames.

Late next morning, in the Trident Hotel down on the quay, Henry looked from their bedroom window up the hill to where the now completely gutted building smoked like a hulk on the horizon. Sheila lay asleep, under sedation, across the room from him. But her hysterical words, before the doctor had come, remained very much alive in him. 'Rape,' she had screamed, among many other bitter things, years of repressed resentment exploding in her. 'I wonder you hadn't thought of that before.'

'But I wasn't in the room, Sheila,' he'd replied. 'It was the curtain – round your neck.'

And he had believed this until afterwards, when the detective from Cork had questioned him downstairs, and told him during the course of their interview that both Captain Jackson and his wife had been found dead in their bedroom.

'In an oilskin – and naval cap?' Henry had asked.

'No. Just in his dressing-gown. Why do you ask?'

'Oh, nothing,' Henry said.

'Did you see anybody?' the detective went on, encouraged. 'Any stranger in or around the hotel last night?'

'No,' Henry lied. 'Why?'

'Well, we have to treat all this as deliberate, I'm afraid. Arson.'

'I don't understand?'

'The Provisionals. The Provisional IRA,' the man said apologetically. 'There've been several other cases recently. Various threats – and attacks on retired British people living over here. Especially from the forces.'

'Oh, yes. I see,' Henry said. 'It's a bad business.'

'Indeed,' the detective agreed. 'A long, bad business. I'm sorry for your trouble.'

JENNIFER JOHNSTON

The Theft

I feel I have to write this down as an explanation of sorts, not that there is anyone remaining who will care much or ask any questions, apart from the authorities and possibly the amiable Mr Moriarty. I am sorry about Mr Moriarty's involvement, but he has been well paid for any inconvenience that he may have to suffer.

It is the 19th of June and we seem to be having one of those spells of beautiful weather that I remember so well as a child. The air is still and golden and warm. It is coming on for evening now and the rays of the sun slant past my window and cast long, graceful shadows on the grass. In the distance someone is cutting grass with one of those old-fashioned machines that whirrs as you push it along, rather than roars. The small garden of the hotel is neat below my window, straight rows of flowers parade in their beds, no weeds provoke the eye. I have asked Mr Moriarty to collect me and take me once more to Beauregard when he has had his tea, a meal they eat in this country around the hour of six, so I have not much time.

I was born in Beauregard in Co Cork on this date eighty-five years ago.

Life was very different then to the way it has become today. That has all been said before. Each generation looks back with regret. 'Things were so much better then,' they sigh. People will never be so brilliant, the sun will never shine as it did then, time, which always seemed to stop at our command, no longer pays heed to our frantic words. I have never been a person for looking over my shoulder, but I remember the simple happinesses of childhood, and always in the back of my mind has been the memory of the unease that drove me at the age of nineteen from Beauregard and which now has drawn me back after all those innumerable years. I don't suppose my childhood was more idyllic than that of any other child brought up in similar circumstances. There may have been bad moments, hours, days, but the mind suppresses them.

I was an only child and passed most of my time, when not being taught, with one of my parents or the other. I grew to be impatient of the children who were invited, from time to time, to keep me company. I despised their chatter, their roughness, their lack of ideas. In short, I was a prig, and, I suppose, may have remained one ever since. Such friends as I have collected through my life became my friends because of the active searching quality of my mind, rather than the warmth of my personality. I digress, seeking perhaps to put off the moment when I must go. I must settle down and tell the story.

One spring afternoon, not long before my tenth birthday, it must have been about the turn of the century, I was sitting alone in the drawing room totally engrossed in a puzzle, that my mother had, not long before, spilled on to a table from a large linen bag. It was warm for May and two of the long south-facing windows were open on to the flagged terrace that ran the length of the drawing room a few feet above the level of the lawn. I had my back to the windows and the sun was warm on my head and shoulders as I leant, concentrating, over the table. I heard no sound, but suddenly became aware of the fact that I was being closely watched. I looked up, with a certain irritation, across the table to see a child of about my own age standing, staring at me. Her appearance was vaguely familiar to me, but I had no idea who she might be.

'Good afternoon,' I said. 'Did you come in through the window?'

She didn't reply.

'Is your mother with you?'

No word.

I fitted another piece into the puzzle before speaking to her again.

'I don't think I remember who you are. What is your name?'

She stared with a certain unfriendliness at me. She remained silent.

Obviously recognising something of myself in her, I smiled grudgingly. 'You can help me do this puzzle if you like.'

She moved towards me and then with an abrupt gesture she leant across the table, scattering the pieces that I had so carefully assembled, and snatched something from beside me. I looked down to see what it was that she had taken and then quickly up, to give her a piece of my mind, but she had gone. The room was empty.

'Come back,' I called. 'Bring it back.'

There was no sound of running feet, no laughter, no rustle of skirts. There was only silence and from the distance the regular click, click, of one of the gardeners clipping a hedge. I got up and went to the window and looked out. There was no one to be seen.

'Do come back.' My voice was filled with anxiety.

I ran back to the table to try and discover what she had taken. The pieces of the puzzle were scattered on the table top and some had spilled on to the floor. There had been nothing else there, nothing to take. I burst into sudden tears. A short while later my mother came into the room and found me crying.

'My darling,' she said with anxiety. 'Whatever is the matter?'

'She took it,' I sobbed.

'Who took it, darling? Who took what?'

'I don't know.'

Sudden hysteria was making my voice shrill. She took my hands in hers, her cool fingers pressing into my skin.

'Darling, stop. Do stop. There's a good girl. Explain. Just explain.'

I tried to stop crying. I tried to speak to her in a coherent voice. My hands in her hands trembled.

'She came in and she took it.'

'She took what, child?'

I shook my head.

'I don't know what she took, but she stood there.'

I pointed to the spot on the other side of the table where the child had been standing looking at me.

'She took something.'

I began to cry again. I had lost something. I had no idea what it was that I had lost, but I was filled with outrage that anyone should treat me as the strange child had done.

My mother looked mildly alarmed. She went to the window

and then out on to the terrace. There was obviously no child to be seen anywhere.

'What did she look like?'

She came back into the room and put a hand on my head, smoothing gently at my hair. She was a very gentle woman and her movements were always graceful and considered.

I described the girl to her. She handed me her handkerchief and smiled. 'Come, dry your eyes. A little moment of the imagination. It happens to many people. Fancy. A little air, my darling, will do us both good. Come.' She took my hand and we went out into the sun. The occurrence was never mentioned again.

The matter slipped, after a few days, into the back of my own mind and quite soon I forgot about the child altogether. We moved through summer and the golden autumn and then Christmas with its amazing excitements was there. On Christmas Eve the gardener and two of his men would carry the tall tree into the drawing room. It would be put standing between two of the windows in a highly-polished brass tub and then my mother would direct Patrick in the decorating of it. She would pick out of the box the blown-glass bubbles and the tiny birds and glimmering bells. Her small hands would put them with care into Patrick's huge hands and he would then attach them to the tree. Then there were the curled candles of red and blue and yellow wax in their gilt holders. I was allowed to watch this magical transformation, and sometimes even allowed to take into my cupped hands some of the less delicate of the glass decorations. The candles were never lit until Christmas Day, nor were the intriguing boxes and parcels heaped under the tree until after I had gone upstairs for my supper and bed, but the tall candle, that always glowed through the night, was placed in the window and I was allowed to light it the moment the tree was dressed. The curtains were then looped back so that the thin light could be seen from the garden after all the other lights in the house had been turned out.

I had awakened early, there was, in fact, only the barest glimmer of light in the sky outside my window. I got out of bed and put on my dressing-gown and, opening my bedroom door with great care, I went down the passage towards the large landing at the top of the stairs. This was lit from above by an ornate dome of glass, through which grey light was now creeping. There was no sound, except for that odd breathing that silence seems to make. I went down the stairs and across the hall and pushed open the drawing room door.

Six pale rectangles and the straight flame of the candle made it possible for me to see the tall tree, the decorations glinting gently in the golden glow and beside the tree the shadowy figure of a child! Slowly she turned towards me as I stepped through the door. For a moment I felt as if my heart had stopped and then, as it thudded back to life again, I turned and ran out of the room, across the hall and up the stairs to the safety of my bed. I lay rigid under the bed-clothes until I heard the early morning sounds of the maids moving around the house, and then, surprisingly, I fell asleep. After that I became more and more aware of her presence. If I were alone in the room I would suddenly become aware of her standing near me, her eyes always fixed on me in an unnerving blue stare. I would leave my book or puzzle or merely my thoughts behind me and go out of the room. She never appeared while there were other people present, so little by little I began to avoid the drawing room when I was on my own. I even made excuses if my mother sent me to fetch something for her that she needed, as I knew that the child would be there, waiting.

When I was about fifteen I was sent to school in England. This was a painful time of my life; I neither appreciated the somewhat dreary disciplines inflicted on us, nor the boisterous friendliness of the other girls after so many years of solitude and freedom. My mind was open to learning however and I learnt what they offered me and in the course of learning forgot about my enemy. She did not forget about me, though, and as I went through the drawing room door on my first day home from England, she rose from a chair by the fire and held out her hand towards me, as if she were the hostess and I the guest. Like myself she was no longer a child, but an attractive-looking girl with a long pale face and searching blue eyes. Without wanting to, I gave a small cry and my mother and her sister, who had paused for a moment in the hall, came into the room and the girl was gone.

My face must have been pale. My mother put her hand on my arm.

'You must be tired, my darling, after all that travelling. Come and sit down and tell us about all your adventures.'

She led me across the room to the chair where the girl had been sitting.

'No,' I said, with, I suppose, a certain shrillness in my voice. 'I'd rather not sit down at the moment.'

'Do what you wish.'

'I feel restless.'

'Overtired,' murmured my aunt. 'The child is overtired. She looks peaky. I'm sure they don't feed her properly in that establishment.'

'Of course they feed her properly,' said my mother, with irritation. 'You can't just pace up and down in here, child, like a caged lion. It makes me nervous.'

'I might just go up to my room for a while. Rest.'

'Anything you want, darling.'

'A little sleep,' my aunt suggested.

'Maybe.'

I left the room.

Upstairs, I lay on my bed and made a promise to myself never to go alone into the drawing room again.

Even so she continued to make her presence felt. Sometimes I would see, out of the corner of my eye, a slight movement, or hear the rustle of a skirt, feel a breath on the side of my face. Sometimes I was even aware of the shape her body had left in a chair in which she had been sitting waiting for me.

I became nervous and irritable. After a year or so, my parents, believing that my moodiness was due to some unhappiness at school, took me away and sent me to a small finishing school near Florence. There, I was happy for the first time, not just the uncaring happiness of childhood. I was filled with a real positive pleasure in being alive, in learning, in moving thoughtfully through the amazing world. I took like a duck to water to the countryside, the clear blue skies and the seamed brown faces of the peasants. I never missed the green rain-softened landscapes around Beauregard, the hedges of thorn and fuchsia, the long quiet evenings when the sun regretfully sighed its way down behind the low hills, leaving a band of gold lingering along the dark land, all those things in fact that make other emigrants sigh. I thrived in my new environment, and only became nervous when I returned home. I became filled with anxiety and my hands plagued me with their inability to rest. My mother would look at me with sad speculation in her eyes. I hated to make her unhappy, but I was unable to bring myself to explain to her or my father the cause of my unease and my very apparent desire to get away from Beauregard as quickly as possible. I think maybe they thought I was touched by some small element of madness and, indeed, maybe I have been all my life. They were gently indulgent towards me, but from time to time my mother became irritated by my behaviour. I would spend most of my time studying in my room, or else setting off for long, solitary walks along the narrow winding lanes and over the hills. Here, I felt safe and almost happy, but each time I approached the house I could feel the tightening of the strings in my head, feel my hands becoming restless once more.

I had a small amount of money of my own at that time and, as the moment came for me to leave my school, I wrote to my parents asking them if I might stay in Florence to continue my studies in my own way. I had the grandiose idea in my mind that I would write over the years and have published a series of books on the various schools of Italian painting. I received an almost angry letter from my mother in reply. She reproached me with indifference towards my parents, with my unconcern for Beauregard, which would after all, as she pointed out, be mine in the future, with her own approaching age and deep affection for me, and with the fact that I seemed to be unaware of what my duties in life might be, but she did not forbid me to stay in Florence, it was, she said, entirely up to me.

I found myself a room in a pensione and stayed. I enrolled myself at the University and studied hard, I felt free and very happy.

I made a brief visit to Ireland to see my parents. It was an unhappy experience for us all. The old weights descended on me again, the fear and constant agitation, the feeling that at any moment some unwanted thing would happen. Their obvious dissatisfaction with me made it all even worse. My father was growing old and needed grandsons, they explained to me. Good intelligent boys who knew about the land and horses and loved the place, not the children of some impossible Italian who would care for nothing but lazing in the sun. A series of young men from all over the country were invited to dinner and picnics and tennis. I left so quickly that even my conscience pricked me, but not for long; the moment my train crossed the border between France and Italy I had forgotten my conscience once more. I was hard, I admit to this, but then, to live alone and as one wishes, one has to be hard.

Over the years I wrote my books and had them published. I became an expert. In Paris, New York and London, apart from Italy where I continued to live, my name became, in the world of art, one to conjure with. Everything went as I had planned.

After the death of my parents I sold Beauregard and bought myself a charming villa on the slope of a hill overlooking my beloved Florence. As the years passed I moved from the field of mediaeval Italian painting to that of modern painting and I built up a fine small collection of the works of painters who are now modern no longer. Braque, Picasso, Matisse, Klee were amongst those whose paintings hang on my walls. I studied, I wrote, I travelled, I lectured. I immersed myself totally in my passion. I made many friends, but had neither time nor inclination to form deep and dependent relationships. In 1938 it became obvious what was going to happen in Europe, so with regret I sold my villa, packed my belongings and moved to New York, where I have lived ever since in great tranquillity. My books on mediaeval and Renaissance painting in Italy have become standard works. I have never had any worries, either financial or intellectual. I have never, until three days ago, returned to Ireland. I have succeeded in sliding over the surface of life with the same ease that a water-skier has as he planes across the seemingly calm surface of the sea.

Most of my closer acquaintances and colleagues have either died in the last few years or become cut off from life by illness. I have found myself that the increase of age and the diminution of respect from the young has made my life less pleasant than it was. I have never been a warm person, a person to whom others are instinctively drawn, irrespective of age or sex, and I have, over the past twenty years or so, found it difficult to change my fairly rigid views. I have become an oddity, a monument to a way of life and thought that no longer appeals to people.

I find the way in which people are choosing to lead their lives distasteful to me. I dislike the incompetence of modern thought, the fading values, the decay of faith. I feel I have no longer any reason for remaining alive.

It was shortly after I had come to this faintly depressing conclusion that thoughts of Beauregard began to creep back into my mind. To begin with, there were dreams; the garden, the smooth lawns, the trees drooping by the bay. The dreams came more and more frequently, evening sunshine sparkling on the granite walls, light moving on the window-panes, the smell of jasmine on the corner of the terrace. I wasn't upset in any way by the dreams, merely filled with nostalgia, something I despised in others. After a while they became daytime dreams. I would enter a room and for a moment I would be back in Beauregard, wrapped completely in the atmosphere of the past. Then the voice began in my head, gentle, courteous, insistent, calling me. There didn't seem to be any point in ignoring it. I knew what she wanted, the child who called. She wanted to give me back whatever it was she had taken so long ago.

I attended to those affairs that needed attending to, papers, settlements, arrangements in general, all tedious. All made more tedious by the fact that I wanted to be finished with them all, to be away.

I arrived at Shannon airport two days ago. It was a beautiful blue day, and the sedate car that I had ordered was waiting for me, with an equally sedate driver, Mr Moriarty by name. He wears a flat black cap when driving me and only speaks when he is spoken to. I appreciate this. He is also a most unostentatious driver.

This hotel is at the opposite end of the village to Beauregard with the neat garden that I have written of sloping down towards the bay. The house, I seem to remember, used to belong to friends of my parents, and is now owned by a retired English couple who run it as an unexceptional, but pleasant hotel. The village street bends gently and then rushes precipitously down to a small harbour. The old stone houses lean companionably together. The Protestant Church sits on one of the small hills at the back of the village, like an old lady, myself perhaps, brooding over the great days of the past and, opposite the wrought-iron gates, are the gates of Beauregard. I thought that to walk up the village street might prove too tiring for me, so I arranged with Mr Moriarty that he should drive me to the house yesterday afternoon before tea. Someone must have removed the massive gates for scrap and we turned in through the high pillars and past the shell of the lodge. The avenue was rutted and sadly overgrown but the tall chestnut trees were elegant as they had always been. The front windows of the house look out across the bay to the sea in the distance. Because of the slope of the hill, the hall door is level with the avenue in front and a narrow balcony runs the whole way round the house, broadening at the back to a terrace outside the drawing room, with steps that lead down to what had once been a lawn. Brambles, ferns and wild fuchsia now grow everywhere and there is a smell of decaying masonry. I turned the handle of the hall door and with a groan it moved. I felt a sudden distaste for entering the dark hall and pulled the door towards me once more. Mr Moriarty watched me with curiosity from the car. I walked around the balcony until I came to the first long window of the drawing room. To the right there was a pattern of roofs and the squat tower of the church, and the rooks were scattering in the sky above the trees as they had always done. I turned towards the window. The glass was thick with dust and salt blown from the sea and I rubbed at it with my sleeve. The room seemed larger than it had ever seemed and I could still see marks on the walls where pictures had hung. Beside the fireplace a tall woman was standing. She was handsomely dressed, her thick grey hair looped back from her face in a chignon. She smiled and held out her hand, in a gesture that I remembered from the past. We stared at each other through the glass for a few minutes and then I turned away and went back to the car.

So, I shall go back. I will open the hall door and walk across the hall. The sun is shining and the drawing room will be filled with golden light. She will be there. She has waited a long time. She must be as tired as I am of the process of living. She will give and I will accept what she took from me so long ago and that will be the end.

I can hear the car on the gravel below. It is time to go. I am very happy.

PATRICK BOYLE

Rise Up, My Love, and Come Away

All graveyards are depressing places. Even the New Cemetery out the Glen Road, with its row upon row of tombstones and statuary set out in orderly files and eyeing each other across railed-in plots containing glass-domed wreaths or carefully tended flowers or pebbled chips of gleaming white marble. That is why I found it so difficult to understand how I came to be in Ballysillon graveyard, soaking wet from head to foot, my stockings laddered, my shoes plastered by muck and clay, my new grey skirt ruined by slimy green stains.

Of course, Ballysillon graveyard would destroy anyone's clothes. Unkempt and neglected, a wilderness of weeds and nettles, briars, and scutch grass, it is the oldest graveyard in the parish, catering alike for Catholic and Protestant and refusing refuge to no one. Rarely used now for burial, there had to be good reason for such an impertinent intrusion on its dead. It was no place to find oneself on a day like this, with overhead a dull leaden sky and a watery sun trying desperately to break through the slowly moving rain clouds.

And yet breakfast – how long ago now? – had been such a gay meal, with John, usually so quiet, chattering to the children, teasing me and clowning like a young fellow, so that he was nearly half an hour late starting off for his work in the bog. Very kind and considerate he was, even remembering not to ruffle my hair when he stooped down to kiss me goodbye. When he was gone and the children packed off to school, I could only sit in happiness at the table and thank God for my good fortune.

So what had gone wrong? I waded aimlessly through the long grass towards a marble angel, leaning dispiritedly against a stubby cross. The angel's nose was chipped off, as was one eye and a large section of the left wing. The face was mottled, the robes disfigured by stains – green, grey, and brown. It was erected, so the legend read, to the memory of James O'Neill, who died March 12, 1878, aged 56. R.I.P.

Even doing the housework, I moved around in a glow of happiness. Clearing away the breakfast things, washing the dishes, making the beds, scrubbing, dusting, tidying – everything I did seemed to have a special significance as if sanctioned and ordained by God. At least, looking back on it now, that is how it seemed. As I went from room to room, picking up soiled clothes from floor or chair or bed, emptying chamber pots into the slop pail, putting away books and comics littering the bedside chairs, I hummed and whistled and sang. I even broke into a few shuffling steps of a dance routine. Not even the discovery of a cigarette butt in the fireplace in Jackie's room, could disturb me. And why should it? John loved me. The children adored me. I was loved and I had a heartful of love to bestow in return. How could I be anything else but happy?

Or was I? It all seemed to have happened so very long ago that you could not be sure of anything. All I knew now was that I felt terribly, terribly tired – as if I had walked for miles. A few yards away was a fallen tombstone. I pushed my way through briar and nettle till I reached it and flung myself thankfully down on the rough granite. Idly I began to spell out the worn inscription.

> *Erected in loving memory of my dear wife*
> *Judith Barnes*
> *Who died June 6, 1844, aged 20*
> *'The Lord giveth and the Lord taketh away'*

What a dreadful tragedy! To be cut down at that age. After only a few months or maybe a year of married life. The poor thing! People are not half thankful enough to have their health and their family and their friends. No matter how bad things are, they could be worse. John was always saying that. And God knows it is a true saying. He is a good man, John. Attends the sacraments regularly. Smokes little and drinks less. Always kind, affectionate, and understanding towards me, when there must have been many times, goodness knows, that I was a trial. I am a lucky woman to have such a husband. So what prompted me to act as I did? What sudden impulse sets a body veering about like a weathercock?

I read on.

> *Also her husband, Amos Barnes*
> *Who died of fever, March 15, 1846, aged 27*

He had not survived her long. Just two years. It must have been the famine fever that carried him off. Some people would say that it was a fitting thing for a husband to follow his wife so soon to the grave. But I think that is wrong. I would like to think of John living happily for many, many years not just to care for the children but to remember me always and ever with love. Never to let my memory wither. That would make me very happy.

The rest of the legend ran:

> Also their son, Matthew Barnes
> Who died May 3, 1928, aged 84.

How awful! Judith must have died in child-bed giving birth to this doddering old monster. How unfair that he should outlive for all those years the person for whose death he was responsible. And now, the fragile brittle crumbling remains of age are heaped on the sturdy bones of youth. I shivered. Got up from the tombstone and wandered off towards the small building, cupola shaped, that must have been used as a kind of mortuary chapel. Tripping over mounds and hollows, climbing grave railings, for no paths were evident, forcing a passage through the dense undergrowth, I reached the building and flopped down on the stone bench running round the inside wall.

What, I wondered, had caused my sudden confusing change of mood? One moment, happily carrying on the housework; the next, sitting morosely in the bedroom gazing down at the laced fingers of my hands. Lonely, depressed, frightened, I sat there and it seemed to me as if every blind in the house were drawn, the carpets up and the furniture gone. I was in a deserted, a forsaken house. My family had abandoned me. Perhaps never to return. I would be forced to spend the rest of my days in this airless gloomy house. With not a sound of shout or of laughter or of scampering feet. Only the creaking of old boards, the squeaking of mice, the rattle of window blinds.

It was then I decided to dress up. After long pondering, I laid out on the bed the grey tweed skirt. My nice pale-blue woollen twin set. My best pair of stockings. And my black court shoes. I decided also on fresh underwear.

Filling a basin with warm water, I stripped off to the pelt and scrubbed myself with sponge and soapy water till my skin glowed. Then I dressed up, taking extra pains over my appearance. I spent a long time at the mirror making up my face, even using a little rouge to put a bit of colour in my pale cheeks. At last, with my wiry dark hair brushed out and a final dab of powder on my nose, I examined myself in the mirror. Satisfied with my efforts, I folded up and put away my discarded clothes and made off for the porch where I slammed behind me the front door. I stood, looking up at the lowering sky with its threat of rain, uncertain what I should do.

Getting up from the stone bench, I wandered restlessly around the mortuary chapel. It was quite small – about six paces wide – with one deeply embrasured window, curtained and clotted with spiders' webs. These were so covered with dust that it was impossible to see out. On the sill of the window I discovered an inscription. It ran:

This graveyard was given and walled in to the people of Ballysillon and the surrounding district by the Rt. Honourable Wm. Conyngham at the expense of twenty pounds and ninepence.

What an absurdly small sum. The stonemasons and the labourers who built the wall must have worked for almost nothing. And yet this great gentleman saw fit to have the cost of his gift chiselled on stone for posterity to wonder at. A skinflint, that's what he must have been.

There was an angry buzzing from the recessed window. A large bumblebee had got itself entangled in the folds of cobweb. It beat its wings frantically, plunged and threshed around, wading, by dint of sheer strength, through clusters of webbing until its whole body was encrusted and wound about with dusty strands of gossamer. Sometimes its wings would become trapped. At once the buzzing would rise to a higher pitch as the insect sought to free itself of the constricting folds. At last, partly freed, it would lurch forward again with long gossamer trailers whirling like spray from its beating wings.

In one corner of the window a large spider crouched, sunk deep in its folded legs. Twice it rose, ran down the webbing and moved cautiously round the entrapped bee. At a safe distance it stayed, watching the struggling insect. Then retreated back to its earlier position at the top left-hand corner of the window.

Meanwhile the bee, by now swathed in a clinging pall of dusty cobweb, had thrust its way downwards towards the bottom of the window. At last it reached the sill where it lay quiescent for a few moments. Its head was smothered in webbing as though in a diver's helmet. From this casque protruded one feeler. Its whole body was festooned with threads of gossamer. Gossamer flapped from its slowly moving wings, twined about the hairy feet, wound itself in chains around the parti-coloured belly.

How long I stood at the front door before deciding to go on

my bicycle, I do not know. But once I had made up my mind, there was no stopping me. I went to the turf house. Rooted out the bike.

The two tyres were flat. I pumped them up. Somebody had lowered the saddle. I found a spanner and shifted it up to the right height. The chain was bone dry. I got an oil can and oiled it. By the time all this was done, the first drops of rain were falling. I had to stand for the most of a quarter of an hour in the turf shed before the rain stopped. Then I started off.

The bee moved forward across the sill, crawling on partly pinioned legs, its outstretched wings trailing at either side. Its body was humped in the effort to propel itself forward. Every so often it blundered against the sucked-dry body of a dead discarded fly. Then it would stop. Investigate the body with the single free feeler. Attempt to nudge the desiccated corpse out of the way. Crawl on once more with the dead fly trailing after it, attached to a strand of gossamer. Sometimes the bee would stagger into a matted cable of tethered cobweb. Push and thrust and bullock its way clear, emerging often with much of its wrappings torn off. Once it rolled over on its back and jerked its legs about, trying to free them from their shackles. Never did it succeed in ripping away the webbing that encased its head. And always it moved blindly towards the edge of the sill. It had not a chance. Stumbling and lurching forward, it toppled over the edge and fell with a squelch on the stone floor. For a few seconds it lay on its back, waving its unentangled legs feebly. I stayed till they had ceased moving. Then I went and stood at the doorway.

I cannot think why I decided to take the Knocklangan road. For it is a hilly road. Very different from the metalled main road. It means pushing the bike up the hills and braking with both hands going down them. Of course the road goes through lovely country. Vivid green pasture land dotted with the pale gold of corn fields and here and there plantations and shelter belts of trees. The rain had brought out a rich heady tang in the air. Larks sang overhead: robins chirped in the bushes: blackbirds screeched as they fled at my approach. The sun was trying to break through the clouds. And yet I was sunk deep in despair as I walked and cycled and walked again.

At Corrigan's Cross I met Mrs Leary coming against me. Driving a herd of Herefords. I had to get off the bike to pass.

'It's turning out nice after the rain,' she said, stopping.

'It is that,' I said, edging forward to get past.

'Though God knows, we could do with a sup of rain. The country's parched for the lack of it. I'm just walking these animals down the road to the Water Field.'

The bullocks had spread across the road and were grazing the grass margins.

'That was a good shower a while back.' I edged a few steps further forward.

'Not worth a curse.' She drew nearer. Her black beady eyes looked me up and down. 'You're all toveyed up. Where are you for, if it's a fair question?'

Another cautious step forward. Where was I bound for anyway?

'I'm heading for the lake. Knocklangan Lake.'

'And what's taking you there, in the name of God?'

'There's a picnic. I'm going to a picnic.'

I was clear now. Up on the bike and away with you.

'I must run now or I'll be late.'

As I pedalled madly away, I heard her exclaim:

'God and his Holy Mother, what's the world coming to?'

Still overcome by depression I pushed and pedalled and braked. With the fields getting scrawnier and scrawnier and the rocks beginning to get above ground and the hedges and bushes and bits of trees all lying the one way on account of the wind that is blowing all the time from the south-west and the day getting darker and darker with the threat of rain. Till at length I reached the foot of Knocklangan. Got off the bike and left it propped against the ditch.

I stood there in the doorway of the mortuary chapel, looking out at the scattered tombstones, almost hidden by the tangled grass. They had the bedraggled appearance of a defeated army. Tombstones sagging wearily forward ready to collapse with exhaustion. Tombstones arched back so that wind and rain and bleaching sun had long since scoured away the chiselled lettering. Tombstones tilted over crazily as though time itself had shrivelled and contracted the muscles of mountain granite. Or sunk to their rounded shoulders in the soft ground. Or sprawled their length in the rank undergrowth, face up or face down it mattered not in their last indignity. And over all the strong musty odour of nettle and briar and scutch grass.

It is a long climb from the road, up through the foothills to the lake. The most of three good miles. There is no recognizable path. Only sheep and rabbit tracks. And these wind their way round rock and bramble patch, pools of water and stunted trees, so that you feel that you are not making an inch of ground. The climbing too is discouraging for no sooner have you struggled to the crest of one hill than you are sliding down the slope on the far side to face once more a panting floundering ascent. At no time can you glimpse the entrance to the lake; all that can be seen is the towering peak of the mountain.

Once in a while you rest, leaning against a boulder. Sucking the cold mountain air into your racked lungs, you look back down the slope and draw some comfort from the tiny figures of man and animal, the ribbon of road and the dolls' houses scattered about below you. Far in the distance, the sea bounds the horizon and the smoke of an unseen ship is pencilled against the sky. All around you stretches the gloomy dun-coloured waste, broken only by mountain tarns and outcrops of grey granite rock. The loneliness was made more lonely by the occasional cry of a seagull muted by height and distance to a pitiable puling wail.

There was a trampling of feet on the road leading towards the cemetery. Many feet. And the low hum of a bevy of slow-moving cars. I waited, listening. As the cars drew nearer and the shuffling footsteps more distinct, it was borne in on me that it was a funeral cortège bound, without doubt, for Ballysillon cemetery. It was only then that I noticed in the far corner of the graveyard, almost hidden by a towering clump of nettles, a mound of freshly dug clay. I moved back inside the mortuary chapel, taking shelter in the corner farthest from the door. There I waited nervously.

The climb up Knocklangan had become steeper. The mossy ground slippery underfoot from the recent rain. Twice I lost my footing, the second time laddering a stocking. Shoes and skirt were mired and stained. My underclothes were sticking to me with sweat. With sweat my eyes were blinded, my lips salty. But still I kept on, gasping and groaning, with the blood thumping in my ears. Up one hill and down the next. Making no apparent headway. Until suddenly, when I had almost given up hope, I was there. Standing at the top of a short slope, dropping sharply down to the lake.

77

It is cupped in a horseshoe of mountain, the slopes of which drop sheerly down to the rim of the lake. Only at the entrance is there any pretence of a beach. This consists of a narrow strip of grey gravelly sand, littered with a confusion of granite boulders. The lake, reputedly bottomless, rarely gets the sun and its smooth surface has the unhealthy pallor of a man who works underground. The immensity, the absolute stillness, the dull grey quality of the light, were awesome and scarey.

I turned away to survey the route I had climbed. Far below me, stretching to the sea, lay the toy landscape of a child. The jumbled up checker board of fields – green, brown, golden. The diminutive houses with their red-roofed barns and sheltering trees. The tiny motionless animals set in position on the nursery floor. The minute figures crawling slowly around intent on their clockwork tasks. It was all so far away and unimportant.

On the horizon, the sea. A broad expanse of grim unpolished silver. At one point – where a cluster of houses indicated Claran Strand – an errant shaft of sunlight burnished the water.

Claran Strand. What a host of happy memories this splash of sunlight evoked. Long summer days stretched out on the beach, the warm wind stroking your limbs with feathery finger tips. The eventual bathe with icy water stinging scorched flesh. The cycle home in the cool of the evening, the wind of your going cooling the sunburn.

Marriage, the move inland, the coming of the children, had changed everything. How many times were we at Claran Strand since we got married? Once. No, twice. The first time, before Jackie was born. John hired a car and the pair of us set off for Claran. We bathed, splashing each other like children. We chased each other around the beach. We walked, arms

78

round each other, along the cliffs where the pounding waves
and the sheer drop alongside the path, made me cling still
closer to him. Until the craving was too much for us. Over the
ditch we went and John, usually so solid and staid, made love
to me in the broad light of day. It was a cornfield. As we lay
back afterwards, eyes closed, hunger slaked, you could hear
the wind whirling through the stalks, cutting a swathe of
rustles like the whirring of a flock of starlings or a long-eared
dog shaking its head. Then sluggishly, linked hands swinging,
we went back along the cliffs. Before we went home we had
one drink each in Lacey's bar. A bottle pint for John: for myself
a glass of sherry wine.

The second time was when? Let me see. Jackie was born. So
was Phil. Marie was on the way. There was a strike on at the
bog and John was at home, eating his heart out. No wages
coming in and the debts mounting up and nothing to be heard
from morn till night but a lot of old trade union talk. The two
of us fought the piece out with rows and arguments that got
worse every day. Eventually I could stick it no longer. I had
over three pounds spogged away. Enough for a day's outing.
The hired car cost two pounds. A picnic lunch was another ten
bob. The remainder went to John for spending money.

We had a marvellous day. The kids took to the water like
ducks. We paddled, bathed, built dykes and sand castles,
played games, slept. At length, tired out, John and I sat on
the rocks, leaving the children to their own devices. John was
filling his pipe. Leisurely, methodically, he tamped down
layer upon layer of tobacco from the shredded heap in his
cupped hand. Suddenly he looked up.

'What have they got now?' he said.

The two children were chasing something along the strand.

Something black and white. And small. That scampered ahead of them in little spurts.

It was a bird. A sea bird of some sort or other. There was a peculiarity about its gait as it ran and fluttered ahead of them. An awkward, unbalanced action that I felt to be unnatural.

John pointed with his pipe.

'That bird,' he said. 'It has got a broken wing, by the look of it.'

He was right. The left wing was trailing the ground whilst the other fluttered bravely in a futile effort to fly. It was this that gave it the lop-sided appearance.

'The poor thing,' I said.

Just then Jackie caught up with it. Stooped down.

'Jackie!' I shouted. 'Don't! Don't touch it, Jackie!'

The bird escaped his clutching hands. Wheeled about. Made for the sea, followed by the two screaming children.

'Jackie! Phil!' I called. 'Come back! Come back here at once!'

By this time, the bird had reached the fringe of the tide and was scuttling through the shallow depths of a receding wave. It had not yet started swimming when the next wave reached it. Caught up in the rushing surf, the bird was carried ashore whirling and tumbling helplessly about. The children rushed to catch it but it evaded them and scurried back in the wake of the retreating wave. Once more it was caught up by the oncoming breaker and swept to the shore.

The children were dancing with glee.

'Oh, Mummy, Mummy, come and look!' they chanted.

'Leave the bird alone, you young rascals!' shouted John.

At the third attempt the bird got through the foaming lather. Swimming strongly, it headed out to sea. But before it got very far, a comber broke over it. I thought it would never reappear. When it rose to the surface, I cheered.

'Oh, you beauty!' I cried.

Soon it was through the breakers and out to the open sea, I turned to John.

'Wasn't it wonderful?' I said. 'I am so glad it got away.'

He struck a match and shielding it, sucked at the pipe. Between puffs, he said:

'It's banjaxed . . . that broken wing . . . it'll banjax it entirely.'

'You mean it was all a waste of effort? That never will it fly again? That the poor thing will have to die? Oh, it can't be. It is too unfair.'

John flung away the burnt match. Drew deeply on the pipe. Blew from pursed lips a slow cloud of tobacco smoke. Shamefacedly, almost furtively, he reached out and caught my hand.

'There's not much fairety in this world, darling,' he said. 'Either for birds or people. If there was, you'd maybe not have had to punch in such a lousy spell as the last few weeks.'

The tears spurted out of my eyes. My throat went dry. A torrent of emotion rose inside me till I thought I would choke. I gripped tight at John's hand. Blinked back the tears. Clamped shut my lips so that I would not disgrace myself by shouting aloud for all the world to hear, that someone I loved still loved me.

I was happy. So very, very happy.

Over Claran the shaft of sunlight was quenched. The world was once more a grey and silent place. Bounded by gloomy mountains and a gloomier sky. So that you are shut in from everything and everybody. No longer able to beat your fists against the invisible barrier that encloses you. Moving further and further away from all you love. You may complete the journey. With your heart turned to stone and the gorge rising in your throat at the thought of turning back, what else is there left to do? Have not the shuffling feet come to a halt outside the cemetery gates? Are not the bearers already shouldering their burden? What need is there to linger? Listening maybe to a voice blown in the wind, intoning sombre, mysterious, terrifying words in an alien tongue? Or to scrape of shovel, clink of stone, thud of clay on hollow wood? Or perhaps watching the stricken desolate faces gazing, not at the open grave, but across at the distant mountains? The sweat of the long climb has put you shivering. Better that you get moving. Scramble down the short incline to the lake shore, your feet sinking in the gravelly sand. At the water's edge, stand a moment to draw breath. But not for long, for hesitation will undo all. Mouth dry and eyes blinded with tears, wade out into the lake, swaying, stumbling, staggering, unmindful of soggy shoes or clinging skirt and jumper, feeling the rising water press against thighs, groin, breasts, ever struggling forward to the final step into bottomless depths that will complete your pilgrimage.

In Ballysillon graveyard, the mourners are beginning to drift away, stopping here and there to gather in groups. Scraps of their conversation come to me, blown on the wind.

'A big turn-out . . . Half the parish must be here . . . Why, in the name of God, did she do it? . . . A shocking business altogether . . . Such a quiet inoffensive creature . . . How could she do such a thing? The husband near demented . . . You'd be sore at heart looking at the childer . . . Och, the poor angashore, what came over her at all? . . . Cycling the most of

ten miles . . . Why? . . . Dressing herself up in all her finery
. . . Why? . . . She shouldn't have had a care in the world . . .
But, why?'

The wind is rising, coming in fresh from the east, flattening
nettle, docken, and scutch grass with the rustle of starlings'
wings. Flurries of rain come in its wake, driving the loiterers
helter skelter through the cemetery gates. I shiver. Better for
you to go now. Why delay? What is there to keep you here any
longer?

DESMOND HOGAN

The Birth of Laughter

Walking through the garden she carefully chided the trees, pulling bushes from her way, distracting leaves from her hair. That she was back here hardly made sense to her. That she was unafraid was not safe to contemplate. Being here was easy. She looked about. Light stole through her hair. She was twenty-two. An observer would have considered her to be very beautiful, hair twisted and knotted in gold pigtails.

A butterfly rose. She stared, haunted by the pallor of its wings. She laughed. The child inside her would be a girl, a brown girl like the black babies in Roman Catholic national schools, nodding on boxes which were filled with money for the foreign missions. The butterfly waved, danced, coaxed. She ran. Her hand reached towards it. Light caught her topaz ring. The colours in it sparkled, green, orange, brown. Catherine laughed. She laughed until the entire garden heard her laughter. Her body froze. Was she really laughing? Was this voice really hers? She waited. Nothing happened. No one took her. A blind aftermath of laughter rang through her. She laughed again, raced again until the entire garden welled with imaginary butterflies and her hair spun imaginary roses.

She stopped. She walked. She felt trees again, bushes again, a Lazarus reborn to sensation. She walked slowly as though in a trance. It was like slow motion in a childhood film. Catherine Findlater you are reborn to the exquisite touch of things she told herself. Catherine Findlater you are saved.

The grass by the stream was already gold. Some straws held themselves high like August wheat. She knelt by the water. Her face glowed. She smiled. She smudged her features with her fingers. She smiled again. Laughter was imminent. This time she did not laugh. She screamed. A figure rose behind her. She looked up quickly. It was Adoe. He embraced her. His skin was stretched and light brown over brittle bones. His arm held her to him. His shirt was white. They strolled through the garden. In lighter moments of remembrance she could recall Aunt Madeleine reciting lines of balmy love poetry by her friend William Butler Yeats or the Song of Solomon, or having recourse to Byron. She strolled now with her Indian lover and husband. Laburnum was bursting, lilac already sheathing bushes with white.

'You're all right. You're fine,' he said.

Sometimes she'd stare at him and ask him why he'd brought her here. 'You must come back. For your own good.' She was frightened and crying. She'd been left the house by her Aunt Madeleine. True she'd grown fond of the lilac there. True she'd placed a big rubber doll among the snowdrops there, left it languishing, sticking pins into it, hoping to draw blood to colour the snowdrops red. In other words she'd been a child here. But the resting place of Aunt Madeleine's shorn-out heart was too close for comfort, grey Wexford stone.

In a Dublin flat she'd said 'No. I can't go back. I can't.' One night when Adoe was out performing in a play – Ghosts by Ibsen – she'd risen screaming. The whole ritual had risen in her. She'd begun sweating. She'd been a month pregnant. She'd gone to the window. It had been in Fitzwilliam Square. She'd pushed up the frame. Sweat was emerging like a shadow from her skin. She'd wished herself dead upon the pavement below. She'd made to throw herself. He'd caught her. He'd forced her on the bed. He'd made love to her. Her mind had given way. She'd dreamt of mice, many mice in the castle long ago. Mice were crawling at her feet. Mice were running beneath and betwixt her. She'd woken as though to scream. He'd been beside her. She'd smitten his nipple with her right forefinger. It had been a butterfly. It had come alive to her. She'd kissed it. She'd slept upon his stomach.

A real butterfly waved by now. 'Look,' she cried delightedly. 'Isn't it pretty?' 'She,' Adoe corrected her. 'It's a she. A she butterfly.' 'How do you know?' 'Isn't it obvious?'

Whereas the previous butterfly had been merely white this one was many coloured. 'Lovely,' Catherine cried. 'Lovely. Lovely. Lovely.' She turned to Adoe. His lips burgeoned with a red like summer raspberries. She kissed him. He held her. Her laughter became tears now; tears shook from her. Again the fear rose in her. She stared into the density of Adoe's chocolate brown eyes. 'Do not forsake me.' 'No,' his voice was a whisper. The French windows behind her held a shadow of lace. Catherine began sobbing and as she did the French windows splintered with red, red from a drawing-room geranium. 'Adoe,' she clutched him. The child started coming. She held him. She collapsed.

Avenues of cypresses in the summer sun; these were her first memories. These cypresses darkened; they held back – like a deluge. Her mother would take her hand, dolled up in grey skirt and white blouse and persuade her through these shadows. Catherine would look – scared. Her mother had been a parson's daughter from Offaly, singularly quiet and inoffensive. She'd married George Findlater after meeting him at a midsummer's party in Tipperary, south of Offaly, north of Wexford. The party had occurred beside a lake. The hills had been lit by fires, burning for St John's Eve, bronzed young men, disgorging themselves of shirts, jumping over the flames, and shadows of flame and evening fire imminent on the lake. The man she'd met had been attractive, rather like one would imagine Emily Brontë's father to have been attractive. He'd been distant and contemplative of the sunset; they'd courted. He'd driven from Wexford in a Ford coupé which resembled a ricocheted funeral car. They'd married when apples had been burnished in the County Wexford glades of George's home. They'd honeymooned in Galway; on a lake beside a convent school where nuns wandered about reading breviaries, draped like blue whales. They'd made love. They'd conceived Catherine there. They'd returned to Wexford.

'There has been much suffering in the Findlater family,' her mother had always said to Catherine. If one looked one could see the offset of such suffering on her mother's face. She'd arrived in Wexford to live in a lowly decaying castle. Portraits had exploded about her like decaying cartoons. Suits of armour had astonished her with their glamour of light. More

than anything she'd been awed by the garden, by the richness
of shade there, by the effervescence of grass. She'd stare as
Madeleine held her parties.

To these parties would be drawn the élite of Ireland and
Britain, young men with faint gladness, neckties and cravats
bursting. These young men came from the hills, from the
Midlands, from castles and fortresses, the last of the Anglo-
Irish peers. They'd come with wolfhounds, with gangling
strides, with fat and expensive cigars whose odours suggested
Berlin and Paris. Madeleine would entertain them with the full
force of the servant population of the house. She'd lay tables
with cakes and strawberries and cream, escalating cakes,
bilberry wines; lavender and roses decorating the sheer white
and the sheer length of the table. One could hear her voice
cackle. 'The horn of plenty,' she'd cry and Catherine's mother
daily becoming more and more aware of local resentment,
realized that Findlaters' access to wealth was based on famine,
on centuries-old greed. Once a Findlater had wandered to
Ireland in dainty pantaloons with Edmund Spenser, recognized this valley with its rolling glades and gossamer-like
hawthorn as being a place of serenity, set up home here,
ransacked the district, drew much wealth to the house. The
Findlaters had lost their title through a row with Queen
Victoria and some of them had taken to the church, a black
whispering Protestantism. During the famine the family was
beset by wraith-like peasants haranguing the door like fam-
ished wolfhounds. They received potatoes, soup. Their eyes
haunted the occupants of the house like the dots on a
peacock's feather. 'Remember 1798,' the eyes seemed to
say. 'Remember the young men who rode into your garden
and died among the apple-blossoms, wounded in Wexford by

the Redcoats.' Maids would firmly replace the leaden locks, shutting out the offending evenings of famine Ireland.

'The horn of plenty!' Madeleine's voice reverberated through the garden even after she'd taken up her bags and flown to Paris in an aeroplane from Shannon airport. 'The horn of plenty!' Catherine's mother had been haunted by Madeleine's silken clothes as she'd wandered about the castle. In the same year her husband had died of a heart attack, she herself had begun to grow weaker and George's two sisters, living in two separate houses in the village, had taken to flights of madness, wandering in the night, both in nightgowns, speaking of ghosts, of wolfhounds, of legendary Irish heroes. Both had been diverted to a mental hospital in Enniscorthy where they ate fresh tomatoes and stared, blissfully, and hauntedly, at the river below. George's third sister, Madeleine, likewise owning a small house in the village, had disappeared to Paris, so as Catherine grew up, holding her mother's hand as she strolled down avenues of cypress trees, all she'd known of Aunt Madeleine was an awesome photograph in the living-room, Madeleine's hair long and black and flowing and her lips, smiling even in middle-age, flushed and shot through as though by blood.

These were her earliest memories, sitting in the living-room in winter or summer, her mother reading her huge handsome volumes of Hans Christian Andersen or the Grimm brothers. If it were summer the windows would be open and bees singing across the patterns of the carpet. If it were winter huge fires would be rumbling and Catherine's mother would occasionally lean towards the blaze and pick chestnuts from the turf. Then her mother died. Catherine had been five. She died almost as gently and as devotedly as ogres came and went in fairy stories or as young women with long golden hair had been carried off to round towers where they waited for handsome princes to free them.

The cause of death – later established – was a lung complaint. Catherine watched her burial. It had been winter. She clutched a doll and shed some tears and watched water springing like seeds from branches. It had been raining. Servants were there in force. Wexford spread. 'If one looked far enough,' Catherine had thought, 'one could see strawberries.'

As a rule strawberries did not arrive in Wexford until June. That year had been no exception. Catherine had waited for strawberries, their seedling red, and knew also that her Aunt Madeleine, previously unidentified, was arriving to look after her. All she'd known of Aunt Madeleine was her books, her photograph. It was known Aunt Madeleine was the author of books. They lingered in the house – like ghosts.

She arrived one afternoon, drawing up in a hearse-like taxi. Her face had seemed blotched and bewildered. Catherine had stared, teddy bear loose in her fingers. Madeleine had beheld her. Her eyes had a lucidity and yet a horror which burnt into memory.

Madeleine Findlater, authoress, author of historical romances, a study of the tarot and a biography of an obscure Rumanian poet who died in 1937.

Catherine's eyes opened – she was in a hospital. Nurses studied her. There was one who held a glass of water. She recognized Adoe behind a black doctor. She reached for him. She collapsed.

Five years old she'd been then and innocent of her aunt's past. The castle was sold to an American millionaire who brought a blue-haired mistress to convalesce there from an attack of polio and who then abandoned it, allowing snow-drops in spring to overshadow its lawns, a lonely cold twirling battalion of incestuous males. Such was the fate of the Findlater castle, a sort of companion to Catherine's growing years. She'd come and look at it, tracing herself a path from the national school, feeding herself on Nestlé's chocolate, finding her hands growing sticky, rubbing them in daisies.

At school, Miss Rafter would recite the poetry of Yeats. 'Though I am old with wandering through hollow lands and hilly lands I will find out where she has gone.' Miss Rafter had pretty blonde hair, a lock of which fell from her forehead. She'd wear blouses as fine as a buttercup and her eyes always seemed shaking and about to flow with tears. Children stared at her, the few Protestant children of the locality. One day she left and years later Catherine saw her again, tempered by age but still lovely.

On going home Catherine would also hear about Yeats. Aunt Madeleine spoke freely on the subject. He used to visit the castle. He would dine there and speak about The Golden Dawn. In the 1930s, in Aunt Madeleine's youth, he would occasionally visit, push white hair from his forehead and recall his own youth and early temptresses as apple-blossom dipped from a bough. Aunt Madeleine would produce photographs in evidence of Yeats's visits. They hadn't been altogether clear but the white lain table on the lawn was in evidence, a shower of strawberries and a poet, leaning on a cane, staring into an unbeckoning afternoon.

Sometimes visitors would come, they also speaking of Yeats. A priest from a strange religion arrived in a long black dress and with a flowing beard. 'Russian Orthodox' was the name of the creed and Aunt Madeleine had expounded with him on the craft of Yeats. One or two visitors arrived from England. They spoke of the Queen. Aunt Madeleine had prepared a jelly dessert and they'd partaken of it, speaking of the Queen's imminent visit to New Zealand. That evening in bed Catherine had recourse to nightmare. She kept seeing her mother; her mother was running through the woods. Her mother was weeping. 'Mother.' She'd woken. She'd aired a slight tremor. She'd run down the stairs. She'd opened the kitchen door. She'd opened the drawing-room door. Inside was dark. Inside Aunt Madeleine was seated by the table, hands outstretched on the table, those of her visitors linking with hers and a candle lighting and a glass on the table, moving.

Her eyes opened once more.

She could hear a nurse saying, 'It will be a while yet.'

Her body slipped. Sleep now was kind; it flowed within her – like a river.

She understood no pain; all that was happening was happening from a force of persuasion. She had worked so hard for this moment, this moment when the past could be reckoned with and the present – for she knew it now – was the birth of a baby.

'Susan.' Madeleine had addressed her mother. She could still hear the voice of Madeleine cutting through the dark. 'Are you unhappy?' Catherine had conceived of that moment many times, a horrific crash, a scream, her scream. Madeleine had taken her and put her to bed. Sweat had oozed.

'Be easy, child,' Madeleine had said. 'Be easy.'

At the door the eyes of the English couple had stared, a point of fixation. They'd seemed so inane that Catherine had quietened, reflecting on the human race. She was ten now. She was growing up.

She'd run in the fields, she'd talk to sheep, she'd sit in the garden eating honey. She'd dance to the music of the gramophone as Aunt Madeleine typed an essay about Bucharest for some English newspaper.

Visitors were scarce now; Aunt Madeleine was drinking port and murmuring to herself and one summer's day in the garden she'd begun weeping as bees hummed about her. That had been one of the first of these flights. Many followed. Her lips were growing redder from port and her voice more cackly. A woman who'd been no more than a guardian for Catherine was emerging as a personality. The shock of seeing Madeleine talk to her mother had given way to curiosity. Catherine would stand at the top of the stairs as Aunt Madeleine recited poetry in a blue nightdress at the bottom. It was not poetry by Yeats but poetry by an obscure Rumanian poet about whom Aunt Madeleine had written a book. Sometimes she'd cackle away in words of Rumanian, mixing them with remarks about wine, about bridges in Paris, about church railings in Trieste. Aunt Madeleine was becoming obsessed.

One day as the gramophone was playing *Tales from the Vienna Woods* Catherine had found Aunt Madeleine sleeping in a chair in the garden, port slipping from her mouth like blood.

The following winter Catherine had trailed to school. Aunt Madeleine was spending much of her time in bed. Catherine would make her cocoa and Aunt Madeleine would speak about the jackdaws outside. 'Such noisy creatures,' she'd remark, 'such noisy creatures.'

Catherine was now in the position of looking after Aunt Madeleine. Sometimes when Catherine entered her room she looked more like a man. One day Aunt Madeleine had risen from bed, put on her good clothes, brought Catherine to Dublin. They'd climbed Nelson's Pillar, they'd munched a strawberry ice-cream in a café beside the bridge. They'd walked avenues sprouting with blossom. Both of them had sometimes stared, bewildered at the beauty of the city. Catherine was now twelve. Having seen enough films at the cinema in Carrick-on-Suir to have become acquainted with devious pasts she was now beginning to realize Aunt Madeleine had a divided history. That day on an avenue near Trinity College an old man with a white beard had called Madeleine. He'd come running towards her. He'd had gold in his white hair and a cap on his head. Madeleine had stared at him. Her eyes had been like frightened butterflies. 'Peter,' he'd kept saying. 'Peter.' Aunt Madeleine had kept babbling. She'd spoken of books, of a novel she had begun writing. Eventually she'd said 'I killed him. I know that.'

The train back to Wexford had taken them through countryside burning with spring. Aunt Madeleine had kept uttering under her breath, 'When all the wild summer was in her gaze.'

As summer approached she worked continuously on her novel, seated by a table in the garden, a silk robe with an orange sun on the back flowing on her, her narrow fingers tapping the typewriter. One day her manuscript had flown away and she'd shrieked, pursuing the leaves until she had the last one, sodden in a pond where a water-lily was about to jump open.

A publisher had arrived from London, a newspaper man. There were photographs of Aunt Madeleine sitting on park benches in Trieste in the English Sunday papers. She had been rediscovered. Her years peeled away in the garden. There was a pink robe she wore that summer and tulips sprung like strangers. Catherine was now growing up in a world of the literary élite.

Madeleine's novel was a huge success. Others of her books were reprinted and one day in autumn some years later Catherine and Aunt Madeleine had packed their bags and left for London. Aunt Madeleine had been awarded a literary prize. Catherine had been grabbed from boarding school and with Aunt Madeleine she crossed the Irish Sea. They'd landed in Wales, taken a train to London and there stayed in a house white as wedding cake in a square where leaves were falling, and Catherine bemoaned the fact she could not appear in *The White Horse Inn* at school.

She hadn't been away in boarding school long enough not to notice that behind the beautiful features which were re-forming on Aunt Madeleine's face was fear. Sometimes on visits to the school those features had seemed blotched and awkward.

What was it Aunt Madeleine was seeking to hide? Where were the secrets? Catherine would have wandered the house demanding answers had she not had a fleeting fancy for a teacher at school who looked like Marianne Faithful.

To the house in the square had come men grown old before their time and women young in years but old in expression. London's literary world had convened. Catherine had attended the odd lesson given by a Rumanian in Bedford Square and returned to find pictures of Yeats on the wall and old men speaking of magic.

She had stopped outside the oak doorway to the living-room one day. 'Peter was a man of remarkable charm,' an old man was saying. 'He was one of the most remarkable poets of his time. Someday that shall be known.'

That evening Aunt Madeleine had stalked about; young men were coming to the house now. They were driving up in red sports cars and Aunt Madeleine was wearing mini-skirts. She'd had power over age. She was as one of the young models of London. She had been seeing a particular young man with hair like summer sunsets, gold and pale and partly blond. He'd been angelic. He'd worn red handkerchiefs in his pockets and occasionally a young woman telephoned, enquiring for him. Aunt Madeleine had taken him to her bedroom more than once. Once they'd screamed at one another. He'd left. Aunt Madeleine had stood on top of the stairs weeping. Catherine had touched her. 'We're going,' she'd said. 'We're going looking for him.'

In the following days Aunt Madeleine had swept along to Greek Orthodox churches, to Russian Orthodox churches. She'd lit candles before ikons. She'd whispered devotions. She'd summoned five older people to the house and performed a seance. This time Catherine had sat in the room next door reading a book by Hans Christian Andersen, realizing for the first time her aunt's all-out preoccupation with the dead. There'd been the seance with her mother when she'd been ten. There'd been the pictures of Isis among the teddy bears of childhood, there'd been chants her aunt had uttered, there'd been herbs she'd chosen on hills in midsummer. All this had been submerged in the stronger occultism of the area, crumbling castles, decaying teachers, whispering flowers.

Aunt Madeleine was now making no secret of it. Catherine had listened that evening. 'It's no good,' her aunt had said next door. Catherine had wandered through the house and picked up her aunt's book on the tarot, opened it on the hanged man, an illustration of a noose about a man's neck. 'The force of tribulation is in this card,' the commentary had read. Catherine had thumbed further through the book. Outside a wind was blowing up and she'd realized, page after page, that herein was contained a history. She'd been fifteen. She'd gone to the window, longed for Ireland, knew her life was beginning.

That evening Aunt Madeleine had announced, 'We're going to Europe.'

'Why?' Catherine had demanded. 'To seek him out?'

'He' was Peter. 'He' no longer was young men who called to the house or dapper princes with red limousines in London who took Aunt Madeleine out. 'He' was Aunt Madeleine's past.

Afterwards she would say to Adoe, what you grow up with you accept.

She'd accepted Aunt Madeleine, she'd lost herself in books, in primroses, in countryside. Now was the time, a sprightly fifteen-year-old she'd demanded questions, she'd asked herself the reason for Aunt Madeleine's extraordinary conglomeration of behaviour.

In later years she would meet young men in Dublin living-rooms who would quote Henry James to her. Certain quotations made sense. Quotations which indicated that there is a moment when personal search commences, search of roots, search of environment, search of past, present and sense of self.

She'd studied the reflection of her hair in a dark taxi which drove through London that evening, blonde on black, autumn outside, a penetrating chill in the leaves, in the faintness of light under a moonless sky.

They'd crossed to Ostend. 'Where are we going?' Catherine had asked. Her aunt had looked at her. She'd been wearing white. Her eyebrows had been defined in black. She'd looked at Catherine and as she had, Catherine had been astounded by the rocking of the ship. 'We're seeking him out. Haven't I told you?'

'Him.' Peter. That moment Catherine had assimilated all. There'd been a man. He'd ruined Madeleine's life. He'd haunted her.

They'd arrived in Brussels. It had been late at night. A shop had been open and they'd indulged in chips with mayonnaise on top. A woman with a kindly face had served them.

'I was in love,' Aunt Madeleine had said. 'I was in love. It was after my first book appeared. I was walking down Southampton Row one day with a rose on my dress when I saw him, I'd seen him in the newspaper the previous Sunday. I said hello. Peter was one of those people who emerge from nowhere. In the twenties there were many. G.I. Gurdjieff was one, men without backgrounds. Peter claimed to be Rumanian. I wrote about him as such. But he wrote in English. He had one of those faces that had registered wine, women, earthquakes, revolutions. He fell in love with me and I fell in love with him. We wrote to one another. We exchanged notes under chandeliers at crowded dinner parties. We confronted something in one another, what would you call it? That not easily defined substance, a soul. In Peter I saw the fruition of my youth, my work, my ability to write. He likewise saw such things in me.

'His work gravitated towards the very fine; there were whispers in his poetry of all kinds of occultism. From my background I was acquainted with the herbs of Wexford, the cards of the tarot, the cult of Isis. I'd spoken to Yeats of seances he'd observed in his youth and despite his warning I partook in the rites – at first but mildly then acquainting myself with the souls of the lonely, those who always came at will to the room wherein a seance is taking place. These were the things of my youth, certain potions for certain ailments, and a deck of cards that read the past as well as the future. But Peter's connections were more intimate with the supernatural. He'd discussed evocation of evil with dignitaries of a certain cult known to touch on a world of which many people were aware at the time, a world wherein were amassing forces of evil which were going to take over the world. These people wished to control these forces. Perhaps out of good, perhaps because of interest in power. Talk of power was everywhere, power over words, power over people.

'Peter and I journeyed up and down the east coast of Ireland; we stopped in houses where we partook of seances and spoke to dead elders. We travelled to Europe; 1936. The year Mussolini rode into Abyssinia I rode into the Mediterranean with Peter on a horse at Saintes Maries de la Mer in the South of France. It was in October, in honour of St Sarah, patroness of gipsies. We were on a voyage, in the heat of autumn we drank wine, smoked Turkish cigarettes; there were cracked mirrors in every little hotel but in our way we knew we were projecting elegance, that extraordinary quality only young people can project, a perfect image of life, a stability the wise can never know. There were bottles of red wine and young men in white suits. Europe was going to pieces but we travelled like patterns on wallpaper to Cairo; we, a poet and a young lady writer, were part of the effulgence of Europe before collapse. We were the cool flowers before the 'blood-dimmed waters' rose. Such knowledge forced us to pray one day; in a church in Sardinia, the two of us on wooden pews.

'Going back on our path, however, we were drawn into knots of Peter's friends, those with contacts in Scotland, England, Ireland. At first our meetings with these people were friendly. Then they were otherwise. Partaking in a seance in Gibraltar I knew our mission was not holy, Peter's friends were trying to control the spiritual rather than allowing the spiritual to control them. They were delving into the interior of a spiritual landscape, a landscape born of evil. They were victims of a desire that surpassed sanity. They desired a say in a new ascendancy, an ascendancy of evil.

'How can I tell you why I became involved? I became involved out of love. I loved Peter. He loved me. He was more victim than I. He'd dabbled in something. It had become his life!'

Catherine had folded her nightdress carefully the following morning. She and Aunt Madeleine had let the light in. They'd boarded a train to Paris. It was to be the location. They were going to try to contact Peter.

'Love,' Aunt Madeleine had explained, 'is a strange thing. It occurs less frequently than we imagine. It is the most surprising and most nourishing thing in life. It is indeed holy. That is why I want to go back and contact Peter. I love him. When we arrived in Paris during the spring of 1937 Peter began thrusting himself into the company of a girl mixed up in his group. This group was making strange wooden instruments. They were preparing for a final evocation of the forces they'd attained to. I recognized waywardness in myself. Though not a Catholic I prayed at the Sacré Coeur. I knew he loved me. About me he'd written the finest of his poetry.

Now this distortion was coming over him. He was leaving me to drink wine alone in a hotel, going off, making love to a Finnish girl. I forgave him twice. The third time I said I was leaving. It was in the hotel room. It was nearly June. There were roses, partly yellow, partly red. He seized them and stuck the thorns on his wrists until the red of his blood commingled with the red of the roses. I took a bag and made to go, stayed with him, made love, knew there couldn't be anything in my life more holy than this.

'I awoke with him in the late evening to dreams of flowering trees in Wexford. We walked by the Seine. We knew we were utterly, utterly in love. Yet it was as though there was a wall in front of us. I said I was leaving the group. There was almost a grotesque look on Peter's face. He continued going to their meetings. He did not see the Finnish girl. I was writing a novel. One day he did not come back. He stayed away three days. I wished to kill myself, not out of love for him but because I knew there'd be no other love. He returned. I knew he'd been with the girl. It was drawing near expiration time for his group. They were about to summon the forces of – of the Anti-Christ. I said goodbye to him. I walked to Gare du Nord. Here, suitcase in my hand before boarding the train, I wished him dead.

'Peter's body was found in a small hotel which had burnt down some days later. There were roses outside, I saw by the newspaper photographs. I returned to Ireland. I told my friends who were Peter's friends I had killed him, but they said his death was an atonement, that the time had not yet come for the intended resurrection of the powers of evil, that there was still time to go. That time I suppose came with the first bombs on Notting Hill Gate. I became like a ghost during

these years. I became unhappy and yet knew that my unhappiness was a source of possible reparation. I wished to
speak to Peter again. There was no card in the tarot which
would speak of him. And I had only myself to talk to. In time I
held parties. Young men came to them and one called Alec I
fell in love with. We went to Paris together. I conceived his
child. The child was born mongoloid and died. I knew I
should not have returned to this city. I went back to Wexford
and there raised you, Catherine. There were times I made to
speak to Peter. I could not contact him. In Paris now I know he
will come. It is best I speak to the dead.'

She should have known the unholiness of the mission. Yet
Aunt Madeleine had convinced her of the exigencies of their
affair, an affair which hung halfway between God and the
devil, an affair which included into its substance fat roses on
spring days in Paris in the temporal haze before the war. 'I
know,' Aunt Madeleine had said, 'that life is short. There are
certain things within one's life one must guard like new
unopened roses. Such was my affair with Peter. It was all such
a terrible mistake, our dabbling in this magic. The young are
wont to make mistakes. It seems like a dream now, the
purpose of our seances in Gibraltar and Paris. But the real
nightmare was in the human heart, the heart which couldn't
distinguish and protect love when it had arrived.'

In Paris they'd made tracks to the house of a Russian woman
whom Aunt Madeleine had conversed with. It had occurred to
Catherine that they were partaking in more than a backward
journey, this was the journey of a soul towards the point of its
possession. She'd chosen cards from the tarot in the following
days. Always the card of the hanged man had attained the most
prominent place.

The Birth of Laughter

In their little hotel Catherine had studied Yeats, had read her aunt's novels and knew there were times in history that were irrevocably evil – such a time was her aunt's time. Aunt Madeleine unknowingly had slipped into dimensions of evil through an innocent affair, and the unfortunate succumbing to things supernatural, things dangerous.

Aunt Madeleine had arranged a seance with the Russian woman as medium. All the time the prominence of youth seemed to ride on her face. Catherine had been frightened. She'd warned her aunt against it, her aunt had insisted. They'd entered a dark room. She needn't have partaken if she hadn't so desired but something in her had insisted. She'd desired to know the darkness of her roots, and the inability of extraordinary and innocent people like Aunt Madeleine to cope with their fates.

The baby was coming. It was pushing forward. Catherine's eyes opened. She thrilled to see Adoe knowing her last sight of him had been in the garden before the baby had begun. His eyes sparkled, ingrained with copper points. She made to reach him, then saw Peter's face as she'd encountered it at that seance in Paris, collapsed writhing, screaming, until the density of hell seemed to burst from her.

Afterwards she'd struggled to know about such phenomena. In some seances it is reported that the medium can take the shape of the spirit she aspires to communicate with. This is called an ectoplasm. That evening in Paris such a strangeness had occurred. The Russian woman's face had transformed into Peter's ashen resemblance.

How much of what Aunt Madeleine had told her was true she'd never know. All she'd known was that Aunt Madeleine's involvement in evil had been greater than she'd admitted; love there may have been between her and Peter but her involvement in the group had been greater than she'd explained.

She'd been a high-priestess in this unfortunate cult. She'd cursed Peter when he'd sought to escape it.

She'd returned to Ireland on his death. Ever since she'd tried to build a shrine of images, of actions to him in order to reach him again. These images, those actions had accumulated in that ghastly seance in Paris when Catherine had screamed and her aunt had shot out of the door, hollering 'I'm evil. I'm evil. I'm evil.'

The truth had emerged, laden with the horror of its homecoming. The ancestral castle had been the starting point in a European cult to aggravate the forces of evil, provoke them to a point of emergence whereby they could be harnessed. This plot was known to few and poets like Yeats and young statesmen had visited the castle, knowing only its jovial side and the effulgence of its roses.

Catherine had never walked its paths again until she'd returned with Adoe. The facts about Aunt Madeleine she'd picked up in a witch hunt among Dublin elders. Aunt Madeleine had been incapacitated since that evening in Paris. When Catherine had taken an overdose of weed-killer in her final year at school Aunt Madeleine had visited her in hospital, an ashen effigy. When she'd fallen in with a theatre group in Dublin to which Adoe had belonged, Aunt Madeleine had appeared, strictly forbidding her against men and especially those involved in theatre. 'They bring wounds,' she'd said, 'they bring your downfall.'

They'd been sitting in one of Bewleys oriental cafés when Catherine had noticed the tears in Aunt Madeleine's eyes and knew her to have repented. She'd been in love once. Wasn't that all you could judge her on? Peter had fallen in love with another woman, a Finnish girl belonging to a circus who had tried to persuade him away from a world of spirits, incantations and words about an apocalypse.

There had been an old man sitting behind Aunt Madeleine. Catherine had asked herself, 'How can I know about a generation other than my own? Above all how can I judge its torments, its fears, its movements – its indulgences?'

She'd been playing the young girl in *A Month in the Country*, her first main role, when she'd learnt Aunt Madeleine had died. It had been the time when yellow tulips would be nosing themselves unsuccessfully around the castle walls. Aunt Madeleine had passed away in her cottage. The funeral had taken place in Dublin. It had been a May day, a day of flowering horse-chestnuts, a day of sunshine. Men of state had gathered, old men, ikons of Irish history. Catherine had wondered, perceiving the few men of literature, the men of state, how close to respectability and respectable quarters Aunt Madeleine's divinations had come.

An elderly gentleman with a beard turned to gold by acute rays of sunshine had read an oration. The puzzle was over. Catherine had turned away from the grave, the past was buried, save for the few intimations old men gave her of Aunt Madeleine's involvement or the questions asked of her by theatre people who presumed her to be an expert in the tarot.

Her eyes grazed with sunshine. She awoke. In front of her Adoe stood, he was holding a child. The child had his circuitous brown eyes. He bent, kissed her. She slept. This time her sleep was easier and her dreams wound with them a trail of January snowdrops, a smile of Aunt Madeleine, one of those extraordinary smiles she gave when she'd made a sponge cake, iced it with caramel and recalled the vibrancy, the possibilities of being young, raven-haired and a woman of talent, of 'exceptional talent' as the blurbs read and the old men stuttered, over whiskeys, at literary parties or on the streets of Dublin, Paris, London a long time ago when fogs descended more easily and circumstances always seemed to point to a world somewhere beyond our own.

ELIZABETH BOWEN

Hand in Glove

J asmine Lodge was favourably set on a residential, prettily
wooded hillside in the south of Ireland, overlooking a river
and, still better, the roofs of a lively garrison town. Around
1904, which was the flowering period of the Miss Trevors,
girls could not have had a more auspicious home – the
neighbourhood spun merrily round the military. Ethel and
Elsie, a spirited pair, garnered the full advantage – no ball,
hop, picnic, lawn tennis, croquet or boating party was
complete without them; in winter, though they could not
afford to hunt, they trimly bicycled to all meets, and on frosty
evenings, with their guitars, set off to soirées, snug inside their
cab in their fur-tipped capes.

They possessed an aunt, a Mrs Varley de Grey, née Elysia
Trevor, a formerly notable local belle, who, drawn back again
in her widowhood to what had been the scene of her early
triumphs, occupied a back bedroom in Jasmine Lodge. Mrs
Varley de Grey had had no luck: her splashing match, in its

time the talk of two kingdoms, had ended up in disaster – the well-born captain from a cavalry regiment having gone so far as to blow out his brains in India, leaving behind him nothing but her and debts. Mrs Varley de Grey had returned from India with nothing but seven large trunks crammed with recent finery; and she also had been impaired by shock. This had taken place while Ethel and Elsie, whose father had married late, were still unborn – so it was that, for as long as the girls recalled, their aunt had been the sole drawback to Jasmine Lodge. Their parents had orphaned them, somewhat thoughtlessly, by simultaneously dying of scarlet fever when Ethel was just out and Elsie soon to be – they were therefore left lacking a chaperone and, with their gift for putting everything to some use, propped the aunt up in order that she might play that role. Only when her peculiarities became too marked did they feel it necessary to withdraw her: by that time, however, all the surrounding ladies could be said to compete for the honour of taking into society the sought-after Miss Trevors. From then on, no more was seen or heard of Mrs Varley de Grey. ('Oh, just a trifle unwell, but nothing much!') She remained upstairs, at the back: when the girls were giving one of their little parties, or a couple of officers came to call, the key of her room would be turned in the outer lock.

The girls hung Chinese lanterns from the creepered veranda, and would sit lightly strumming on their guitars. Not less fascinating was their badinage, accompanied by a daring flash of the eyes. They were known as the clever Miss Trevors, not because of any taint of dogmatism or book-learning – no, when a gentleman cried, 'Those girls have brains!' he meant it wholly in admiration – but because of their accomplishments, ingenuity and agility. They took leading parts in theatricals,

lent spirit to numbers of drawing-room games, were naughty
mimics, and sang duets. Nor did their fingers lag behind their
wits – they constructed lampshades, crêpe paper flowers and
picturesque hats; and, above all, varied their dresses marvel-
lously – no one could beat them for ideas, nipping, slashing or
fitting. Once more allowing nothing to go to waste, they had
remodelled the trousseau out of their aunt's trunks, causing
sad old tulles and tarlatans, satins and *moiré* taffetas, to appear to
have come from Paris only to-day. They re-stitched spangles,
pressed ruffles crisp, and revived many a corsage of squashed
silk roses. They went somewhat softly about that task, for the
trunks were all stored in the attic immediately over the back
room.

They wore their clothes well. 'A pin on either of those two
would look smart!' declared other girls. All that they were
short of was evening gloves – they had two pairs each, which
they had been compelled to buy. *What* could have become of
Mrs Varley de Grey's presumably sumptuous numbers of this
item, they were unable to fathom and it was too bad. Had
gloves been overlooked in her rush from India? – or, were
they here, in that *one* trunk the Trevors could not get at? All
other locks had yielded to pulls or pickings, or the sisters
found keys to fit them, or they had used the tool-box; but this
last stronghold defied them. In that sad little soiled silk sack,
always on her person, Mrs Varley de Grey, they became
convinced, hoarded the operative keys, along with some
frippery rings and brooches – all true emeralds, pearls and
diamonds having been long ago, as they knew, sold. Such
contrariety on their aunt's part irked them – meanwhile,
gaieties bore hard on their existing gloves. Last thing at nights
when they came in, last thing in the evenings before they

went out, they would manfully dab away at the fingertips. So, it must be admitted that a long whiff of benzine pursued them as they whirled round the ballroom floor.

They were tall and handsome – nothing so soft as pretty, but in those days it was a vocation to be a handsome girl; many of the best marriages had been made by such. They carried themselves imposingly, had good busts and shoulders, waists firm under the whalebone, and straight backs. Their features were striking, their colouring high; low on their foreheads bounced dark mops of curls. Ethel was, perhaps, the dominant one, but both girls were pronounced to be full of character.

Whom, and still more when, did they mean to marry? They had already seen regiments out and in; for quite a number of years, it began to seem, bets in the neighbourhood had been running high. Sympathetic spyglasses were trained on the conspicuous gateway to Jasmine Lodge; each new cavalier was noted. The only trouble might be, their promoters claimed, that the clever Trevors were always so surrounded that they had not a moment in which to turn or choose. Or otherwise, could it possibly be that the admiration aroused by Ethel and Elsie, and their now institutional place in the local scene, scared out more tender feeling from the masculine breast? It came to be felt, and perhaps by the girls themselves, that, having lingered so long and so puzzlingly, it was up to them to bring off (like their aunt) a *coup*. Society around this garrison town had long plumed itself upon its romantic record; summer and winter, Cupid shot his darts. Lush scenery, the oblivion of all things else bred by the steamy climate, and perpetual gallivanting – all were conducive. Ethel's and Elsie's names, it could be presumed, were by now murmured wherever the Union Jack flew. Nevertheless, it was time they should decide.

Ethel's decision took place late one spring. She set her cap at the second son of an English marquess. Lord Fred had come on a visit, for the fishing, to a mansion some miles down the river from Jasmine Lodge. He first made his appearance, with the rest of the house party, at one of the more resplendent military balls, and was understood to be a man-about-town. The civilian glint of his pince-nez, at once serene and superb, instantaneously wrought, with his great name, on Ethel's heart. She beheld him, and the assembled audience, with approbation, looked on at the moment so big with fate. The truth, it appeared in a flash, was that Ethel, though so condescending with her charms, had not from the first been destined to love a soldier; and that here, after long attrition, her answer was. Lord Fred was, by all, at once signed over to her. For his part, he responded to her attentions quite gladly, though in a somewhat dazed way. If he did not so often dance with her – indeed, how could he, for she was much besought? – he could at least be perceived to gaze. At a swiftly organised river picnic, the next evening, he by consent fell to Ethel's lot – she had spent the foregoing morning snipping and tacking at a remaining muslin of Mrs Varley de Grey's, a very fresh forget-me-not-dotted pattern. The muslin did not survive the evening out, for when the moon should have risen, rain poured into the boats. Ethel's goodhumoured drollery carried all before it, and Lord Fred wrapped his blazer around her form.

Next day, more rain; and all felt flat. At Jasmine Lodge, the expectant deck chairs had to be hurried in from the garden, and the small close rooms, with their greeneried windows and plentiful bric-à-brac, gave out a stuffy, resentful, indoor smell.

The maid was out; Elsie was lying down with a migraine; so it devolved on Ethel to carry up Mrs Varley de Grey's tea – the invalid set very great store by tea, and her manifestations by door rattlings, sobs and mutters were apt to become disturbing if it did not appear. Ethel, with the not particularly dainty tray, accordingly entered the back room, this afternoon rendered dark by its outlook into a dripping uphill wood. The aunt, her visage draped in a cobweb shawl, was as usual sitting up in bed. '*Aha*,' she at once cried, screwing one eye up and glittering round at Ethel with the other, 'so what's all this in the wind today?'

Ethel, as she lodged the meal on the bed, shrugged her shoulders, saying: 'I'm in a hurry.'

'No doubt you are. The question is, will you get him?'

'Oh, drink your tea!' snapped Ethel, her colour rising.

The old wretch responded by popping a lump of sugar into her cheek, and sucking at it while she fixed her wink on her niece. She then observed: 'I could tell you a thing or two!'

'We've had enough of *your* fabrications, Auntie.'

'Fabrications!' croaked Mrs Varley de Grey. 'And who's been the fabricator, I'd like to ask? Who's so nifty with the scissors and needle? Who's been going a-hunting in my clothes?'

'Oh, what a fib!' exclaimed Ethel, turning her eyes up. 'Those old musty miserable bundles of things of yours – would Elsie or I consider laying a finger on them?'

Mrs Varley de Grey replied, as she sometimes did, by heaving up and throwing the tray at Ethel. Nought, therefore, but cast-off kitchen china nowadays was ever exposed to risk; and the young woman, not trying to gather the debris up, statuesquely, thoughtfully stood with her arms folded, watching tea steam rise from the carpet. Today, the effort required seemed to have been too much for Aunt Elysia, who collapsed on her pillows, faintly blue in the face. 'Rats in the attic,' she muttered. 'I've heard them, rats in the attic! Now where's my tea?'

'You've had it,' said Ethel, turning to leave the room. However, she paused to study a photograph in a tarnished, elaborate silver frame. 'Really quite an Adonis, poor Uncle Harry. From the first glance, you say, he never looked back?'

'My lovely tea,' said her aunt, beginning to sob.

As Ethel slowly put down the photograph, her eyes could be seen to calculate, her mouth hardened and a reflective cast came over her brow. Step by step, once more she approached the bed, and, as she did so, altered her tune. She suggested, in a beguiling tone: 'You said you could tell me a thing or two. . . ?'

Time went on; Lord Fred, though forever promising, still failed to come quite within Ethel's grasp. Ground gained one hour seemed to be lost the next – it seemed, for example, that things went better for Ethel in the afternoons, in the open air, than at the dressier evening functions. It was when she swept down on him in full plumage that Lord Fred seemed to contract. Could it be that he feared his passions? – she hardly thought so. Or, did her complexion not light up well? When there was a question of dancing, he came so late that her programme already was black with other names, whereupon he would heave a gallant sigh. When they did take the floor together, he held her so far at arm's length, and with his face turned so far away, that when she wished to address him she had to shout – she told herself this must be the London style, but it piqued her, naturally. Next morning, all would be as it

was before, with nobody so completely assiduous as Lord Fred
– but, through it all, he still never came to the point. And
worse, the days of his visit were running out: he would soon
be back in the heart of the London Season.

'Will you ever get him, Ethel, now, do you think?' Elsie
asked, with trying solicitude, and no doubt the neighbourhood wondered also.

She conjured up all her fascinations. But was something
further needed, to do the trick?

It was now that she began to frequent her aunt.

In that dank little back room looking into the hill, proud
Ethel humbled herself, to prise out the secret. Sessions were
close and long. Elsie, in mystification outside the door, heard
the dotty voice of their relative rising, falling, with, now and
then, blood-curdling little knowing laughs. Mrs Varley de
Grey was back in the golden days. Always, though, of a
sudden it would break off, drop back into pleas, whimpers and
jagged breathing. No doctor, though she constantly asked for
one, had for years been allowed to visit Mrs Varley de Grey –
the girls saw no reason for that expense, or for the interference
which might follow. Aunt's affliction, they swore, was confined to the head; all she required was quiet, and that she got.
Knowing, however, how gossip spreads, they would let no
servant near her for more than a minute or two, and then with
one of themselves on watch at the door. They had much to
bear from the foetid state of her room.

'You don't think you'll kill her, Ethel?' the out-of-it Elsie
asked. 'Forever sitting on top of her, as you now do. Can it be
healthy, egging her on to talk? What's this attraction, all of a
sudden? – whatever's this which has sprung up between you
two? She and you are becoming quite hand in glove.'

Elsie merely remarked this, and soon forgot: she had her own fish to fry. It was Ethel who had cause to recall the words – for, the afternoon of the very day they were spoken, Aunt Elysia whizzed off on another track, screamed for what was impossible and, upon being thwarted, went into a seizure unknown before. The worst of it was, at the outset her mind cleared – she pushed her shawl back, reared up her unkempt grey head and looked at Ethel, unblinkingly studied Ethel, with a lucid accumulation of years of hate. 'You fool of a gawk,' she said, and with such contempt! 'Coming running to me to know how to trap a man. Could *you* learn if it was from Venus herself? Wait till I show you beauty. – Bring down those trunks!'

'Oh, Auntie.'

'Bring them down, I say. I'm about to dress myself up.'

'Oh, but I cannot; they're heavy; I'm single-handed.'

'Heavy? – they came here heavy. But there've been rats in the attic. – I saw you, swishing downstairs in my *eau-de-nil*!'

'Oh, you dreamed that!'

'Through the crack of the door. – Let me up, then. Let us go where they are, and look – we shall soon see!' Aunt Elysia threw back the bedclothes and began to get up. 'Let's take a look,' she said, 'at the rats' work.' She set out to totter towards the door.

'Oh, but you're not fit!' Ethel protested.

'And when did a doctor say so?' There was a swaying: Ethel caught her in time and, not gently, lugged her back to the bed – and Ethel's mind the whole of this time was whirling, for tonight was the night upon which all hung. Lord Fred's last local appearance was to be, like his first, at a ball: tomorrow he left for London. So it must be tonight, at this ball, or never!

115

How was it that Ethel felt so strangely, wildly confident of the outcome? It was time to begin on her coiffure, lay out her dress. Oh, tonight she would shine as never before! She flung back the bedclothes over the helpless form, heard a clock strike, and hastily turned to go.

'I will be quits with you,' said the voice behind her.

Ethel, in a kimono, hair half done, was in her own room, in front of the open glove drawer, when Elsie came in – home from a tennis party. Elsie acted oddly; she went at once to the drawer and buried her nose in it. 'Oh my goodness,' she cried, 'it's all too true, and it's awful!'

'What is?' Ethel carelessly asked.

'Ethel dear, would you ever face it out if I were to tell you a certain rumour I heard today at the party as to Lord Fred?'

Ethel turned from her sister, took up the heated tongs and applied more crimps to her natural curliness. She said: 'Certainly; spit it out.'

'Since childhood, he's recoiled from the breath of benzine. He wilts away when it enters the very room!'

'Who says that's so?'

'He confided it to his hostess, who is now spitefully putting it around the country.'

Ethel bit her lip and put down the tongs, while Elsie sorrowfully concluded: 'And your gloves stink, Ethel, as I'm sure do mine.' Elsie then thought it wiser to slip away.

In a minute more, however, she was back, and this time with a still more peculiar air. She demanded: 'In what state did you leave Auntie? She was sounding so very quiet that I peeped in, and I don't care for the looks of her now at all!' Ethel swore, but consented to take a look. She stayed in there

116

in the back room, with Elsie biting her thumb-nail outside the door, for what seemed an ominous length of time – when she did emerge, she looked greenish, but held her head high. The sisters' eyes met. Ethel said, stonily: 'Dozing.'

'You're certain she's *not* . . . ? She *couldn't* ever be – you know?'

'Dozing, I tell you.' Ethel stared Elsie out.

'If she *was* gone,' quavered the frailer sister, 'just think of it – why, we'd never get to the ball! – And a ball that everything hangs on,' she ended up, with a scared but conspiratorial glance at Ethel.

'Reassure yourself. Didn't you hear me say?'

As she spoke Ethel, chiefly from habit, locked her late aunt's door on the outside. The act caused a sort of secret jingle to be heard from inside her fist, and Elsie asked: 'What's that you've got hold of now?' 'Just a few little keys and trinkets she made me keep,' replied Ethel, disclosing the small bag she had found where she'd looked for it, under the dead one's pillow. 'Scurry on now, Elsie, or you'll never be dressed. Care to make use of my tongs, while they're so splendidly hot?'

Alone at last, Ethel drew in a breath, and, with a gesture of resolution, retied her kimono sash tightly over her corset. She shook the key from the bag and regarded it, murmuring, 'Providential!', then gave a glance upward towards where the attics were. The late spring sun had set but an apricot after-glow, not unlike the light cast by a Chinese lantern, crept through the upper storey of Jasmine Lodge. The cessation of all those rustlings, tappings, whimpers and moans from inside Mrs Varley de Grey's room had set up an unfamiliar, some-what unnerving hush. Not till a whiff of singeing hair announced that Elsie was well employed did Ethel set out on the quest which held all her hopes. Success was imperative – she must have gloves. Gloves, gloves . . .

Soundlessly, she set foot on the attic stairs.

Under the skylight, she had to suppress a shriek, for a rat – yes, of all things! – leaped at her out of an empty hatbox; and the rodent gave her a wink before it darted away. Now Ethel and Elsie knew for a certain fact that there never *had* been rats in Jasmine Lodge. However, she continued to steel her nerves, and to push her way to the one inviolate trunk.

All Mrs Varley de Grey's other Indian luggage gaped and yawned at Ethel, void, showing its linings, on end or toppling, forming a barricade around the object of her search – she pushed, pitched and pulled, scowling as the dust flew into her hair. But the last trunk, when it came into view and reach, still had something select and bridal about it: on top, the initials E. V. de G. stared out, quite luminous in a frightening way – for indeed how dusky the attic was! Shadows not only multiplied in the corners but seemed to finger their way up the sloping roof. Silence pierced up through the floor from that room below – and, worst, Ethel had the sensation of being watched by that pair of fixed eyes she had not stayed to close. She glanced this way, that way, backward over her shoulder. But, Lord Fred was at stake! – she knelt down and got to work with the key.

This trunk had two neat brass locks, one left, one right, along the front of the lid. Ethel, after fumbling, opened the first – then, so great was her hurry to know what might be within that she could not wait but slipped her hand in under the lifted corner. She pulled out one pricelessly lacy tip of what must be a bride-veil, and gave a quick laugh – must not this be an omen? She pulled again, but the stuff resisted, almost as though it were being grasped from inside the trunk – she let go, and either her eyes deceived her or the lace began to be drawn back slowly, in again, inch by inch. What was odder was, that the spotless finger-tip of a white kid glove appeared for a moment, as though exploring its way out, then withdrew.

Ethel's heart stood still – but she turned to the other lock. Was a giddy attack overcoming her? – for, as she gazed, the entire lid of the trunk seemed to bulge upward, heave and strain, so that the E. V. de G. upon it rippled.

Untouched by the key in her trembling hand, the second lock tore itself open.

She recoiled, while the lid slowly rose – of its own accord.

She should have fled. But oh, how she craved what lay there exposed! – layer upon layer, wrapped in transparent paper, of elbow-length, magnolia-pure white gloves, bedded on the inert folds of the veil. 'Lord Fred,' thought Ethel, 'now you're within my grasp!'

That was her last thought, nor was the grasp to be hers. Down on her knees again, breathless with lust and joy, Ethel flung herself forward on to that sea of kid, scrabbling and seizing. The glove she had seen before was now, however, readier for its purpose. At first it merely pounced after Ethel's fingers, as though making mock of their greedy course; but the hand within it was all the time filling out . . . With one snowy flash through the dusk, the glove clutched Ethel's front hair, tangled itself in her black curls and dragged her head down. She began to choke among the sachets and tissue – then the glove let go, hurled her back, and made its leap at her throat.

It was a marvel that anything so dainty should be so strong.

So great, so convulsive was the swell of the force that, during the strangling of Ethel, the seams of the glove split.

In any case, the glove would have been too small for her.

The shrieks of Elsie, upon the attic threshold, began only when all other sounds had died down . . . The ultimate spark of the once-famous cleverness of the Miss Trevors appeared in Elsie's extrication of herself from this awkward mess – for, who was to credit how Ethel came by her end? The sisters' reputation for warmth of heart was to stand the survivor in good stead – for, could those affections nursed in Jasmine Lodge, extending so freely even to the unwell aunt, have culminated in Elsie's setting on Ethel? No. In the end, the matter was hushed up – which is to say, is still talked about even now. Ethel Trevor and Mrs Varley de Grey were interred in the same grave, as everyone understood that they would have wished. What conversation took place under the earth, one does not know.

JOHN B. KEANE

'You're on Next Sunday'

Y ou'll find more than a few to tell you that there isn't a
  word of truth in the following story and the nearer you
come to the place where it happened you'll find a lot more.
When I taxed the man who told me the story with these facts
he took his pipe from his mouth, spat into the fire and looked
me between the eyes for an embarrassingly long spell. He did
not speak but when he returned the pipe to his mouth I knew
that the tale was true and that those who belied it were either
knaves or fools.

It happened on the fifteenth day of August in the year of our
Lord, as they say in these parts, nineteen hundred and thirty-
four. It was a fair year for primroses, a better one for hay and a
woeful year for funerals.

The Fifteenth as it is still called locally is the annual Pattern
Day in the lovely seaside resort of Ballybunion. From all
quarters of Kerry, Cork and Limerick would come thousands
of country people in every mode of conveyance from bike to

omnibus to Shanks's mare and pony cart. They still come but in nothing like the vast numbers of yore.

That particular Fifteenth, as I recall, broke fair and clear. Skies were blue. The air was fresh and wholesome and there was a hearty trace of fine breeze from the west. At the creameries and dispensaries that morning man, woman and child wore happy faces.

' 'Tis a great day for the Fifteenth,' they would say to each other and back would come the reply, 'Ah sure 'tis a great day entirely.' At quarter to eleven in the noon of the day my grand-uncle Morrisheen Digley went forth to the haggard to catch the pony and at the turn of the noon he set forth for Ballybunion in his newly varnished trap. It would do your heart good to see the dancing legs of the pony and the squinting sparks on the flinty road when his iron-shod hooves made light of the long haul. I did not go on the occasion. He said I was too young. Instead he called for his old crony Thady Dowd of Lacca. Neither of the two was under seventy but none gamer set out that day for Ballybunion.

They untackled the pony in the back yard of Mikey Joe's American Bar and celebrated their arrival at the Pattern with two glasses of potstill whiskey. This was followed by a brace of pints, pints of creamy black porter. These were consumed so that the remains of the whiskey might be entirely scoured from the gullet, a most advisable practice this if one is to believe those who are fond of indulging in such procedural drinking.

Towards evening they walked as far as the beach to savour the salt sea air and to partake of a paddle near the shore. According to the old people there was nothing the equal of a paddle in the salt water to cure what might be wrong with you. It was pleasant on the shore. The fresh Atlantic breeze was sharp and bracing but as yet without its late autumnal sting. There were hundreds like themselves pacing up and down, ankle deep in the water, content to dawdle aimlessly until the anxiety for drink returned.

In the village they met neighbours from the townland of Lacca and between them they started a sing-song in one of the public houses. When darkness fell a great hunger for meat seized them. They repaired to a café where they were served with succulent steaks and roast potatoes. This was followed by two dishes of rich trifle and the lot was washed down by several cups of strong, well-sugared tea.

'This will make a handy base for more drink,' my grand-uncle announced to Thady Dowd. Dowd nodded agreement happily. So far the pair had enjoyed themselves thoroughly and the night was still but a starry-eyed child in swaddling clothes. The best was to come. After the meal they embarked on a grand tour of the village pubs and they had a drink in every single one.

At this stage the reader will begin to raise an eyebrow or two and wonder what is the purpose in the retelling of such a commonplace narrative. Was not their visit to the Pattern but a replica of other years, a common jaunt indulged in by thousands of others and all following the same predictable course?

Patience, dear reader, and bear with me. As soon as the time came to close the pubs three pairs of well-made civic guards appeared on the street and by their presence ensured that every tavern was cleared. The publicans were grateful enough for theirs had been a long and arduous day. By this stage Thady Dowd and my grand-uncle had more than their share of strong drink but for the purpose of shortening the road home they invested in a half pint of whiskey apiece at Mikey Joe's American Bar.

Earlier they had plied the pony with a sufficiency of oats and when they came to tackle him they found him in excellent fettle. Like all animals who have spent a long day away from the green pastures of home he was full of taspy for the task before him. As soon as he found the open road free from obstacles he started to jogtrot in real earnest. Overhead a full moon lit up the countryside and the sky, its full complement of stars visible in all its quarters, shone like a treasure-house. In the body of the trap the semi-drunken companions sang at the top of their voices to the steady accompaniment of the pony's clopping hooves.

They sang song after song and from time to time they would uncork their whiskey bottles and partake of wholesome slugs. This made them sing all the louder and soon every dog in the countryside was responding. There was an unholy cacophony as the miles fell behind them.

Then, suddenly, for no reason whatsoever the pony stopped in his tracks and despite their most earnest entreaties would not be coaxed into moving a single, solitary inch.

'What's the matter with the creature anyway?' Thady Dowd asked indignantly.

'Beats me,' said my grand-uncle. All around there was an unearthly silence save for the chuckling of the Gale River which lay just ahead of them spanned by a narrow bridge. It was the same Gale that poor Spenser the poet did not forget when he wrote about Irish Rivers. On the left the crosses and tombstones of Gale Churchyard stood pale and grey in the drenching moonlight. The pony stood rooted to the roadway, head bent, his whole frame taut and tense. There was white foam at the corners of his mouth and a look of abject terror, terrible to behold, in his bloodshot eyes.

'I don't like the look of things,' my grand-uncle whispered.

'A rattling damn I don't give,' Dowd shouted, 'I'm getting out of here to see what the matter is.'

'Stay as you are,' my grand-uncle counselled but there was no stopping the headstrong Dowd. He jumped on to the roadway and walked round trap and pony several times.

'There's nothing here,' he called out. He then proceeded towards the river thinking that some calamity might have overtaken the bridge and that the pony, with its animal instinct, might have sensed this. The bridge was in perfect order. Dowd looked over its twin parapets into the shallow, warbling water. He could see nothing unusual.

He retraced his steps and with a scornful toss of his grey head went towards the graveyard of Gale. As soon as he entered the little by-road which led to the gateway the pony lifted its head and followed slowly. It is well to remember that at no time did my grand-uncle leave the trap. He sat stiffly, holding the reins, carefully following his friend's every move.

When Dowd leaned across the gate of the graveyard he emitted a loud yell of genuine surprise. There before him were two hurling teams dressed in togs, jerseys and slippers. Every hurler had a hurley in his hand and at one side sitting on a low tombstone sat a small inoffensive-looking, bald-headed man. He wore a white jersey as distinct from the two teams who wore red and green respectively. He had a sliotar or hurley ball in one hand and in the other he held an ancient, burnished, copper hunting horn.

The pony had stopped dead a second time opposite the gateway over which Dowd was leaning.

'Come away out of that,' my grand-uncle called out, 'and leave the dead to themselves.'

'What's the use?' Dowd called back, 'the pony won't budge till it suits these people.'

'What's the matter?' he called out to the hurlers who stood about as if they were waiting for something special to happen. At first no one heeded him but when he called out belligerently a second time a tall player with a face the colour of limestone approached the gate. He explained to Dowd that he was the captain of the red-jerseyed hurlers but that the game could not start because his team was short a man.

'Who are these teams anyway?' Dowd asked cheekily. The captain explained that his team was Ballyduff and the other team Ballybawn.

'Ho-ho,' cried Dowd exultantly. 'I'm your man. My mother, God be good to her, was a Ballyduff woman. If you have no objection I will play with your team.'

The captain nodded silently and when my grand-uncle called to Dowd to abandon his arrant foolishness the captain turned and addressed him where he sat in the trap.

'Not an inch will you or your pony move,' said he in a hollow, haunted voice, 'until the final horn is sounded in this game of hurling.' My grand-uncle said no more. The pony stood now like a statue and the sounds of the river were no longer to be heard. Overhead the moon shone brightly and the pitch which was the length and breadth of the graveyard, was illuminated as though it were floodlit. Forms appeared from the ground and sat themselves on the graveyard wall. The referee looked upwards at the moon and after a few moments wait blew upon the hunting horn. Then he threw in the ball.

The exchanges started slowly enough with Dowd's team, Ballyduff, getting the worst of it from a faster Ballybawn side. The first score came when the referee awarded a free puck to

Ballybawn. He also cautioned a number of the Ballyduff players, notably Dowd and the captain, for abusive language towards himself and for dirty play in general.

The Ballybawn skipper drove the ball straight between the uprights. On the graveyard walls the partisans went wild and a fist fight broke out near the gate. Somebody flung an empty cocoa canister at the refereee and he threatened to call off the game if the crowd did not behave themselves. There were a number of fistic exchanges on the field of play but by and large the standard of hurling was as good as my grand-uncle had seen for many a day. There were many fluent movements and excellent long-range scores. The wrist work and pulling left little to be desired. Half time came and went and now the two teams were playing for all they were worth. Time was slipping away and with five minutes to go the sides were level.

Neither would yield an inch. Every player strove manfully to register the single score that would put his own team ahead of the other. The ghostly forms jumped up and down on the walls egging the players on to greater deeds.

It seemed as if the game must end in a draw and the grand-uncle noted that from time to time the referee looked nervously at the full moon and feverishly fingered his hunting horn, anxious for full time to roll round so that he might wash his hands of the whole affair. There is nothing a referee loves so dearly as a drawn game. The hopes of both sides are kept alive and it is unlikely that he will be assaulted as he leaves the pitch. With less than a minute remaining there was a mêlée at midfield in which Dowd was involved. Fists flew and hurleys were raised. More than once could be heard the clash of ash against doughty skulls.

The referee intervened and taking a scroll from his togs'

pocket he commenced the business of taking names. It was during this lull that Dowd sat on a convenient tombstone to savour a richly-merited breather. He withdrew the half pint bottle from his trousers pocket and dolefully surveyed the remnants of his whiskey. The bottle was still quarter full. He raised it to his lips and without once taking it from his head swallowed the contents. Almost immediately he heaved a great sigh which could be heard all over the graveyard. Then he tightened his trousers' belt and waited for play to resume.

With seconds remaining the hunting horn was sounded yet again and the ball was thrown in. Dowd it was who won possession. With a fierce and drunken yell he cut through his opponents like a scythe through switch-grass with the ball poised on the base of his hurley. There were times when he darted like a trout and times when he bounded like a stag. He leaped over gravemounds and skirted crosses and tombstones at breakneck speed. All the time he edged his way nearer the opposing goal line.

Seeing an opening on the left wing he seized his chance and headed straight for the goal with the entire Ballybawn team on his heels like a pack of hungry hounds. Thirty yards out he stopped dead and took a shot. The ball went away to the right but if it did it passed through the eye of a Celtic cross and rebounded off the head of a plaster angel. The rebound was deflected towards the goal by the extended hand of the figure of Michael the Archangel. It skimmed the left upright and found its way to the back of the net. Need I mention that while the ball was travelling so was the empty whiskey bottle which Dowd, with sound foresight, had flung at the Ballybawn goalkeeper as soon as the referee's back was turned. The crowd went wild. The Ballyduff team and supporters milled around Dowd and embraced him. Then they lifted him aloft and trotted round the graveyard on a lap of victory. Finishing the lap the Ballyduff captain called for three cheers for their visitor. Three eerie ullagones went heavenwards and died slowly till the muted river sounds took over once more. The teams had suddenly vanished save for the tall, ghostly presence of the Ballyduff captain. For the first time in over an hour the pony stirred. He pawed the dirt roadway, anxious for the high road.

'Come on at once,' my grand-uncle called. Dowd, escorted by the captain, made his way towards the gate where the pony was now prancing and difficult to restrain. Dowd shook hands with the captain and was about to depart when a ghostly hand was laid firmly on his right shoulder. The captain leaned forward and whispered into Dowd's ear. Whatever it was he said Dowd's face underwent a terrible change. The glowing red nose was now puce-coloured and the rosy, whiskey-tinted cheeks were ashen grey. Slowly, almost painfully, he climbed across the gate while the captain faded like a breeze-driven mist behind him.

In the trap Dowd was silent and thoughtful. On his face was a woebegone look that struck a chill in my grand-uncle's heart. The pony highstepped his way homewards, his dark mane flowing loosely behind him, his firm rump bobbing up and down as the miles passed by.

Finally my grand-uncle popped the question.

'What in heaven's name did he say to you?' he asked. Dowd shook his head sadly before he replied. Then he spoke slowly and deliberately with a crack in his voice.

'He informed me,' Dowd announced, 'that because of the way I played tonight I would be on for good next Sunday.'

PETER SOMERVILLE-LARGE

Rich and Strange

Jack Colley's eldest child had known our daughter in playgroup years, then at school. They had been in and out of each other's houses, tongues orange from ice lollies, sharing roller skates, bicycles and felt pens. Deirdre came to our house more than Rachel went to hers; in winter we ran our central heating regularly and our place never smelt of nappies. They played upstairs or in the garden as weather dictated; they slumped over the same homework and skimped it to watch the children's programmes. Deirdre's cheeks bulged a little into her jaw like a bloodhound or a pear. Her flaxen hair was beginning to have dark streaks, and would end up mousy or dark brown. She had round eyes like one of her dolls, making her look surprised.

From time to time she brought over her sleeping bag to spend the night, usually, it seemed, when she was about to acquire another sibling. On those occasions Jack and his aptly-named Breda distributed their children among friends and relatives for the duration of Breda's stay at the Rotunda.

Relationships with the parents of children's friends have an element of gradual coercion. Our acquaintance with the Colleys progressed from shared school runs to female coffee mornings to formal entertainment to an exchange of small Christmas presents. In roughly the same time that the Black Death took to cross Asia and Europe, we found ourselves friends. Jack wasn't a bad fellow. He worked in local government, where his job, though not all that well paid, was inflation-proof and promised an adequate pension. The boys had their names down for Gonzaga. He ran a big car, while Breda drove an ancient Morris Minor. Morris Minors have acquired a disreputable image, and tend to be driven by mountainy men or delinquent teenagers; but the Colleys' was grey and clean with a respectability that belonged to a previous decade. Both cars, like ours, were insured with the Private Motorists Protection Association. We didn't have all that much more in common.

For several summers running we took our holidays in rotation, since we lived in the same neighbourhood. In this way we could watch each other's houses and feed the other family's cat. The Colleys used to go abroad to some place like Benidorm or Lido di Jesolo, leaving behind a baby or two with Breda's mother. Then came the year when, like a lot of other people, they were kept at home by the falling pound. Jack bought a second-hand Sprite caravan and planned to take the whole family to Kerry. Breda's people came from there, and she had memories of holidays on relatives' farms.

Our holiday occurred first. We were back at the end of July, and a week later the Colleys made their ponderous departure, starting early in the morning. We waved from the bedroom as

the Sprite passed, rattling over the concrete on its way towards
the Limerick road.

That summer was exceptionally hot. In our suburb the long
spell of glittering weather became a time to be endured.
During August I escaped the office fairly often, and we drove
to beaches south of the city. The Colleys sent us a postcard
from Dingle with a picture of two currachs. But there were
other things to think about besides the Colleys and after they
returned we didn't see them until school began. The first days
of September ended the hot weather abruptly so that the
children went back in rain. On the Friday of the second week
of September when I came home from work I found a sleeping
bag in the hall.

'Deirdre's staying,' Anne told me.

'What's wrong?'

'Breda's not well.'

'Miscarriage?'

Anne's voice took on the hush of scandal.

'A bit of a breakdown. Dr Byrne's sending her to the
psychiatric unit at Elm Park. I feel terrible not having once
seen them since they got back . . .'

'Will we be stuck with Deirdre for weeks?'

'Not at all. Only a couple of days. Breda's mother is coming
up to take charge.'

'Poor old Jack. I'll give him a ring later on.' These things
have become less embarrassing. In our suburb psychiatric
troubles are more common than adultery.

'You won't get anything out of him.'

'I didn't mean that. I just feel sorry for the poor bastard.'

'All he would say when I asked him was that she was under
a bit of stress.'

'Anyone who takes five children off in a caravan is looking for stress.'

In the end I left Jack and his troubles to himself. Over tea I noticed that the children were all in bad form. There was none of the usual giggling among the girls, no nudging or back-chat or teasing Tommy. In fact, hardly any conversation at all. I knew that Anne wanted to pump Deirdre about her mother, but there was something formidable about the child's reserve. I tried to ease things up with a few knock knock jokes and questions about school, and Miss Synott's boy friend, a subject that usually promoted ribald laughter. Not a stir from either of them. Deirdre turned down her eyes like a propositioned nun.

Anne laid out her sleeping bag as usual on our safari bed which was set up in Rachel's room. The girls didn't play or talk late. After midnight Deirdre woke us with screams. She couldn't remember, she said, when I asked, what the bad dream had been about.

Ten minutes after we had all settled down I found Rachel standing beside my bed.

'Go back to your room at once.'

'She's at it again.' We listened. We could hear her across the passage, not so loud, more like groans.

'The same silly word,' Rachel said.

As usual Anne had closed her eyes again with a deter-minedly sleepy grunt. I have always been the one to get up and cope with the children. I put on my dressing-gown again and walked over into Rachel's room, half-lit by the light on the landing. Deirdre thrashed about in her sleeping bag, mutter-ing.

'Misericordia, misericordia . . .'

'That's what she was saying before.'

Her face was covered with perspiration. I debated whether to wake her, when she solved the problem by waking herself.

'Another dream?' She nodded and put her thumb in her mouth. I went down to the kitchen to fetch a couple of mugs of hot milk, knowing that Rachel would insist on having one too. When I got back upstairs, both of them were lying quite silently in their respective beds. As I gave Deirdre two Junior Aspirin, I asked her, 'What's all this about misericordia? Is it a word that you hear in church?' Her upper lip, its line emphasised by a white moustache of milk, drew back like an angry cat. Her round eyes didn't have a look of surprise, but of terror.

'Never mind . . .' Rules were suspended, and I read aloud a soothing passage from *A Bear Named Paddington*. Then we went back to sleep. I remembered that Mass has been said in English for the past decade or so.

Next morning the girls seemed fine, as is so often the case after a wicked night, while Tommy had slept through it all. Anne wanted to drive to Superquinn for Saturday's big shopping. In the usual way we would have all gone together so that I could help with the bags of groceries and the children could spend their pocket money. But the rain was pouring down, and after all the excitements Anne and I both felt that it might be better if the children and I stayed at home and she managed on her own. The girls seemed indifferent while Tommy was persuaded with a promise of extra sweets. None of them really wanted to go out in the wet.

After I had washed the breakfast things I settled down in the kitchen with the paper. When the yells came from the playroom I only felt annoyance. They were of a type instantly recognisable, the unmistakable sounds of resentful children in unison making a noise like angry sheep.

'What's going on up there?' Rachel seemed to be siding with her brother, something I had hardly known her to do since the time Tommy began to speak. In the end I went storming upstairs.

Tommy keeps his Action Man meticulously, far better than Rachel maintains her dolls. His model has a beard, a fair pelt moulded to his rubbery little face. His wardrobe includes the uniforms of a Commando, a tank commander, a Red Devil and a storm trooper, while he possesses accessories like a rifle rack, a mortar and a belt-feed machine-gun.

He was not dressed in his Commando clothes that Saturday, or in any of his other outfits. He wore a long shirt, borrowed from a teddy bear.

He had been hanged.

It gave me quite a shock to see him. The gallows, made out of Lego, was on two legs with a bar across like a football goal without the net. His hands were tied behind him with knitting wool and the noose was also made out of wool which had been strengthened by being plaited. Rachel and Tommy stood crying, but they didn't touch him. They let him hang, his plastic toes a couple of inches above the cork tiles of the playroom floor. Deirdre looked on serenely.

She didn't object when I cut the Action Man down with nail scissors. Tommy stopped crying, to test his soundbox by pulling a string and listening to him give orders in an American accent, telling his men to go over the top or something similar. Thankfully Anne came back soon after to sort things out. After lunch the rain was still coming down, so they chose to look at television. But that also ended in a row.

'What was it this time?'

Anne said, 'They wouldn't agree on what to watch. Deirdre is becoming impossible. She wouldn't look at the film on RTE and she and Rachel were struggling with the knobs – they almost had the set over. There's only racing or wrestling on the English channels.'

'What was it about? Something horrific? She seems in such a funny state.'

'It was only an old pirate film. Stewart Granger. Deirdre's seen far more grisly things in her time. Remember when we all went to *Jaws*?'

The children continued to bicker so that several times Rachel came to Anne and tried to win her sympathy with a whining tale. Then the television improved, and they sat down silently watching it. I gave Jack a ring, but there was no reply; we concluded that he must have gone down to Naas to fetch his mother-in-law. Anne rang round her friends to find out what their opinion was about giving Deirdre a spot of Valium. I don't know what the verdict was, but the night passed more or less undisturbed. Although the child called out several times, she didn't wake the others, and was deeply asleep the couple of times I went across to her.

When I took her home on Sunday morning Breda's mother was there to greet us. In the kitchen there was a smell of roasting meat, and three of the younger children were seated on the windowseat in front of a table littered with crisp bags, Blu-tack, Playdough, paper and felt pens. After giving her grandmother a kiss Deirdre went straight upstairs to the chilly bedrooms above. I accepted a cup of coffee and made stilted conversation with the old lady while I drank. When I finished I said, 'I'd like a word with Jack sometime.'

'He's out front,' she said.

'Oh?'

She let me go and seek him out myself while she attended to the cooking. He was slumped in an armchair in the sitting room, a couple of unopened Sunday papers beside him. He held a drink and stared out through the double-glazed windows at the rain. He half-turned when he heard the door opening.

'Is that you, Brian? Help yourself.'

'I've had coffee with Mrs Gorman. I brought Deirdre back.'

'She all right?'

I hesitated. 'A bit off colour, we thought.'

'In what way?' His voice was sharp.

'She seemed to be having quite a few nightmares.'

'Anything else?'

'Nothing really. Just one or two little things that seemed to indicate she isn't quite herself.'

He wanted to know exactly. He was insistent, so I told him.

'I thought if she got away from the family she might be better . . .'

'What's the matter with her?'

'Do you really want to know?' He immediately began to tell me at length the things he hadn't discussed with the family doctor, the psychiatrist or the priest. (But later on I ran into a couple of people who had heard the same story from him.) After he had talked for a bit I accepted a drink, and by the end of the morning we had killed the bottle.

He said that the holiday had gone very well – for most of the time. No problems going down, apart from the odd child getting car sick. They went right to the west end of the Dingle peninsula where a farmer near Dunquin rented them a site in a small stonewalled field. There was a view of the sea across the

Blaskets towards the pointed peaks of the Skelligs eight or nine miles to the south. The same view they kept showing in *Ryan's Daughter*. The Sprite was a great success – the interior very clean, made more so by Breda. Deirdre and the babies slept in it with their parents, while the two boys had a tent. The weather was perfect and they worked out a routine. Every morning Jack would take all the children down the lane to Krugers to shop while Breda made up the bunks, cleaned the sinkful of Tupperware and put the washing to soak. After that most days they went to some beach for a picnic. Jack fitted in a good bit of golf. The boys played football while Deirdre spent a lot of time on a school project – collecting shells, or wild flowers which she put in jam-jars or pressed in books.

The sun never stopped shining. A couple of days before they left, the wind died altogether and it became too hot, even in the early morning. The air was stagnant, the sea looked like glue, the Blaskets were turned into sea monster's humps. As they sat round the greasy breakfast plates, the curtains were drawn to keep out the sun.

The boys were shouting for football, while Deirdre wrote neat labels. Breda had a naggy look similar to Deirdre's air of concentration. She was needling Jack about his golf and the round of drinks afterwards that kept him away from his beloved family which would soon be going back to school. Once term began they would see less of their Daddy. He gave in without too much reluctance, because of the heat. He'd made no firm commitment to play. So they got off quite early that day on their picnic.

They left Dunquin, driving past the little mound that is known as Uaig Ri na Spainne – the Grave of the Sun of the King of Spain – under Mount Eagle and the black claw of

Dunmore Head to Coumeenole Bay. About a half dozen other holiday families were there already. They joined them, taking down the baskets, rugs and newspapers. Jack put up canvas chairs for himself and Breda and erected the canvas windbreak, more to create a patch of shade than anything. The little white beach, facing south-west, shimmered against the glaring blue of the sun-lit water.

Jack and the children swam while Breda cut the bread and divided up the ham and tomatoes and hardboiled eggs, and poured orange squash into plastic mugs. After they had eaten, the parents had their flask of coffee while the children received their daily handout of sweets. Then the elder ones drifted off.

'No more swimming for now,' Jack called as they made their way down to the limp wave line. Breda, wearing dark glasses, read the paper. The babies, in sun hats, pottered near her. Jack slapped lotion on himself.

When he first heard Deirdre's cries he knew it was her straightaway. Sitting up in the glare he looked over the wind-break; he could only pick out two members of his family from the figures strewn along the beach. The boys were standing beside their football which was only visible against the sand because of its hexagonal black markings.

He thought she must be drowning. 'My God, where is she?' He looked seawards; in the distance he could see the fuzzy shape of the Great Blasket, and between it and him the oily current flowing over the Stromboli rocks in a way that seemed to set them moving. He searched the shore line. The cries were difficult to pinpoint, but people were looking round.

'There!' Breda shrieked. He felt nothing but relief when he located her at last. In fact she was well away from the water, up above the tide mark, a plump little figure standing with her hands over her eyes making this terrible racket. He ran over, Breda gathering up babies and following more slowly. When he got to where she was, her mouth was still wide open in a gape and her eyes were still covered with her hands.

'What is it, darling?' Taking her in his arms, he looked for cuts from broken glass. He had to shout to make himself heard. He couldn't see any blood.

'Stop them!'

'Stop what, treasure?'

'Stop the killing.'

He carried her back towards Breda. A couple of people looked up curiously as Deirdre's wails, making a counterpoint to the song on their transistor, passed them. Gradually her sobs subsided into sniffs and gasps. Once, though, she cried out suddenly, 'They're screaming, Daddy.'

Breda could do nothing with her. She'd be quiet for a bit and then start crying again. She was attracting attention so that in the end they collected everything and drove back. Jack gave up the idea of golf and endured the atmosphere in the stifling caravan for the rest of the day. The babies were fractious, the boys quarrelled and Deirdre sat huddled on a bunk. Breda thought she might have a spot of sunstroke, but her temperature was normal. Between the fits of sobbing she was almost silent, answering her parents in monosyllables without even a 'Mummy' or 'Daddy' tacked on. If they tried to question her the crying was worse. That night was the first in which she kept calling out in her sleep.

Next day Jack took the boys off, leaving Breda to pack. Deirdre insisted on staying behind with the babies. She did her own version of packing by taking her jam-jars of shells and carrying them over to a ruined cabin that stood on the edge of the field. She threw them all in among the nettles. When Jack was collecting his things together he missed the good leather-handled hammer from his tool-box. He found it easily enough not far from the Sprite, lying beside a stone on which there were the crumbling remains of a substance which he identified as coral from a big piece Deirdre had found on a beach a week before. Stuck to some of it was a piece of lead that had once been round, but was now flattened by blows of the hammer.

When they got back to Dublin Deirdre continued to be difficult. Sometimes she seemed to improve, but then it would be the same thing all over again. The night the weather broke with a thunderstorm she screamed so loudly that a neighbour heard and complained. Her teacher telephoned specially to enquire what was wrong. The family doctor recommended a psychiatrist; there was something of reproach in the hectoring questions he asked them.

'I think his hint that it was all our fault finally drove Breda over the edge.' Jack filled up our glasses. 'He couldn't even make anything out of the drawings.'

'What drawings?'

'I'll show you.' He went over the nylon carpet with its bright pattern of pinwheels to the book shelf on the right of the rough stone fireplace. Searching among the Reader's Digest condensations, Leon Uris's Trinity reverently displayed as if it were indeed a holy book, and the Harold Robbins and Arthur Haileys, he pulled out a stack of library books and finally the AA Book on Ireland which had a wad of papers in it.

'When she got home she did nothing for a few days and then she began to draw. The same thing, time and again. Of course drawings are meat and drink to these boys and he was very interested. He said to encourage her – that drawing would provide a form of therapy which would help her work out her trauma. He asked if Deirdre was a particularly imaginative child in my opinion. Would you say Deirdre was imaginative?'

'No.' He had spread out a number of papers on the coffee table. They showed a crude child's version of an old-fashioned sailing ship with four masts, a high poop, gun-ports and flags. It looked very battered.

'He was particularly interested in the torn sails and the crack in the hull. He said that distressed children often convey their feelings in drawings. Most kids like to draw trees and houses. If they do a tree . . . the roots represent the id, the trunk the ego, and the top the super ego.'

'What's that supposed to mean?'

'Jung and his people worked it all out. If the tree is emphasised rather than the roots the child is living in a fantasy world. Look at these ships, the way they float over the waves.'

I looked at them carefully. 'She might just have been trying to convey the effects of a storm.'

'You or I might think so. Not that laddo. He said that a child who has had a traumatic experience within its own family will often draw its house with a crack in it. And sometimes it will put in curtained windows – or cover the windows completely – that is another distress signal. And if it draws trees, another very common theme, they will often have boles which are very much emphasised. Often they will have smoke coming out of them. So your man interpreted these black portholes, and the little bit of smoke at the end of the cannon here and there, and the broken mast and torn sails and all the rest as interesting variations on usual run of the mill disturbed drawings. And he kept asking if Breda and I had had any significant disagreements over the holiday which might have affected the child. It wasn't until a couple of days after I saw him that I realised what nonsense he was talking and that what Deirdre was drawing was a lot of pictures of the Santa Maria de la Rosa.'

The books he had with him were Garrett Mattingly's Defeat of the Spanish Armada, Evelyn Hardy's Survivors of the Armada and Robert Stenuit's Treasures of the Armada. He first opened up the AA book and found an article on marine archaeology which had a clear little diagrammatic illustration. 'For a time I thought Deirdre was just copying from here. Look, she has the same details, the flags and pennant of the Vice Flag Ship of the squadron. And all the different shapes of the sails are right – I've checked. You can make them out, even though she has them torn. All except the foresail. And one mast broken. In every picture.'

His eyes looked glazed. 'She got it all right.' Now he was referring to passages in the library books marked with dog-eared pages. 'On September 15, 1588 two great ships came down the west coast to just off the Blaskets. They were galleons called the San Juan de Portugal and the San Juan Bautista. These were two that got away. They anchored for a time, and later set off again, and in the end they got back to Spain. But before that could happen there was a hell of a storm.'

He was referring to another book. 'This storm was on the 21st of September. It swept two other Spanish ships into the sound. One of them was the Santa Maria de la Rosa. She was a Mediterranean merchantman that had been specially con-verted for the Armada. She displaced 945 tons and carried

26 guns. She had a complement of 64 sailors and 233 soldiers. Plenty of gentlemen and proud Spanish hidalgos among them.'

I accepted another glass. He was taking his neat. 'At midday on the 21st she came into the sound nearer land on the north-west side. She fired a shot on entering as if seeking help, and another further on. All her sails were in pieces except the foresail. She anchored, but the anchor dragged and she struck the Stromboli rocks. She sank with all hands, just about.'

'How do they know all this?'

'The captain of the *San Juan Bautista* gave a deposition when he got home to Spain.' He paused. 'I'll tell you a thing about Deirdre. If you try and question her directly it's all dreams and nightmares. But if you ask her about the drawings she doesn't mind. She's usually quite pleased to answer. What do you make of this one?'

He pushed over another sketch of a sailing ship drawn with bright felt pens, the same as the others except that in the wavy blue sea was a black figure with its arms raised.

'When I asked her about him she said, "That's Juan." And I said, "One what?" And she said, very angry, "Not one. Juan. Hoo-an. He's not going to be drowned." That's when I went to the library.' He opened up another reference. 'Seemingly there was just one survivor. They captured him, and before they hanged him he gave evidence.' He read out: 'His ship broke against the rocks in the sound of the Bleskies a league and a half from land upon the Tuesday at noon, and all in the ship perished saving this examinate, who saved himself upon two or three planks . . .'

'Oh come on, Jack, she's having you on . . . She's read about it somewhere.'

'She can only just read.'

'Well then, she's learnt about it at school.'

'Breda and I have had to have a couple of sessions with Miss Synott. I asked her specifically if the class had learned anything about the Armada. No, nothing.'

'What about television then?'

'It's possible.' He hardly considered it. 'Here's another, just to show you.' The ship with its torn sails and shattered hull was drawn with a curve of shore line on which some big curly waves were breaking. The sand, violently yellow, was scattered with what seemed to be piles of black sticks or seaweed.

'No, not seaweed. I asked her. Bodies, she said.'

The last picture he showed me was done with a black pen, and the lack of colour gave it an odd authenticity. This time the little figures had been drawn with great care, and some of them were good enough to put you in mind of Derricke's engravings in the *Image of Ireland*. Jack pointed out details as if it were a holiday snapshot.

'Here's poor old Giovanni or Juan on his gallows in this corner. And this is a group of local militia. These are the Spaniards they are killing.'

The two groups took up the centre of the page, the people on the right thrusting swords into those on the left. Several of the left-hand people were lying prone, within reach of a couple of men bending over them.

'They're stripping them of jewels and weapons.'

'But who are the ones being killed? I thought you said that Giovanni was the only survivor from the *Santa Maria de la Rosa*?'

'He's the only one mentioned in the history books.'

'Who are these supposed to be then?'

'They're more survivors. Deirdre saw them. They went

unrecorded. There were thousands of Spaniards off Armada ships being slaughtered all round the west coast, right? When it came to writing down what happened plenty of incidents like this must have been missed out. Giovanni gave evidence that a party went ashore from the *Santa Maria* to try and find water. There's not definite mention of their return. And the captain of the *San Juan Bautista* testified that two days before the storm Admiral Recalde who was on board his ship put fifty men ashore in an attempt to get supplies, but they were turned back by some soldiers. He wrote: "100 arquebusiers were marching, bearing a white standard with a red cross. It was concluded that they were English." '

'It seems unlikely they would have waited around for two days.'

'Not at all. We happen to know that there was a detachment of English soldiers at the west end of the Dingle peninsula. It was commanded by a man called James Trent, one of the Sovereign of Dingle's officers. His job was to watch over the Spanish ships anchored off Great Blasket Island. He actually wrote a letter in which he said. "We have two hundred men watching upon the shore every day. We stand in no fear of them" – he meant the Spanish – "for they are so much afraid for themselves." It's clear that Captain Trent's men did a little killing that never made the lists. Look.' Jack showed me another of Deirdre's pictures – a small group of soldiers, three of whom held old-fashioned guns with trumpet-like barrels. 'Arquebuses.' Another carried a standard with a red cross. It was the only bit of colour in the whole picture.

'I must go,' I said. 'Lunch will be waiting.'

AODH DE BLÁCAM

'Top of the Morning'

L ike the prodigal son, I suddenly found the whole glamour of my Bohemian life faded. I felt disinclined to go to the café that evening to hear my friends Gaston and Arsène arguing over their drinks, using the worn counters of pseudo-science and amateur philosophy in a profitless contest. Arsène would provoke the controversy with some new blasphemy of his idol, Stephen Mallarmé, and Gaston would reply with the stock answers of that Catholicism of which he talked of, but never practised.

'*Mais non*,' he would say 'all the ideals, see you, for which one makes sacrifices have objective realization in the spiritual world.'

That was his favourite dogma (and I'm not sure that it wasn't nearer to Platonism in his working out than to orthodoxy) – he thought it summarized all religion, and to him, religion, like art and politics, had no *raison d'être* but to serve as a topic for polemics.

I remembered all this with some disgust, though once I had found it amusing. Unbidden, my fancy turned homeward, and brimmed with familiar and alluring images, as if I had met my former self like a friend who has grown almost a stranger. I seemed to smell the Atlantic wind and feel it beat my face; I saw the huge clouds hosting from the sea to the haunted grey hills of Donegal; I saw the white cabins, the stone walls round the fields. . . . Desire surged up in me to see again the rainy island, to hear once more the homely Irish tongue.

When I landed in Dublin and tasted the Irish air, boarded the north-bound train, and travelled past the rich Midlands, with their borders of ancient hills, I seemed to pick up my life where I left it five years before, when I voyaged forth with my patrimony. It seemed but yesterday that I had seen these fields, for Ireland's countenance changes nothing through years and generations. But in that brief space my youth had burned away.

When I changed for the last time, now in the county of the peat-reek, I bought the local sheet. 'Twas as gay and gossiping as ever. It still printed an unreadable sermon in Irish and a column of Leaguer's personalities in English. It pleased me to read the familiar names. So old Pat Gallagher of Cashelbeg was dead: Lord have mercy on him. And Marie McGonagle married: the happy man's name was strange – I hoped for the best. And what was this? – Garret O'Malley's little schooner lost off Connemara, all on board reported drowned! . . . Well, well; I remembered Garret well, and his Quixotic character; how he thought his boat would be the nucleus of an Irish coasting marine. (Each of us had thought his hobby of vital import to Ireland in those days. It was odd, that people who remained in this forsaken place took so long to grow out of their ideals.) . . . When I reached my destination there was no one to welcome me. I splashed my way through the mud and darkness to the house that once had been my home. It was now an hotel, and I hired the very room in which I had seen my father lying dead five years ago.

I awoke next morning at daybreak, and looked forth from my window. The shadow lay before me to the foot of the slope, where the village rose in tiers of houses, clear and mellow in the morning light. It seemed as if God had just pencilled it upon the sky. The hills were banked at either hand, the cliffs showing at their broken edges. No blue segment bit the horizon, yet I knew that there behind my ken the ocean lay reflecting the same fleecy clouds that backed my picture. Then, where the houses were low, I saw the topmasts and tackle of some vessel, and strangely moved by the simple sight, I set out for the sea.

Now, as I went down the bohareen, through the outskirts of the little port, I seemed to enter a new Ireland. The place had a fresh, vigorous air, like that of a young colony, as if it were the Gael's 'Oileán Ur'. There lay a chain of neat, new villas where had reeked the squalid cabins; a sturdy hall stood on the place of the old 'hotel'. Over the houses, looming on the blue, was the lofty tripod structure of a crane over some big building operations. A train, with an immense load of timber, had just come down the line. And as I passed shops, I saw no English at all; every announcement that caught my eye was in Gaelic. Therewith I turned into a lane between the ware-houses, and, through the slender vista, saw the green glitter of the Atlantic under lifting haze.

When I reached the quay I beheld a spectacle fairer than any in Tir na n-Og. For in the harbour that was void from ancient times, rode many brave ships, all mirrored in the drifting, pearly tide. Against the sky that was flaked with clouds like a mirage of unseen beaches, flew the flags of France and Spain, and amongst them the Irish flag, as it was before our island and our peace were robbed from us. I stood awhile before the French ship, *L'Espérance*, watching the writhing figures of eight upon the water, listening to the creak of the busy derrick as the merchandise was swung into the hold, and wondering at the prosperity I had found. 'Surely the "cause" has prospered,' I thought. It was then that someone clapped my shoulder, and I looked up into Eoin Gallaher's blue earnest eyes, something, as it were, tightening within me.

'You've come back, too, at last, a Sheoirse?' says he, in cordial speech.

I began uncomfortably to ask his pardon for that insult that once estranged us. But he answered: '*Ní thuigim*. I remember no quarrel,' and, as if to change the subject, quoted the line: 'And did you see the *Cuilfhionn*?'

I looked up the quay with him, and saw a pigtailed cailin cycling recklessly near the dangerous edge. She passed a group of artisans going to their labours. One and all they saluted her, the foreman lifting his cap with the Tartarinesque pomp of your stout man, and loftily kissing the tips of his fingers.

'*Ce hí an cailin?*' I asked. 'She was like Noreen O'Cryan, but the O'Cryans are in the States.'

'Then they are in two places at once, for that is Noreen. Padraic Og is getting his learning at Clonmacnoise, and The O'Cryan himself is doing a thriving trade in timber here and at

Sligo. We're not the only folk at home, Vanity. Clery is expected daily, and O'Malley came last night . . .'

'O'Malley? But *An Deagh-Run* is reported sunk in last week's gale, and he carrying some cargo in her.'

'Indeed?' said Eoin, idly, pointing a thumb over his shoulder. 'But *bi gasta*, I'm coming to breakfast with you.'

Looking where he had pointed, I saw a newly-anchored vessel, sails drooping on the yards, and read on the stern, *An Deagh-Run*. 'Twas the *Good Intention* herself.

Then Eoin led me through the town that now was growing busy, and many there were that greeted us as they hurried to their duties in a way hitherto undreamed of in Portabeg. Some faces were familiar, but I could not give a name to one. There was a man like Tarlach of the Pipes, but he was only in the prime of life, not aged, like Tarlach. So I went through the crowd like a phantasmagoria, till we reached the foot of the bohareen to the house. Then Eoin fell back a little, cour- teously, as if to let me enter alone; almost, I thought, as one stands back from the meeting of lovers, or from the orphan, and he standing by the grave. The door opened, and against the dark interior a patient, familiar figure stood. I heard, as in the distance:

'*Dia do bheatha*, Eoin, Come in, come in . . . I wish you had my boy with you.'

I tried to cry the name of 'Father,' but was dumb. My eyes were darkened for a moment, and, when I saw again, the door was shut, the bohareen empty, and deathly clouds were hurrying over the sky.

My slatternish host came out. 'Where is Eoin Gallaher?' I asked, 'and where . . .'

'I am sorry, sir,' he said, gravely, and leading me to the

wall, pointed down to the churchyard. Amongst the white leaves men were toiling, digging a grave . . . I took his meaning.

That is my only ghost story. But there are dreams whose matter may be silly or incredible, yet their glamour clings about our waking life, as if, in them, the soul had gone through real experience, and had seen, in their quaint symbols, some vivid truth. I have wondered since whether Gaston's dialectics might not be in some sense true, and whether the vessels of our hopes that sink here may not sometime, somewhere, rise in happier seas.

MARY LAVIN

The Dead Soldier

W hen he was going away his mother and his sister Solly went up to Dublin to see him off. When they got off the train the sun still shone in the spaces between the city buildings, but by the time they had found their way to the docks it was dark. They stood under a lamp-post so they would be sure to pick him out from the other men as he marched past. When they heard the band in the distance they stood very close together, and when a crowd of children came running along in the dark, the old woman began to tremble. The soldiers would not be far behind.

The soldiers were marching four abreast. They advanced steadily, rank after dark rank, like the waves of the sea. And under the lamp-post, where the women stood, the black ranks foamed into faces, for a moment, and then went onward again, rank after rank, into the darkness where the river sirens wailed.

The women knew instinctively when Matty's rank was

coming near, and when his face shone in the light they took the full advantage of their eyes in staring at him. They smiled, and they put their hands to their lips. They waved at him. But they couldn't be sure if Matty saw them.

In the train going home again the old woman was desolate.

'If we ran as far as the next lamp-post we would have seen him again!'

'Now, Mother!' said Solly. 'You know yourself that Matty would not have wanted us to do that. He'd only be saying afterwards that we made a laughing stock of ourselves before the other men, two women running along the street thinking they were fit to keep up with the soldiers.'

'That's like what a daughter would say,' said the old woman. 'A son would never say the like of that. A son would never see anything to laugh at in his own mother, no matter what she did.'

'All the same, I'm glad we stayed where we were. We might have lost the way, and missed the train, if we went any farther from the station.' She looked out the carriage window at the pattern of the lighted city that was fading into the black sky, and she wondered what got into men that they wanted to go off to fight in a foreign country that meant nothing to them, one way or another. Matt was a real Irishman, if ever there was one, and yet he was one of the first in the country to give his name and go off to France, although the old woman cried and screamed and threw herself down on the floor and begged him not to leave her.

'Women don't understand,' was all Matty said.

'Leave the way!' he said to Solly, who had gone over to stand between him and the door.

'Stay where you are, Solly!' the old woman cried.

'I can't stop him, Mother, if he's set on going,' Solly said, and she had to stand aside and let him pass.

That was only four days ago, and now he was gone; and in a few hours the two of them would be back in the empty house, making up the fire that had never been let die out before, since the day the old woman came into the house as a young bride in a blue dress. Solly knew all about the blue dress. It had cerise bows down the front. The old woman was always talking about it. I suppose she'll never talk about it again, thought Solly. She'll talk about nothing but Matty now till the day he comes home again.

The talk about Matty began the minute they got into the house. As they made up the fire the old woman told Solly stories about the time he was a child. Even when Solly went out to the well she could hear the old woman talking to herself: laughing over some things and sobbing over other things. When she thought of the times she had been hurt and worried while Matty was growing up, she laughed, because those times were gone; but when she thought of the gay times, and the happy times, she sobbed, and wiped her eyes with her skirt, because those times were gone as well.

Both the chaff and the grain had gone on the wind, and the barren days had begun. In the house where seven men sat down to be served by the two women, there was no one now to sit down but the servers. Matty was the last of the men to leave home, and what lured him away was beyond the comprehension of any woman.

Week after week there was no other talk in the cottage, but talk about Matty. And when the priest called, he had to stay for an hour listening to an account of the time that Matty played hurley for the county. But when he was going he called Solly out into the yard.

'Let her talk about him all she wants. Don't stop her,' he said. 'It will be an ease to her mind.'

So when they got the news that Matty was killed, Solly knew she'd have to let the old woman talk away, day and night. So she went around the house all day listening to her and encouraging her. And when there was another death in the parish, she took the opportunity to try and console her mother.

'Murty Glynn is dead, Mother. He had a hard death. He was dying for three day and three nights. They said it was agony to look at him. Isn't any death better than that? Isn't a blow of a bullet a grand death compared with that?'

'I don't know. It's a great thing to die in your bed,' the old woman said.

'It's a great thing to die quick! You wouldn't want to think Matty was lying inside there in the room, twisting in agony, would you? Isn't it better to think of him maybe laughing one minute and maybe lying at peace the next?'

'I suppose you're right,' said the old woman. 'But it's a nice thing to be able to lay a body out, and see that he gets the best in candles and linen. It's nice to get a last look at it before it's put down into the grave.'

'It's not right to talk like that, Mother. It's flying in the face of God's goodness. I think it's nice to remember Matty like we last saw him, marching along to the sound of the band with a smile on his face. I'm glad I don't have to remember him as a corpse. All corpses look alike in my opinion.'

'You don't know what you're talking about, Solly,' the old woman said. 'Your own father was the handsomest corpse that was ever stretched. People that never knew him when he was alive came from miles just to see him laid out, he was such a handsome sight then. I can see him to this day, when I close my eyes, looking as fierce as when he was a living man. You'd think to look at his hands that he'd raise up one of them any minute, and brush away a fly that was flying around his face.'

'I'm glad I don't remember him,' Solly said, 'and I'm glad I didn't see Matty dead. I'm glad I remember him alive.' She took up a picture from the mantelpiece, a picture of two swans standing in a clump of bulrushes. The frame was engraved steel and there was no glass in it.

'I was thinking we could take out this picture, and put in one of Matty,' she said, and she took a prayer book from a shelf under the mantelpiece and pulling out a photograph, began to put it into the frame instead of the picture of the two swans.

'Be careful you don't tear that photograph while you're putting it in,' the mother said, leaning anxiously over Solly's shoulder and watching her every action. When she was satisfied that Solly was doing it carefully she picked up the picture of the swans in the bulrushes and put it into the prayer book, and put the prayer book back on the smoky shelf. 'Give me that frame, I'll shine it up a bit,' she said, wiping it in her skirt by rubbing it back and forth. Then looking at it, she wiped it back and forth again, until, apparently, she saw some improvement in it, and satisfied, put it back on the mantelpiece. She stared into the eyes of the photograph.

'I often saw him looking just like that,' she said. 'Didn't you?'

Solly took the picture and looked hard at it. 'Isn't it funny the different looks a person can have on his face, from one time to another, and yet when you think of them you think of them with the one look only on them. I always think of Matty the way he looked when he was passing under the lamp-post the night he went away.'

'If you were his mother you'd remember every look he ever had on his face from the day he was born to the last day you saw him. Do you mean to say you don't remember the way he looked when he came running in with the blood pouring down his face the time he fell on the broken pie dish in the yard and cut his head open?'

'No,' said Solly, 'I don't remember that day.'

'Don't you?' The old woman was surprised. 'Well, surely you remember the day he came racing up the yard with the geese after him, and his face red as the jersey on his back?'

'No,' said Solly, 'but now I come to think of it I do remember the way he looked in his uniform the first day he put it on, when he was showing us the map and marking out where France was. He had his cap pushed back on his head, and the track of it was across his forehead in a big red weal.'

'It's my opinion that that cap was too small for him,' said the mother. 'It was too tight across the forehead. It should have been a half-size larger.'

'He told you himself, Mother, that they don't look into half-sizes in the army!'

She smiled into the eyes of the photograph, thinking Matty would be pleased if he could hear her now consoling their mother. But the words had not penetrated far into the old woman's sorrow.

'No matter how many memories I have,' she said, 'it doesn't make up for not seeing him laid out in his own house. I don't like to think of them burying him in a hurry, along with a lot of other poor young fellows. I think to myself that, for all we know, it may have been night-time, and raining at that, and the place too dark and wet for them to kneel down and say a prayer for him!'

'Now, Mother, stop crying. You may be sure they knelt down and said a prayer for him, no matter how wet or dark it was, when they didn't know which of themselves would be the next to be shot.'

'I suppose you're right,' said the old woman. 'Anyway I thought by the letter the officer wrote that he wasn't the kind of man to throw down the spade out of his hands after burying a boy, and not wait to kneel and say a prayer.'

'You may be sure he said many a prayer,' said Solly, 'but of course, I don't suppose it was the officer himself who buried Matty!'

'He said in the letter that he did! "We buried him under a little ash tree," he said. "I know his mother will be glad to hear that." I was very glad to hear it. I say a prayer for that officer every night after I've said prayers for Matty and for his father, and for my own poor mother and father – God be good to them. I always say a special prayer for that officer who buried my son.'

'I suppose he was there at the time,' Solly said, 'but I think it likely he got someone else to do the digging for him!'

'I wouldn't give in to that,' said the mother. 'Matty was a nice lad. Everyone liked him. I never knew anyone yet that didn't take a liking to him, specially when he smiled. He had a lovely smile.'

Solly took up the frame and looked again at her brother's face. 'I couldn't get him to smile when I was taking this picture of him,' she said. 'He kept telling me to hurry up all the time. "Take the picture, can't you, if you're going to take it?'' he said. "I'm not aiming to stand here all day with the sun in my eyes!''

'I hope he wasn't lying in the sun when he was wounded,' the mother said suddenly. 'I heard Marg Mack and Maggie Cullen talking in the shop yesterday about a young lad who was wounded. Maggie's son wrote home to say that that young lad, whoever he was, was lying in the blazing sun for six hours before they found him, and they only got time to pull him over under a bit of a tree or a bush before the poor fellow died. "I'm glad I'm not going to die looking up at the bloody sun" was the last thing he said. They stopped talking when they saw I was listening. I suppose they thought I'd feel bad on account of my boy being killed in the war too. But I'd only love to hear them talking. You like to hear about other people's troubles when you have trouble of your own.'

'All the same, I wouldn't like to listen to those old gossips,' said Solly, 'they love to talk about people that are dead or dying, just to make themselves important.'

'You don't understand. You don't understand at all,' her old mother said. 'When I was walking home along the road, I was thinking of what they said, and I was wondering what was the last thing our Matty said. The officer didn't think to tell us that.'

'I'm sure Matty was praying,' Solly said, 'but maybe if the officer wasn't a Catholic himself he wouldn't think to put a thing like that in a letter.'

'That's right. I'm sure he was praying. He was a good boy. Still it's a great consolation for a mother if she has to lose a son, to see him slipping out of this world with his grip on a crucifix, and his lips moving at least, if he wasn't able to repeat the prayers of the priest.'

'Don't talk like that now, Mother,' said Solly. 'I've often heard tell that a soldier gets a special grace when he's dying. Many a one, they say, is saved at the last minute, just by thinking of the Judgment.'

'That's right. God is good,' said the old woman. 'I hope I won't have too long to wait now till I'm called myself to meet my dear ones.'

'And what about me?' said Solly. 'Have you no consideration for me, Mother, that you sit there talking about dying, and not remembering that I'd be all alone then, with no one at all to care what becomes of me or whether I get a bit to eat for myself or not?'

The old woman was staring into the fire and she didn't hear Solly. It was getting late and the fire was dying down. Solly took out a candle from the drawer of the dresser. She paid no attention to the fact that the old woman didn't answer her. She didn't expect an answer. Her own remark was an old one, well worn, and brought into use every time the old woman began to talk about dying.

'I think sometimes when I'm half asleep I see his face in the fire,' said the old woman, again, after a few minutes' silence.

'Take heed would you fall into the fire some night, staring into it like that, and you half asleep,' Solly said. 'Will I get your pillow, Mother, and put it by the fire, for a spell, to take the chill off it before you go to bed? It's getting late.'

The old woman looked up.

'I'm not going to bed yet,' she said. 'Do you not know what night it is?'

'I do,' Solly had hoped her mother had forgotten. It was All Souls' Night.

'My own poor mother, God be good to her,' said the old

woman, 'used say that the dead are sometimes allowed come back to their own fireside tonight, and sit down by the hob until the first light steals up through the trees.'

Solly went into the other room and came out with the pillow in her arms. 'Here's your pillow. Hold it to the fire for a bit, Mother, and then we'll go to bed. Don't be talking about ghosts. Listen to the wind under the door! I wish there was a man in the house to put a bit of cement on the floor, there by the hinge. That's where the wind is coming in.'

'My father used to laugh at my mother,' the old woman continued, as if she had not been interrupted. 'He used to tell her that if it was as easy as all that to come back from the grave, there wouldn't be such a dread on people at the thought of going into it.'

'That's what I say too,' Solly said.

'When I was a child, old people had strange notions.'

'Old people are always the same. I wouldn't wonder to hear that you were thinking of sitting up all night yourself to see if Matty would come back!' Solly said, and she gave an awkward laugh, and stood back out of the circle of the lamp so that she could look at the old woman. She had an idea her mother might have a notion of staying up and she wanted to laugh her out of it. The old woman threw a big sod of turf on the fire.

'Why are you putting on turf at this hour of the night, when we're going to our beds?' Solly asked.

'It's raking down the fire every night that has this house as damp as it is,' said the old woman. 'It's no harm to have a good blaze on the hearth during the night in damp weather. The wall over there, by the dresser, is dripping wet. The lime is washed off it. There'll be a hole in it after another winter.'

'A man would mix up a bit of plaster for that wall while

you'd be looking around you,' said Solly. 'Is your pillow warmed?'

'It is,' said the old woman, 'but don't light the candle yet awhile.'

All the same, Solly stuck a bit of paper in between the red sods of turf on the hearthstone, and when it lit with a pout of flame, she held the flame to a candle-butt that she took out of her pocket.

'Are you coming to bed, Mother?' she said, going into the next room and standing the candle in a cup on the table beside the tufty bed with its white counterpane.

The old woman hoisted herself out of the chair by leaning on the arms and drawing herself up with a jerk.

'Stop that candle from guttering and spluttering,' she said.

Solly squeezed the burnt end of the wick with her finger and thumb, and the candle blazed freshly and cleanly along the new piece of wick.

'Do you know what it is?' she said. 'The moon is so bright tonight you'd hardly want a candle at all.'

Through the small window, the rim of a hill behind the house could be seen against the bright moonlit sky. The light of the candle, the lamp, and the fire, all burning at their brightest, was not strong enough to keep out the light of the moon. Even an odd star, that shone brighter than the other stars, could be seen as clearly from where they stood as if the cottage were in darkness.

'The moon is in full bloom,' said the old woman.

Solly stood looking out and listening. The wind had risen, and somewhere away behind the cottage it sounded in the trees.

'It's odd for the wind to be so high on a moon-bright night,' she said.

The old woman went into the inner room and Solly turned down the lamp in the kitchen. She kicked in a sod that had fallen out from the hearth and lit another butt of a candle for herself.

'If you feel cold, Mother, be sure to give a rap on the wall, and I'll come down and put another blanket over you,' she said as she went up the steps of the loft. 'Give a good loud rap,' she repeated when she got to the top step.

'I won't want any more over me than I have every night,' the old woman said. 'Put another blanket over yourself. Young people nowadays haven't as good blood in their veins as we had in our day.'

Solly closed the door of the loft. The old woman left her door open and she went on talking to herself. Solly listened to her for a few minutes and then she took off her clothes, and lay down on a trestle bed with her face to the gable window where she could see the moon high in the bright sky. But she was asleep before a travelling cloud had crossed the bright face of the moon.

Down below the old woman was still talking to herself.

'I don't know why Solly is so cold,' she muttered. 'Every one of my children felt the cold worse than me, but Solly and Matty were the worst. Perhaps it's because they came last of the family.' She sat on the edge of the bed, and it sank under her with a creak. 'Matty could never get socks thick enough to suit him.' She stood up again and the bed sprang up with a rusty whinge. She went over to the yellow chest of drawers in the corner and pulled out the top drawer. She took out a thick grey sock and another unfinished sock that dangled from four steel needles. 'There's no harm in finishing a thing once it's begun,' she said. And she went over to the open door that led into the kitchen and listened to Solly's breathing. 'Who knows?' she said. 'Matty might come back. There was a lot of sense in the things my mother said. I don't believe that everyone that dies has the power to come back, but a poor harmless boy like Matty, that died so far away from his home, might be allowed to come as far as the door, and step inside for a minute just to please his old mother.' She put the finished sock back in the drawer, and then on second thoughts she took it out again. 'If he came back he might like to see I was still knitting for him, even after he was gone,' she said. 'But of course it's only nonsense thinking that he'll come back.' She put her hand under the bolster, and drew out a pair of worn rosary beads that were polished from a lifetime of handling. 'Poor Matty!' she said. 'Poor Matty! Your old mother would give her senses for one sight of your darling face!' Then she went back out into the kitchen, talking to herself. 'He won't come, I know that. But it's no harm to stay up awhile. I couldn't sleep anyway. My father was right when he said that people wouldn't get it so hard to leave this world if there was any chance of getting back to it. He had good sayings. He wore my poor mother out with his talk, but she cried herself into a fit the day he died. It is a strange thing the way you value a person when he's gone from you. But it's a strange thing too that I never had any hankering to see my father or mother again, once they went from me – nor any of the other children either, not the way I hanker to see Matty.' She left the lamp unlit, finding her way in by the light of the fire that darkened and brightened every other minute, and pausing to feel the edges of the furniture like a blind person, with gentleness and timidity – yet with a kind of loving gratitude in the touch of her fingers. 'If I had seen him laid out I might have been satisfied,' she said as she sat down by the fire.

For a long time, then, there was no sound, as the old woman's fingers went silently up and down the knitting needles, except when the tips of the needles came together, accidentally, with a little knocking sound. Then a sod fell with a thud, and the bitter smell of smoke threaded the air. She let the sod burn out where it lay, until the bitter fumes made her eyes sore. When she stirred in her chair, to lift it, the chair made a harsh sound as it grated on the rough flagstones, and she looked anxiously up at the loft to see if Solly had wakened. But Solly slept on.

The clock on the dresser seemed to get louder and louder as she listened, and she could barely make out its face because of the way the clouds were passing over the moon every minute, darkening the kitchen. She could imagine that she saw the clock, but she could not possibly have been looking at it, because she imagined it as it was, when she was first married. Then the paint was fresh and bright. It was red, with blue and yellow flowers stencilled up the sides, and a cuckoo that came out on the platform with his beak open and called out the hours. But of course there was no paint on it now. It was as smoky as a pot, and there'd been no cuckoo in it since the day Matty knocked him off with a catapult, when he was a little lad. She was very angry with him that day. She was going to raise her hand to him, but he pleaded with her like a little girl.

'I wouldn't have touched him if he was alive, Mother, but I knew he was only made of cardboard and feathers,' he said, and he picked up the cuckoo, and plucked out the feathers to show her the cardboard body.

She put out her hand and groped along the mantelshelf till she found the framed photograph, and she lifted it carefully and held it low down near the flames to see the features more clearly.

'If you come back, Matty, you'll find your old mother waiting for you,' she said. 'But God is an obstinate man. He has his own ideas, but it's very hard on the like of me.'

The wind dropped suddenly. Then it rose again in a gust. Soot loosened in the chimney and fell down into the fire. From under the door there came a thin, whistling sound and then the clouds broke and the moon slipped out like a nut from the kernel. All at once the room was as bright as if a light had been flashed in through the window again.

And then there was a step outside the door.

The old woman remained where she was, crouched low over the flames with the picture in its steel frame in her hands.

'Good Christ,' she said. 'Good Christ deliver us!'

She didn't move. Then the moon was covered again, and the steps came nearer. They paused outside the window. They went past the window. Then they came back again – came to stand outside the window.

'Christ and His Blessed Mother,' said the old woman. She raised her eyes without raising her head. I can't be seen from here, she thought. If I was sitting between the fire and the window it would be another thing; but I can't be seen from here.

The wind dropped again. Now there was no sound.

Maybe I only thought I heard a step, the old woman thought.

Then the steps sounded again – this time outside the door.

The door is bolted she thought, staring at it, and as she stared her upper lip raised so that her yellow teeth, and her gapped gums, were to be seen. Her face looked like a mask with a hole for breathing cut out of the lower part.

Then a hand pressed down the latch.

'Good Christ deliver me! Matty, go back where you belong! Go back where you belong for the love of God and His Holy Mother, and leave me in peace to live out the bit of life that is left to me. Good Christ deliver me! Holy Mother ward off from us all wicked spirits who wander through the night!' She longed to scream out for Solly, but she couldn't raise her voice beyond a whisper. Then the steps went away from the door. But they paused again at the window and she could make out a dark form. 'Good Christ keep the clouds travelling,' she implored, and she raised her eyes again as high as she could, without moving her head, till she felt the veins swelling and throbbing at the back of her eye sockets. She saw a great rent coming in the clouds. 'Good Christ!' she said, over and over again, and then the clouds broke and once more the moon slipped out.

There was no one at the window.

The old woman put her hands over her eyes and ran over to the step that led up to the loft, knocking into a bench at the foot of the steps. But she didn't feel the pain in her hurry to touch the warm and living body of Solly.

Solly didn't feel her crawling in across her either, but she wasn't surprised in the morning when she found her in the bed.

'I often wondered why you didn't sleep up here,' she said. 'It's warmer here than down below. Were you cold? Did you rap on the wall?'

'I didn't rap,' said the old woman. 'I wasn't cold. I was only lonesome thinking of Matty.' She looked at Solly with a sly look, but Solly was drawing on her stockings and didn't notice anything unusual.

'Will I make you a nice cup of tea, Mother, before you put your feet out on the floor?'

'No,' said the mother. 'I'll get up. What time is it by that clock?'

'It's ten minutes past eight.'

'I think I'll go to Mass,' said the old woman. 'The only way you can help the dead is by praying for them.'

Solly looked at her.

'Why are you raising your lips like that, Mother?' she said sharply. 'You look as if you'd seen a ghost!'

'Nobody ever saw a ghost. Stop your nonsense!' said the old woman.

'Last night I was afraid you were going to stay up all night to see Matty,' said Solly.

'What would be the use of that?' said the old woman, irritably. 'If he came, I wouldn't see him!'

'How do you know?' said Solly, throwing down the broken comb on the chair. She was thinking more of what she had to do than of what she was saying. She had to go to the well and fill the bucket. She had forgotten to do it the night before. She had to gather a few twigs to blaze up the fire, and she had to put the pig's mash to boil on the fire.

'If Matty came back, and walked in that door,' said the old woman, 'you wouldn't have the strength to lift your eyes to look at him. It isn't that the dead can't come back, but that we haven't the strength to face them. We don't want them to come back! That's the truth. It all comes to the same thing in the end! They might as well be gone for ever. When they're gone, they're gone.'

'There's no need to shout, Mother, I'm not deaf,' Solly said, and she looked at her mother again, more sharply. 'Didn't I tell you not to drag your lips back across your gums like that, Mother, you look terrible. I don't think you ought to go to Mass this morning. It's quarter past eight already. You wouldn't be down to the chapel before the middle of Mass. Get back into bed and I'll bring you a nice cup of tea.'

When Solly went downstairs there was a sound of sticks breaking and a sound of crockery hitting against crockery and a sound of a door opening and shutting. There was a sound of a pail being left down on the floor with a clatter and a sound of water splashing into an empty vessel. Then there was a sound of voices in the yard. Soon after that Solly came to the foot of the stairs leading up to the loft.

'The kettle is beginning to talk, Mother. The tea will be ready in a minute.' The sound of the cup could be heard wobbling in the saucer as Solly came up to the loft with the tea. The spoon was in the cup, sticking up straight because there was so much sugar in the bottom. 'Here's your tea, Mother, the way you like it, boiling hot with plenty of sugar, and the top off the milk.' The old woman put out her hand and took the cup. She began to drink.

'Don't get the spoon in your eye, Mother,' Solly said, looking nervously at the shaking hand.

'Give me the saucer so,' said the old woman, and she poured a thin stream of the tea into the saucer and held it to her lips, holding it with both hands and tilting it like a shallow goblet. 'Who was that I heard talking to you below?' she asked.

'It was Packy Reilly. He stepped across the fields to tell me that he was passing here late last night and the cottage was so bright he looked in the window. There was a fire on the hearth big enough to roast an ox, he said. He thought surely there was something wrong. He tried the latch but the door was bolted. He looked in the window a second time, but he could see nothing. I said we didn't hear him. At least, I didn't hear him. Did you hear anything, Mother?' The old woman stared into the pool of tea in the bottom of the saucer. 'Did you hear me asking you a question, Mother?' Solly asked sharply.

'Go down and drink your own tea. It's getting cold while you're standing there talking.'

Solly went to go down but she didn't. 'Is there anything wrong with you, Mother?' she said, standing over the ladder-hole and looking back at the old woman. She got no answer. She was no sooner at the foot of the ladder though than she came running up it again.

'Mother, Mother! Look what I found in the ashes when I was throwing them out in the ash pit.' She held out the steel picture frame. It was blackened and twisted from the heat of the fire. 'The wind must have blown it off the mantelpiece,' she said.

'It will shine up again,' said the old woman, and she reached out her hand for it.

'But the photo of Matty is burnt out of it!' Solly said.

The old woman took the frame. She stared at it and Solly stared at her. Then Solly stamped her foot.

'Mother! will you stop drawing back your lips from your gums like that? If you could only see how awful you look!'

The old woman's face returned to normal at once, but when Solly went downstairs the corners of the mouth lifted and the face became a mask again.

LENNOX ROBINSON

A Pair of Muddy Shoes

I am going to try to write it down quite simply, just as it happened. I shall try not to exaggerate anything.

I am twenty-two years old, my parents are dead, I have no brothers or sisters; the only near relation I have is Aunt Margaret, my father's sister. She is unmarried and lives alone in a little house in the country in the west of county Cork. She is kind to me and I often spend my holidays with her, for I am poor and have few friends.

I am a school-teacher – that is to say, I teach drawing and singing. I am a visiting teacher at two or three schools in Dublin. I make a fair income, enough for a single woman to live comfortably on, but father left debts behind him, and until these are paid off I have to live very simply. I suppose I ought to eat more and eat better food. People sometimes think I am nervous and highly strung: I look rather fragile and delicate, but really I am not. I have slender hands, with pale, tapering fingers – the sort of hands people call 'artistic'.

I hoped very much that my aunt would invite me to spend Christmas with her. I happened to have very little money; I had paid off a big debt of poor father's, and that left me very short, and I felt rather weak and ill. I didn't quite know how I'd get through the holidays unless I went down to my aunt's. However, ten days before Christmas the invitation came. You may be sure I accepted it gratefully, and when my last school broke up on the 20th I packed my trunk, gathered up the old sentimental songs Aunt Margaret likes best, and set off for Rosspatrick.

It rains a great deal in West Cork in the winter: it was raining when Aunt Margaret met me at the station. 'It's been a terrible month, Peggy,' she said, as she turned the pony's head into the long road that runs for four muddy miles from the station to Rosspatrick. 'I think it's rained every day for the last six weeks. And the storms! We lost a chimney two days ago: it came through the roof, and let the rain into the ceiling of the spare bedroom. I've had to make you up a bed in the lumber-room till Jeremiah Driscoll can be got to mend the roof.'

I assured her that any place would do me; all I wanted was her society and a quiet time.

'I can guarantee you those,' she said. 'Indeed, you look tired out: you look as if you were just after a bad illness or just before one. That teaching is killing you.'

The lumber room was really very comfortable. It was a large room with two big windows; it was on the ground floor, and Aunt Margaret had never used it as a bedroom because people are often afraid of sleeping on the ground floor.

We stayed up very late talking over the fire. Aunt Margaret came with me to my bedroom; she stayed there for a long time, fussing about the room, hoping I'd be comfortable, pulling about the furniture, looking at the bedclothes.

At last I began to laugh at her. 'Why shouldn't I be comfortable? Think of my horrid little bedroom in Brunswick Street! What's wrong with this room?'

'Nothing – oh, nothing,' she said rather hurriedly, and kissed me and left me.

I slept very well. I never opened my eyes till the maid called me, and then after she had left me I dozed off again. I had a ridiculous dream. I dreamed I was interviewing a rich old lady: she offered me a thousand a year and comfortable rooms to live in. My only duty was to keep her clothes from moths; she had quantities of beautiful, costly clothes, and she seemed to have a terror of them being eaten by moths. I accepted her offer at once. I remember saying to her gaily, 'The work will be no trouble to me, I like killing moths.'

It was strange I should say that, because I really don't like killing moths – I hate killing anything. But my dream was easily explained, for when I woke a second later (as it seemed), I was holding a dead moth between my finger and thumb. It disgusted me just a little bit – that dead moth pressed between my fingers, but I dropped it quickly, jumped up, and dressed myself.

Aunt Margaret was in the dining-room, and full of profuse and anxious inquiries about the night I had spent. I soon relieved her anxieties, and we laughed together over my dream and the new position I was going to fill. It was very wet all day and I didn't stir out of the house. I sang a great many songs, I began a pencil-drawing of my aunt – a thing I had been meaning to make for years – but I didn't feel well, I felt headachy and nervous – just from being in the house all day, I suppose. I felt the greatest disclination to go to bed. I felt afraid, I don't know of what.

Of course I didn't say a word of this to Aunt Margaret.

That night the moment I fell asleep I began to dream. I thought I was looking down at myself from a great height. I saw myself in my nightdress crouching in a corner of the bedroom. I remember wondering why I was crouching there, and I came nearer and looked at myself again, and then I saw that it was not myself that crouched there – it was a large white cat, it was watching a mouse-hole. I was relieved and I turned away. As I did so I heard the cat spring. I started round. It had a mouse between its paws, and it looked up at me, growling as a cat does. Its face was like a woman's face – was like my face. Probably that doesn't sound at all horrible to you, but it happens that I have a deadly fear of mice. The idea of holding one between my hands, of putting my mouth to one, of – oh, I can't bear even to write it.

I think I woke screaming. I know when I came to myself I had jumped out of bed and was standing on the floor. I lit the candle and searched the room. In one corner were some boxes and trunks; there might have been a mouse-hole behind them, but I hadn't the courage to pull them out and look. I kept my candle lighted and stayed awake all night.

The next day was fine and frosty. I went for a long walk in the morning and for another in the afternoon. When bedtime came I was very tired and sleepy. I went to sleep at once and slept dreamlessly all night.

It was the next day that I noticed my hands getting queer. 'Queer' perhaps isn't the right word, for, of course, cold does roughen and coarsen the skin, and the weather was frosty enough to account for that. But it wasn't only that the skin was rough, the whole hand looked larger, stronger, not like my own hand. How ridiculous this sounds, but the whole story is ridiculous.

I remember once, when I was a child at school, putting on another girl's boots by mistake one day. I had to go about till evening in them, and I was perfectly miserable. I could not stop myself from looking at my feet, and they seemed to me to be the feet of another person. That sickened me, I don't know why. I felt a little like that now when I looked at my hands. Aunt Margaret noticed how rough and swollen they were, and she gave me cold cream, which I rubbed on them before I went to bed.

I lay awake for a long time. I was thinking of my hands. I didn't seem to be able not to think of them. They seemed to grow bigger and bigger in the darkness; they seemed monstrous hands, the hands of some horrible ape, they seemed to fill the whole room. Of course if I had struck a match and lit the candle I'd have calmed myself in a minute, but, frankly, I hadn't the courage. When I touched one hand with the other it seemed rough and hairy, like a man's.

At last I fell asleep. I dreamed that I got out of bed and opened the window. For several minutes I stood looking out. It was bright moonlight and bitterly cold. I felt a great desire to go for a walk. I dreamed that I dressed myself quickly, put on my slippers, and stepped out of the window. The frosty grass crunched under my feet. I walked, it seemed for miles, along a road I never remember being on before. It led up-hill; I met no one as I walked.

Presently I reached the crest of the hill, and beside the road, in the middle of a bare field, stood a large house. It was a gaunt, three-storeyed building, there was an air of decay about it. Maybe it had once been a gentleman's place, and was now occupied by a herd. There are many places like that in Ireland. In a window of the highest story there was a light. I decided I would go to the house and ask the way home. A gate closed the grass-grown avenue from the road; it was fastened and I could not open it, so I climbed it. It was a high gate but I climbed it easily, and I remember thinking in my dream, 'If this wasn't a dream I could never climb it so easily.'

I knocked at the door, and after I had knocked again the window of the room in which the light shone was opened, and a voice said, 'Who's there? What do you want?'

It came from a middle-aged woman with a pale face and dirty strands of grey hair hanging about her shoulders.

I said, 'Come down and speak to me; I want to know the way back to Rosspatrick.'

I had to speak two or three times to her, but at last she came down and opened the door mistrustfully. She only opened it a few inches and barred my way. I asked her the road home, and she gave me directions in a nervous, startled way.

Then I dreamed that I said, 'Let me in to warm myself.'

'It's late; you should be going home.'

But I laughed, and suddenly pushed at the door with my foot and slipped past her.

I remember she said, 'My God,' in a helpless, terrified way. It was strange that she should be frightened, and I, a young girl all alone in a strange house with a strange woman, miles from any one I knew, should not be frightened at all. As I sat warming myself by the fire while she boiled the kettle (for I had asked for tea), and watching her timid, terrified movements, the queerness of the position struck me, and I said, laughing, 'You seem afraid of me.'

'Not at all, miss,' she replied, in a voice which almost trembled.

'You needn't be, there's not the least occasion for it,' I said, and I laid my hand on her arm.

She looked down at it as it lay there, and said again, 'Oh, my God,' and staggered back against the range.

And so for half a minute we remained. Her eyes were fixed on my hand which lay on my lap; it seemed she could never take them off it.

'What is it?' I said.

'You've the face of a girl,' she whispered, 'and – God help me – the hands of a man.'

I looked down at my hands. They were large, strong and sinewy, covered with coarse red hairs. Strange to say they no longer disgusted me: I was proud of them – proud of their strength, the power that lay in them.

'Why should they make you afraid?' I asked. 'They are fine hands. Strong hands.'

But she only went on staring at them in a hopeless, frozen way.

'Have you ever seen such strong hands before?' I smiled at her.

'They're – they're Ned's hands,' she said at last, speaking in a whisper.

She put her own hand to her throat as if she were choking, and the fastening of her blouse gave way. It fell open. She had a long throat; it was moving as if she were finding it difficult to swallow. I wondered whether my hands would go round it.

Suddenly I knew they would, and I knew why my hands were large and sinewy, I knew why power had been given to them. I got up and caught her by the throat. She struggled so feebly; slipped down, striking her head against the range; slipped down on to the red-tiled floor and lay quite still, but her throat still moved under my hand and I never loosened my grasp.

And presently, kneeling over her, I lifted her head and bumped it gently against the flags of the floor. I did this again and again; lifting it higher, and striking it harder and harder, until it was crushed in like an egg, and she lay still. She was choked and dead.

And I left her lying there and ran from the house, and as I stepped on to the road I felt rain in my face. The thaw had come.

When I woke it was morning. Little by little my dream came back and filled me with horror. I looked at my hands. They were so tender and pale and feeble. I lifted them to my mouth and kissed them.

But when Mary called me half an hour later she broke into a long, excited story of a woman who had been murdered the night before, how the postman had found the door open and the dead body. 'And sure, miss, it was here she used to live long ago; she was near murdered once, by her husband, in this very room; he tried to choke her, she was half killed – that's why the mistress made it a lumber-room. They put him in the asylum afterwards; a month ago he died there I heard.'

My mother was Scotch, and claimed she had the gift of prevision. It was evident she had bequeathed it to me. I was enormously excited. I sat up in bed and told Mary my dream.

She was not very interested, people seldom are in other people's dreams. Besides, she wanted, I suppose, to tell her news to Aunt Margaret. She hurried away. I lay in bed and thought it all over. I almost laughed, it was so strange and fantastic.

But when I got out of bed I stumbled over something. It was a little muddy shoe. At first I hardly recognised it, then I saw it was one of a pair of evening shoes I had; the other shoe lay near it. They were a pretty little pair of dark blue satin shoes, they were a present to me from a girl I loved very much, she had given them to me only a week ago.

Last night they had been so fresh and new and smart. Now they were scratched, the satin cut, and they were covered with mud. Some one had walked miles in them.

And I remembered in my dream how I had searched for my shoes and put them on.

Sitting on the bed, feeling suddenly sick and dizzy, holding the muddy shoes in my hand, I had in a blinding instant a vision of a red-haired man who lay in this room night after night for years, hating a sleeping white-faced woman who lay beside him, longing for strength and courage to choke her. I saw him come back, years afterwards – freed by death – to this room; saw him seize on a feeble girl too weak to resist him; saw him try her, strengthen her hands, and at last – through her – accomplish his unfinished deed . . . The vision passed all in a flash as it had come. I pulled myself together. 'That is nonsense, impossible,' I told myself. 'The murderer will be found before evening.'

But in my hand I still held the muddy shoes. I seem to be holding them ever since.

JOYCE CARY

A Private Ghost

A s soon as he waked in the morning, Peter, aged eight, felt a difference. Then he remembered that his father and mother were away – they had gone to Dublin very suddenly for the week-end – and that Grand-aunt was also away. His grand-aunt lived close by, and always when his parents had been away she had come to stay and watch over the children. But now she was in a Dublin hospital. No one had come to hear his prayers last night. This was why, he thought, he felt a difference.

His sister Noni, in the next bed, did not notice a difference. As soon as she waked, she proposed to come into his bed, as usual; but he refused her firmly. He was devoted to Noni, and she adored him, but at the moment he did not want adoration. He was preoccupied, listening intently to the household. Noni at six was too young to notice the difference.

Certainly, the household *was* different. It was so different that he could hardly recognise it. The cat next door in the day nursery was miaowing loudly in a despairing voice; it had not been let out yet. Down in the kitchen, below the night-nursery window, someone with a very deep hoarse voice, some old beggar, perhaps, was talking to a dog. And this strange dog was padding round the floor, rattling its claws on the linoleum, and uttering now and then a little whine.

What was stranger still on this strange day was that when Annie the nurse came in five minutes later to get the children up, Lizzie the housemaid came with her. Lizzie and Annie had not been speaking for weeks past. But now they came in laughing, and Lizzie whispered something. Then she ran out of the nursery and shouted down the well of the stairs to the cook, 'I told Annie on you, Maggie.' Even her voice was a new voice, more like Maggie's when she was drunk. But Lizzie didn't drink.

Breakfast in the day nursery was delayed, and Noni grew impatient. She climbed into her chair and beat on the table with a spoon. Annie, however, was down in the kitchen telling some tale to the beggar, and what was still queerer, she had left the nursery doors wide open. The nurseries, usually so jealously kept aloof, now seemed as public as the back stairs, through which all these peculiar noises were piped direct to the children. Peter sat at the table listening. He frowned. He did not like the difference in the house. He felt a certain nervousness, and he also felt a certain responsibility, but for what, he did not know.

Suddenly he took the spoon out of Noni's hand and said, 'Don't do that – it's rude.' This was unexpected to Noni. Peter was usually kind to her. She flushed with pain and surprise. Her forehead crinkled and the corners of her mouth turned down; she was about to cry. But Peter's glance daunted her. He said severely, 'You're not a baby any more.'

Lizzie came in again when Annie brought the tray. The two were giggling together again at something that had happened in the kitchen. And then Lizzie shouted from the window at Mrs Conor, the gardener's wife, slopping past in the rain with a sack over her head and her skirt turned up to the knees. Mrs Conor answered with cheerful yells, and soon she, too, came up to the nursery. She spent the whole morning there, drinking tea and telling stories that made the usually dignified Annie explode through her nose with protesting cries, 'Oh, Mrs Conor, you're killing me!'

Mrs Conor stayed all day. After the children's dinner, at noon, all the staff gathered in the day nursery, and there was great laughter when Lizzie was persuaded to ride the rocking horse – not that Lizzie needed much persuading. She was a pale, high-breasted girl, with big grey eyes and a little round mouth, who was dancing mad, and even when the family were there she would go bouncing through the rooms as if she were late for a ball. When she was on the horse, she laughed so much that she nearly fell off. Then Maggie pushed the horse to make it rock harder, and Lizzie gave a shriek like an engine and began to be angry. But when they all laughed she stopped being angry and proposed a dance.

So Annie played the gramophone. They did not dance, however; they were tired of the idea already. And they began to make much of the children. All of them were devoted to Peter and Noni, and now in the exuberance of their holiday, they were demonstrative, they competed in affection. Lizzie tickled Noni till she laughed herself crimson, and this almost provoked a scene. For Annie, the nurse, taken suddenly jealous, snatched the child away and said, 'That's enough.' Lizzie turned upon her and laughed in her nose, saying, 'You,

Annie—' At that moment, Mrs Conor, the hanger-on, who was not quite of the inner household but earned her cups of tea by her good stories and her flattery, made a quick diversion. She lifted Peter to her lap and stroked his hair, which was as pale as flax. 'Oh, the pet – the spit of his grandda. And do you know, my prince, that I've seen him? I've seen your grandda with my own eyes.'

The maids gazed at her. Annie's breast was still heaving, and Lizzie's little mouth was still pushed out in scorn, but they were attentive. They knew that Mrs Conor had some trick in hand.

'Come now, Mrs Conor,' said Annie in her downright way. 'The old master is dead this forty years.'

'Wasn't that the one that drowned himself in the river?' Lizzie asked.

'Forty-three years,' said Mrs Conor, 'and that was before I was born, but I've seen him.' And looking at the child, she said to him, 'And how do you think that was, my pet? How do you think I saw him that was dead?' Peter gazed earnestly at Mrs Conor, and Noni, who had come to lean against her brother, made big eyes round his arm. They knew the question was not meant to be answered; it was simply an introduction to Mrs Conor's story. 'It was when I was eight – just your age, my pet – that I saw him walk. He was all in white, and while he walked he kept shaking his hands and the water was dripping from him. And, bless you, I didn't know who he was then, or what it meant. But I was frightened, and I ran to my mother, and it was then she told me about the old master. And she said if I was to see him again I must cross myself.'

There was a short silence. All four of the servants were gazing at the two children to see the effect of this tale.

'And they say,' said Mrs Conor, 'they say that it's only a child has ever seen the old master walk.'

'Was it a ghost?' Noni asked in a loud voice.

'Yes, indeed. You wouldn't see him living when he was dead, would you, pet?'

'Ghosts are only stories,' Noni said. 'Pappy told me.'

Peter opened his mouth to say the same thing. But as he glanced up he caught the maids' eyes fixed upon him, and suddenly he was not so sure that they were playing a trick upon him. When Annie or Maggie codded him about potatoes that grew on trees or the man in the moon, they had a laugh in them. They might look grave, but you could feel the laugh. But now there was no laugh, and their grave faces had a different gravity. All at once, he was not so confident of his father's assurances, even about ghosts. Did his father know that things could be so different at home when he was away?

'There aren't such things,' Noni said indignantly. But Peter looked at her severely, and she turned red.

'Well, now,' Mrs Conor said, 'do you tell me I'm telling you lies?'

The children looked at her, and Peter said, 'Grandda fell in when he was fishing.'

'I wouldn't know that,' Mrs Conor said. 'But if he only fell in, why would he walk?'

'Why, indeed?' Lizzie said. 'And why only for children?'

'Well now,' Mrs Conor said, 'I wouldn't know that either, but isn't it the same with the fairies? They say it's only children and naturals can see the wee folk. And so you never saw the like of him, Master Peter?'

Peter shook his head, and Mrs Conor looked round at her audience. 'If anyone were to see the old master, it would be this one that's so like him.' And suddenly she winked. Mrs Conor was a good winker; she could close either eye without the slightest change of expression on the other side of her face. That's why Peter saw only her grave good-natured countenance, while Maggie and Lizzie and Annie had a glimpse of enormous slyness. Mrs Conor once more turned her grave mild face towards Peter. 'Yes, my dear, you would be the one, for aren't you the spit of him? It's a wonder that you haven't seen him yet, for it's my belief he crosses that back-yard every day of the week on his way from the water to the cemetery.'

'What, Mrs Conor?' Lizzie said. 'Every day of the week? I wouldn't like to think that.'

'No, indeed,' said Maggie, coming into the game. Maggie was old and tired, and slow in her mind, but still she was ready to take her part in a good game. 'No, indeed,' she said. 'Why, I'd be afraid to go into the yard if I thought that.'

'But then you wouldn't see him,' Annie said. 'It would be only Master Peter here that would see him.'

'It was about six o'clock in the evening that I saw him,' said Mrs Conor. 'And they said that was the time that he went into the water.'

There was another long pause, and then Lizzie said, 'Well now, I wonder, would Master Peter see him if he looked at six o'clock?'

'It'd be a bit dark at six,' Maggie said.

'It'd have to be,' said Mrs Conor. 'You don't think that ghosts will walk in daylight? But there, I'm not saying that Master Peter would see his grandda on any day of week, dark as it might be.'

'No,' Maggie said. 'It's only that he might take a look some evening if he wouldn't be afraid.'

'It's well he might be,' Lizzie said. She gave a deep sigh and gazed into the air with her big grey eyes, imagining the terror of ghosts.

'He would not!' Annie cried. 'Would you, my darling? Would you now?'

Peter made no answer to this. He understood the challenge. He had been challenged before, and usually in a trick, as when Maggie had dared him to open a parcel, which, so she said, might have a bomb in it, and it had let out a jumping jack, which hit him on the nose. But he had not really believed that there would be a bomb in a parcel. Who would put bombs in parcels? Ghost were quite another thing. And it was true that his grandfather had died young, and tragically.

'Oh, he's the brave boy always,' Mrs Conor said, and Maggie came in hastily, 'Sure. There never was any of the family afraid of anything.'

'Would you look for your grandda?' Lizzie asked, staring at the boy with her big eyes.

Peter, staring back and wondering at this strange excited Lizzie, answered, 'You mean in the yard?'

'You wouldn't have to go in the yard,' said Mrs Conor. 'You could see from the kitchen window. Aye, it would be better from the window.'

'And what better day than today, when themselves is out of it?' Lizzie said.

'It's stopped raining,' Peter said, as if he had not noticed Lizzie's suggestion. 'Can I go to Willy?' Willy was the garden boy, a close friend of Peter's, but Annie did not always approve of their meetings which, she considered, were often too exciting for Peter and kept him wakeful at night.

'There now,' Lizzie muttered. 'I knew he'd get out of it.'

187

'Of course you can go to Willy,' Mrs Conor said quickly. 'He'd be in the cabbages this minute. And I tell you, why wouldn't ye have supper in the kitchen, too – for a treat? I'm sure Annie wouldn't mind just for today.'

'Oh, yes!' cried Noni. 'Oh, yes, yes please.'

And even Peter, disturbed as he was by the confusion in the house, was pleased by this suggestion. 'Oh, do, Annie. I'd like that very much,' he said.

'Sure, my pet,' Annie said.

'Indeed, and ye shall,' said Maggie, winking at Mrs Conor, but so clumsily that Noni noticed and stared at her eye. Maggie was very red, and seemed about to burst.

'And as for ghosts, Miss Noni,' said Mrs Conor, 'sure your pappy may be right after all. Why, I wouldn't be too sure myself. It's so long since I saw one that indeed your grandda mightn't have been one at all. There now, Maggie, don't I hear your kettle?' And the four rushed suddenly out of the room so violently that they jammed on the narrow back stairs and Lizzie gave a squeak of laughter. Then, below, the kitchen door banged shut behind them.

Peter paid no more attention to their nonsense. He was too pleased with himself for eluding Mrs Conor's embarrassing proposal. Joyfully he hurried off to see Willy in the garden. He even allowed Noni to take his hand and go with him, stipulating only that she should not speak to Willy.

Noni was perfectly satisfied to be beside her darling and listen to his conversation with Willy, while the party moved from the cabbages to the byre, the byre to the pigsty, the pigsty to the pump, where Willy completed his last duty by filling the house tanks, so that, as he said thoughtfully, 'You wains have your baths the night.'

Peter provided most of the talk, giving, for instance, a full account of the mammoth found in Russia under the ice and explaining that whales were really animals, and had milk. He hadn't had so good a day with Willy for a week, and he started back to the kitchen in the highest spirits. The reason the children loved supper in the kitchen was that the maids, and especially Lizzie, were such good company with their gossip and their jokes. They were always playing some trick on each other and laughing. Last time, Lizzie had pulled Annie's chair away and caused her to sit down hard on the floor. The children had laughed until they could not eat, and Lizzie herself had had to say that they must behave themselves better or they would not be asked again.

They were laughing in recollection of this performance when they came into the kitchen. But what a surprise! There was no one there but old Maggie, and the table was not by the stove, but pushed into the window embrasure, close against the window itself. And when Maggie had placed them in their chairs, at opposite ends of the table, she made for the door.

'Oh, Maggie,' Noni wailed, 'I want to have supper with you all.' But Maggie muttered something about the storeroom, and went out, shutting the door after her.

Almost at the same moment, there was a moaning cry from the yard, and Peter, who had been put facing the yard gate that led from the front lawn and the river, looked up and saw the ghost. It was just coming through the gate.

The lamp in the kitchen was turned low, and the yard was lighted only by the sky, which was a pale-green colour. The yard, surrounded by barns and stables, by the byre and garage, all in dark-reddish bricks, was paved with dark-blue cinders; these dark buildings and the dark cinders soaked up the light from above. The air in the yard seemed to be without light, so that the whiteness of the ghost was as bright as a swan's feathers on a dark evening. The ghost was all in white; a short thick figure in a sheet, which was pulled over its forehead in front, and which covered its body and fell to the ground so that the creature did not seem to have feet.

When it passed the gardener's shed, it turned towards the kitchen window. And now Peter could see, under the white fold of the sheet, a face as white, except that its eyes were like enormous black holes, and its mouth was grey. This mouth was moving all the time as if crying.

Peter was fixed in such fear, such horror, that he could not take his eyes off this face with its weeping mouth. He got down slowly from his chair and retreated a pace backwards; but this brought him up against the end of the embrasure. And he stood there, fixed, helpless, unable to move, speak, or think.

'What are you doing, Peter?' Noni said, surprised at his getting down from his chair. Then the ghost moaned again, more loudly. Noni looked round, gave a shriek, and ran to her brother. Peter held her tight and drew her to one side – she hid her face against his ribs.

The ghost was now four or five yards from the window. Peter could see long leaves of river weed glistening wet on its shoulders and the water pouring down the white folds to the ground – the eyes were shining palely in the middle of their great black holes. It was staring at him and shaking its hands all the time as if in grief. He thought, 'It's crying – it wants to tell me something.' He was shivering in terror that the creature would speak to him, and yet he could not run away. He felt he had to wait for the message.

The ghost took one more step towards him and gave another long deep heartbreaking moan. Noni gripped Peter convulsively and uttered shriek after shriek. But the ghost's next move was to its right. With a wavering, wobbling motion, it glided slowly towards the back corner of the house, where it suddenly vanished behind the porch of the scullery.

Almost at the same moment, Annie, Lizzie, and Maggie burst into the kitchen. Peter, mechanically patting and stroking Noni, gazed at them with wide vague eyes as if he had forgotten their existence. Noni stopped screaming and ran towards Annie. 'It came – it came – we saw it!' she cried. But the maids were staring at Peter, with eyes nearly as wide as his own – half curious, half alarmed at the child's fearfully white face and crazy expression.

'What – what happened then?' said Annie in a stammering voice.

And now Mrs Conor, rather breathless, came darting into the kitchen from the scullery. She still had some burnt cork under her right eye, but she covered it with her hand, so that the children could not see it. 'What's wrong?' she said. 'Was that Miss Noni I heard?'

'They saw him, Mrs Conor!' Lizzie exclaimed. 'They saw the old master in the yard – did you ever hear the like of that?'

Peter came to himself, walked out of his corner, and took Noni's hand. 'It was nothing,' he said. And his face turned very red.

'A ghost, nothing?' said Mrs Conor. 'Weren't you afeared?'

'We didn't see anything,' he said. 'It was only Noni being silly. You didn't see anything, did you, Noni?'

Noni stared at him. Then she slowly shook her head. She

191

didn't know why Peter was telling this enormous lie, but she was glad to support him.

He then walked her slowly and with great dignity towards the hall door. The maids parted and let him go. Even Mrs Conor was taken aback by this strangely aloof Peter. He led Noni through the hall into the drawing-room. He seldom went to the drawing-room except on state occasions, in his best clothes. For him, it was a place of ceremony, where grown-up persons of distinction conferred together in quiet tones and a reserved manner upon important matters – births, deaths, marriages, money, family affairs.

As soon as they entered the room, Noni protested that it was a ghost. 'I *saw* it.' Peter shut the door firmly behind them and cut off the excited chatter of the maids. Then he led Noni to the middle of the carpet and explained to her, kindly but gravely, 'Yes, it was grandpapa. But don't talk to them about it. They'd only laugh and he's our own grandpapa.'

WILLIAM TREVOR

The Death of Peggy Meehan

L ike all children, I led a double life. There was the
ordinariness of dressing in the morning, putting on shoes
and combing hair, stirring a spoon through porridge I didn't
want, and going at ten to nine to the nuns' elementary school.
And there was a world in which only the events I wished for
happened, where boredom was not permitted and of which I
was both God and King.

In my ordinary life I was the only child of parents who
years before my birth had given up hope of ever having me. I
remember them best as being different from other parents:
they were elderly, it seemed to me, two greyly fussing people
with grey hair and faces, in grey clothes, with spectacles. 'Oh,
no, no,' they murmured regularly, rejecting on my behalf an
invitation to tea or to play with some other child. They feared
on my behalf the rain and the sea, and walls that might be
walked along, and grass because grass was always damp. They
rarely missed a service at the Church of the Holy Redeemer.

In the town where we lived, a seaside town thirty miles from Cork, my father was employed as a senior clerk in the offices of Cosgriff and McLoughlin, Solicitors and Commissioners for Oaths. With him on one side of me and my mother on the other, we walked up and down the brief promenade in winter, while the seagulls shrieked and my father worried in case it was going to rain. We never went for walks through fields or through the heathery wastelands that sloped gently upwards behind the town, or by the river where people said Sir Walter Raleigh had fished. In summer, when the visitors from Cork came, my mother didn't like to let me near the sands because the sands, she said, were full of fleas. In summer we didn't walk on the promenade but out along the main Cork road instead, past a house that appeared to me to move. It disappeared for several minutes as we approached it, a trick of nature, I afterwards discovered, caused by the undulations of the landscape. Every July, for a fortnight, we went to stay in Montenotte, high up above Cork city, in a boarding-house run by my mother's sister, my Aunt Isabella. She, too, had a grey look about her and was religious.

It was here, in my Aunt Isabella's Montenotte boarding-house, that this story begins: in the summer of 1936, when I was seven. It was a much larger house than the one we lived in ourselves, which was small and narrow and in a terrace. My Aunt Isabella's was rather grand in its way, a dark place with little unexpected half-landings, and badly lit corridors. It smelt of floor polish and of a mustiness that I have since associated with the religious life, a smell of old cassocks. Everywhere there were statues of the Virgin, and votive lights and black-framed pictures of the Holy Child. The residents were all priests, old and middle-aged and young, eleven of them usually, which was all the house would hold. A few were always away on their holidays when we stayed there in the summer.

In the summer of 1936 we left our own house in the usual way, my father fastening all the windows and the front and back doors and then examining the house from the outside to make sure he'd done the fastening and the locking properly. We walked to the railway station, each of us carrying something, my mother a brown cardboard suitcase and my father a larger one of the same kind. I carried the sandwiches we were to have on the train, and a flask of carefully made tea and three apples, all packed into a sixpenny fish basket.

In the house in Montenotte my Aunt Isabella told us that Canon McGrath and Father Quinn were on holiday, one in Tralee, the other in Galway. She led us to their rooms, Canon McGrath's for my father and Father Quinn's for my mother and myself. The familiar trestle-bed was erected at the foot of the bed in my mother's room. During the course of the year a curate called Father Lalor had repaired it, my aunt said, after it had been used by Canon McGrath's brother from America, who'd proved too much for the canvas.

'Ah, aren't you looking well, Mr Mahon!' the red-faced and jolly Father Smith said to my father in the dining-room that evening. 'And isn't our friend here getting big for himself?' he laughed loudly, gripping a portion of the back of my neck between a finger and a thumb. Did I know my catechism? he asked me. Was I being good with the nuns in the elementary school? 'Are you in health yourself, Mrs Mahon?' he inquired of my mother.

My mother said she was, and the red-faced priest went to

join the other priests at the main dining-table. He left behind him a smell that was different from the smell of the house, and I noticed that he had difficulty in pulling the chair out from the table when he was about to sit down. He had to be assisted in this by a new young curate, a Father Parsloe. Father Smith had been drinking stout again, I said to myself.

Sometimes in my aunt's house there was nothing to do except to watch and to listen. Father Smith used to drink too much stout; Father Magennis, who was so thin you could hardly bear to look at him and whose flesh was the colour of whitewash, was not long for this world; Father Riordon would be a bishop if only he could have tidied himself up a bit; Canon McGrath had once refused to baptize a child; young Father Lalor was going places. For hours on end my Aunt Isabella would murmur to my parents about the priests, telling about the fate of one who had left the boarding-house during the year or supplying background information about a new one. My parents, so faultlessly regular in their church attendance and interested in all religious matters, were naturally pleased to listen. God and the organization of His Church were far more important than my father's duties in Cosgriff and McLoughlin, or my mother's housework, or my own desire to go walking through the heathery wastelands that sloped gently upwards behind our town. God and the priests in my Aunt Isabella's house, and the nuns of the convent elementary school and the priests of the Church of the Holy Redeemer, were at the centre of everything. 'Maybe it'll appeal to our friend,' Father Smith had once said in the dining-room, and I knew that he meant that maybe one day I might be attracted towards the priesthood. My parents had not said anything in reply, but as we ate our tea of sausages and potato-

196

cakes I could feel them thinking that nothing would please them better.

Every year when we stayed with my aunt there was an afternoon when I was left in charge of whichever priests happened to be in, while my parents and my aunt made the journey across the city to visit my father's brother, who was a priest himself. There was some difficulty about bringing me: I had apparently gone to my uncle's house as a baby, when my presence had upset him. Years later I overheard my mother whispering to Father Riordon about this, suggesting – or so it seemed – that my father had once been intent on the priestly life but had at the last moment withdrawn. That he should afterwards have fathered a child was apparently an offence to his brother's feeling of propriety. I had the impression that my uncle was a severe man, who looked severely on my father and my mother and my Aunt Isabella on these visits, and was respected by them for being as he was. All three came back subdued, and that night my mother always prayed for much longer by the side of her bed.

'Father Parsloe's going to take you for a walk,' my Aunt Isabella said on the morning of the 1936 visit. 'He wants to get to know you.'

You walked all the way down from Montenotte, past the docks, over the river and into the city. The first few times it could have been interesting, but after that it was worse than walking on the concrete promenade at home. I'd have far preferred to have played by myself in my aunt's overgrown back garden, pretending to be grown up, talking to myself in a secret way, having wicked thoughts. At home and in my aunt's garden I became a man my father had read about in a newspaper and whom, he'd said, we must all pray for, a thief who broke the windows of jewellers' shops and lifted out watches and rings. I became Father Smith, drinking too much stout and missing the steps of the stairs. I became Father Magennis and would lie on the weeds at the bottom of the garden or under a table, confessing to gruesome crimes at the moment of death. In my mind I mocked the holiness of my parents and imitated their voices; I mocked the holiness of my Aunt Isabella; I talked back to my parents in a way I never would; I laughed and said disgraceful things about God and the religious life. Blasphemy was exciting.

'Are you ready so?' Father Parsloe asked when my parents and my aunt had left for the visit to my uncle. 'Will we take a bus?'

'A bus?'

'Down to the town.'

I'd never in my life done that before. The buses were for going longer distances in. It seemed extraordinary not to walk, the whole point of a walk was to walk.

'I haven't any money for the bus,' I said, and Father Parsloe laughed. On the upper deck he lit a cigarette. He was a slight young man, by far the youngest of the priests in my aunt's house, with reddish hair and a face that seemed to be on a slant. 'Will we have tea in Thompson's?' he said. 'Would that be a good thing to do?'

We had tea in Thompson's café, with buns and cakes and huge meringues such as I'd never tasted before. Father Parsloe smoked fourteen cigarettes and drank all the tea himself. I had three bottles of fizzy orangeade. 'Will we go to the pictures?' Father Parsloe said when he'd paid the bill at the cash desk. 'Will we chance the Pavilion?'

I had never, of course, been to the pictures before. My

mother said that the Star Picture House, which was the only one in our town, was full of fleas.

'One and a half,' Father Parsloe said at the cash desk in the Pavilion and we were led away into the darkness. THE END it announced on the screen, and when I saw it I thought we were too late. 'Ah, aren't we in lovely time?' Father Parsloe said.

I didn't understand the film. It was about grown-ups kissing one another, and about an earthquake, and then a motor-car accident in which a woman who'd been kissed a lot was killed. The man who'd kissed her was married to another woman, and when the film ended he was sitting in a room with his wife, looking at her. She kept saying it was all right.

'God, wasn't that great?' Father Parsloe said as we stood in the lavatory of the Pavilion, the kind of lavatory where you stand up, like I'd never been in before. 'Wasn't it a good story?'

All the way back to Montenotte I kept remembering it. I kept seeing the face of the woman who'd been killed, and all the bodies lying on the streets after the earthquake, and the man at the end, sitting in a room with his wife. The swaying of the bus made me feel queasy because of the meringues and the orangeade, but I didn't care.

'Did you enjoy the afternoon?' Father Parsloe asked, and I told him I'd never enjoyed anything better. I asked him if the pictures were always as good. He assured me they were.

My parents, however, didn't seem pleased. My father got hold of a *Cork Examiner* and looked up the film that was on at the Pavilion and reported that it wasn't suitable for a child. My mother gave me a bath and examined my clothes for fleas. When Father Parsloe winked at me in the dining-room my parents pretended not to notice him.

That night my mother prayed for her extra long period, after the visit to my uncle. I lay in the dimly lit room, aware that she was kneeling there, but thinking of the film and the way the people had kissed, not like my parents ever kissed. At the convent elementary school there were girls in the higher classes who were pretty, far prettier than my mother. There was one called Claire, with fair hair and a softly freckled face, and another called Peggy Meehan, who was younger and black-haired. I had picked them out because they had spoken to me, asking me my name. I thought them very nice.

I opened my eyes and saw that my mother was rising from her knees. She stood for a moment at the edge of her bed, not smiling, her lips still moving, continuing her prayer. Then she got into bed and put out the light.

I listened to her breathing and heard it become the breathing which people have when they're asleep, but I couldn't sleep myself. I lay there, still remembering the film and remembering being in Thompson's and seeing Father Parsloe lighting one cigarette after another. For some reason, I began to imagine that I was in Thompson's with Father Parsloe and the two girls from the convent, and that we all went off to the Pavilion together, swinging along the street. 'Ah, isn't this the life for us?' Father Parsloe said as he led us into the darkness, and I told the girls I'd been to the Pavilion before and they said they never had.

I heard eleven o'clock chiming from a nearby church. I heard a stumbling on the stairs and then the laughter of Father Smith, and Father Riordon telling him to be quiet. I heard twelve chiming and half past twelve, and a quarter to one, and one.

After that I didn't want to sleep. I was standing in a

classroom of the convent and Claire was smiling at me. It was nice being with her. I felt warm all over, and happy.

And then I was walking on the sands with Peggy Meehan. We ran, playing a game she'd made up, and then we walked again. She asked if I'd like to go on a picnic with her, next week perhaps.

I didn't know what to do. I wanted one of the girls to be my friend. I wanted to love one of them, like the people had loved in the film. I wanted to kiss one and be with one, just the two of us. In the darkness of the bedroom they both seemed close and real, closer than my mother, even though I could hear my mother breathing. 'Come on,' Peggy Meehan whispered, and then Claire whispered also, saying we'd always be best friends, saying we might run away. It was all wrong that there were two of them, yet both vividly remained. 'Tuesday,' Peggy Meehan said. 'We'll have the picnic on Tuesday.'

Her father drove us in his car, away from the town, out beyond the heathery wastelands, towards a hillside that was even nicer. But a door of the car, the back door against which Peggy Meehan was leaning, suddenly gave way. On the dust of the road she was as dead as the woman in the film.

'Poor Peggy,' Claire said at some later time, even though she hadn't known Peggy Meehan very well. 'Poor little Peggy.' And then she smiled and took my hand and we walked together through the heathery wastelands, in love with one another.

A few days later we left my Aunt Isabella's house in Montenotte and returned on the train to our seaside town. And a week after that a new term began at the convent elementary school. Peggy Meehan was dead, the Reverend Mother told us, all of us assembled together. She added that there was diphtheria in the town.

I didn't think about it at first; and I didn't connect the reality of the death with a fantasy that had been caused by my first visit to a cinema. Some part of my mind may passingly have paused over the coincidence, but that was all. There was the visit to the Pavilion itself to talk about in the convent, and the description of the film, and Father Parsloe's conversation and the way he'd smoked fourteen cigarettes in Thompson's. Diphtheria was a terrible disease, my mother said when I told her, and naturally we must all pray for the soul of poor Peggy Meehan.

But as weeks and months went by, I found myself increasingly remembering the story I had told myself on the night of the film, and remembering particularly how Peggy Meehan had fallen from the car, and how she'd looked when she was dead. I said to myself that that had been my wickedest thought, worse than my blasphemies and yet somehow part of them. At night I lay in bed, unable to sleep, trying hopelessly to pray for forgiveness. But no forgiveness came, for there was no respite to the images that recurred, her face in life and then in death, like the face of the woman in the film.

A year later, while lying awake in the same room in my aunt's boarding-house, I saw her. In the darkness there was a sudden patch of light and in the centre of it she was wearing a sailor-suit that I remembered. Her black plaits hung down her back. She smiled at me and went away. I knew instinctively then, as I watched her and after she'd gone, that the fantasy and the reality were part and parcel: I had caused this death to occur.

Looking back on it now, I can see, of course, that that feeling was a childish one. It was a childish fear, a superstition that occurring to an adult would cause only a shiver of horror. But, as a child, with no one to consult about the matter, I lived with the thought that my will was more potent than I knew. In stories I had learnt of witches and spells and evil spirits, and power locked up in people. In my games I had wickedly denied the religious life, and goodness, and holiness. In my games I had mocked Father Smith, I had pretended that the dying Father Magennis was a criminal. I had pretended to be a criminal myself, a man who broke jewellers' windows. I had imitated my parents when it said you should honour your father and your mother. I had mocked the holiness of my Aunt Isabella. I had murdered Peggy Meehan because there wasn't room for her in the story I was telling myself. I was possessed and evil: the nuns had told us about people being like that.

I thought at first I might seek advice from Father Parsloe. I thought of asking him if he remembered the day we'd gone on our outing, and then telling him how, in a story I was telling myself, I'd caused Peggy Meehan to be killed in a car accident like the woman in the film, and how she'd died in reality, of diphtheria. But Father Parsloe had an impatient kind of look about him this year, as if he had worries of his own. So I didn't tell him and I didn't tell anyone. I hoped that when we returned to our own house at the end of the stay in Montenotte I wouldn't see her again, but the very first day we were back I saw her at four o'clock in the afternoon, in the kitchen.

After that she came irregularly, sometimes not for a month and once not for a year. She continued to appear in the same sudden way but in different clothes, and growing up as I was growing up. Once, after I'd left the convent and gone on to the

Christian Brothers', she appeared in the classroom, smiling near the blackboard.

She never spoke. Whether she appeared on the promenade or at school or in my aunt's house or our house, close to me or at a distance, she communicated only with her smile and with her eyes: I was possessed of the Devil, she came herself from God. In her eyes and her smile there was that simple message, a message which said also that my thoughts were always wicked, that I had never believed properly in God or the Virgin or Jesus who died for us.

I tried to pray. Like my mother, kneeling beside my bed. Like my aunt and her houseful of priests. Like the nuns and Christian Brothers, and other boys and girls of the town. But prayer would not come to me, and I realized that it never had. I had always pretended, going down on my knees at Mass, laughing and blaspheming in my mind. I hated the very thought of prayer. I hated my parents in an unnatural manner, and my Aunt Isabella and the priests in her house. But the dead Peggy Meehan fresh from God's heaven, was all forgiveness in her patch of light, smiling to rid me of my evil spirit.

She was there at my mother's funeral, and later at my father's. Claire, whom I had destroyed her for, married a man employed in the courthouse and became a Mrs Madden, prematurely fat. I naturally didn't marry anyone myself.

I am forty-six years old now and I live alone in the same seaside town. No one in the town knows why I am solitary. No one could guess that I have lived with a child's passionate companionship for half a lifetime. Being no longer a child, I naturally no longer believe that I was responsible for the death. In my passing, careless fantasy I wished for it and she, already dead, picked up my living thoughts. I should not have wished for it because in middle age she is a beautiful creature now, more beautiful by far than fat Mrs Madden.

And that is all there is. At forty-six I walk alone on the brief promenade, or by the edge of the sea or on the road to Cork, where the moving house is. I work, as my father worked, in the offices of Cosgriff and McLoughlin. I cook my own food. I sleep alone in a bed that has an iron bedstead. On Sundays I go hypocritically to Mass in the Church of the Holy Redeemer; I go to confession and do not properly confess; I go to Men's Confraternity, and to Communion. And all the time she is there, appearing in her patch of light to remind me that she never leaves me. And all the time, on my knees at Mass, or receiving the Body and the Blood, or in my iron bed, I desire her. In the offices of Cosgriff and McLoughlin I dream of her nakedness. When we are old I shall desire her, too, with my shrunken, evil body.

In the town I am a solitary, peculiar man. I have been rendered so, people probably say, by my cloistered upbringing, and probably add that such an upbringing would naturally cultivate a morbid imagination. That may be so, and it doesn't really matter how things have come about. All I know is that she is more real for me than anything else is in this seaside town or beyond it. I live for her, living hopelessly, for I know I can never possess her as I wish to. I have a carnal desire for a shadow, which in turn is His mockery of me: His fitting punishment for my wickedest thought of all.

MARY BECKETT

A Ghost Story

T he house was a cause of dissension between them from the first. Fiona said her father would buy them a house for their wedding present, as he had done for her three sisters. He was a builder, of the kind who drove round in a polished Rover and wore gloves while he inspected his sites. He not only had money now, but his people had been rich for generations which was a source of wonder to Fintan. It was one of the things that attracted him to Fiona. She appeared to him as some aureate butterfly that he hoped to pin down. But he was not going to sponge on his father-in-law. He insisted they must buy their own house.

'Don't be ridiculous,' Fiona said. 'All your money will go on paying for the house and mine will go on housekeeping and we'll have nothing to spend. I thought we'd have a lovely life together, but not if you insist on this.'

'We have to pay our way first if I'm to have any self-respect,' Fintan said, surprising himself.

'Such a peasant attitude,' she teased.

'Oh well you can take the man out of the bog but not the bog out of the man,' Fintan quoted his father, a big handsome school-inspector who was given to such dicta.

'I'm not discussing turbary rights,' Fiona laughed, and he laughed back, but the problem remained, holding up their wedding until an agent told him one day that he could sell him a house for twenty-five thousand pounds. It had been on his hands for several years – he just wanted rid of it. He'd settle for twenty-five thousand. It was a modest detached house built in the sixties and never lived in for more than a few months at a time because it was said to be haunted. But since Fintan was a modern young man who wouldn't heed such womanish nonsense he could pick up a bargain. Fintan said he'd have to consult Fiona and the agent raised his eyebrows and turned down the corners of his mouth.

Fiona thought the house was cute in a way but the rooms were smaller and the ceiling lower than anything she'd been used to. Besides, the kitchen was just a small square with a sink unit and the main bedroom had doors across one alcove by way of a built-in wardrobe. Fintan thought she was using these complaints as excuses, that she was really worried about the ghosts. He pointed out that if the house had been old he could have understood ghosts, but since the house the two old ladies were supposed to have lived in had been completely razed and this one built on the site he didn't see how ghosts could have survived. If it would make Fiona any easier in her mind they could get a priest, he was sure, to come and bless the place. Fiona scoffed at him, 'You know I don't go along with all that mumbo-jumbo.'

'I'm never too sure about you,' Fintan said. 'You roll out with your family every Sunday like a dutiful daughter.'

Fintan himself lived in a flat, having been asked by his father to leave home because he wouldn't go to Mass. 'I'm not criticising your religion or the lack of it,' his father had said. 'It is your own affair. And as far as the Almighty is concerned I'm sure you are just one of the flies flattened on the wind-screen. But your mother sees things differently and I'm not going to have you worrying her Sunday after Sunday.'

'I can't be dishonest,' Fintan protested. 'I've got to make my own statement. I can't pretend, just to please my mother.'

'There's many a better man than yourself did just that all his life and maybe got to heaven at the heel of the hunt. But if you won't, just take yourself off quietly to a flat of your own. Say it's to leave more room at home for your brothers. But leave her in peace and don't have her saying Rosaries night after night in bed when she thinks I'm asleep.'

'She was always religious. It's not just for me.'

'Until you began troubling her she never said Rosaries when I was in the bed,' his father stated, and Fintan had moved out with no recriminations anywhere.

He found the wedding awkward from that angle – a huge number of guests, a plethora of priests, and Fintan had to explain beforehand that he would not receive Holy Communion. Fiona did, devoutly to all appearances, but during the honeymoon she neglected Mass, not mentioning it at all. It was their economic approach to life that provided a series of surprises for both of them. Even though they earned similar salaries, prices meant entirely different things to each. Fintan looked forward to coming back to his own house where he was sure their lives would blend better.

He had had no objection to presents of carpets and furniture from his rich in-laws, but his tastes were different and he saw no reason to keep quiet about that. Fiona wanted him to accept gifts quietly, whether the suites were too big or the patterns too striking. He complained that he had to live with them and she'd have to adjust herself to smaller rooms. He went round auction rooms and bought small pieces of old furniture. One he had especially loved was a walnut desk with moss-green leather on the writing place, and little drawers with wooden handles all delicately turned and never a nail or a rough edge to be seen. He gave it to Fiona for a present but her offhand acceptance hurt him. He borrowed a spade from a brother-in-law and tackled the front garden. It was stony and grey. A neighbour stopped in passing and advised him that he'd never grow anything in that barren patch unless he got a few loads of topsoil and manure as everyone else had done. 'What is topsoil?' Fintan wondered, but assured the neighbour that he'd see about it and stood the spade in the garage with relief.

When the house was more or less painted and furnished they decided to have a house-warming. They agreed that a brunch party some Sunday would suit and they'd have their own friends, leaving out all the middle-aged people who were at the wedding. On the Friday before the party they got an anonymous letter in the post telling them they ought to know that their house was haunted by the two old ladies knitting. They laughed, passed the letter to each other across the table, relishing it, and argued over who should bring it into work to share the joke there. In the end Fintan took it, with Fiona agreeing to wait until Monday.

The brunch was not really a success. They had thought that the party would begin around noon and end about four in the afternoon, but nobody went home until all the wine had been drunk and by then it was nearly eleven o'clock at night. Fintan enjoyed that, but Fiona was annoyed because things didn't turn out as she had expected. Besides, a close friend of Fintan's, whom she was meeting for the first time, disliked her and took every opportunity to sneer at her cooking, her decorating, her wealth and her father's wealth. Fiona laughed it off so that nobody else felt uncomfortable and to divert them she produced the anonymous letter and handed it around. People started talking about haunted houses they had heard of, at a distance. They all agreed a new house could not possibly be haunted, although somebody said, 'How about the air waves?' One girl had heard her grandfather tell of a cottage in the bog. The man who lived alone there brought in his friend to visit after they left the pub. They drew up their chairs to the fire and a third chair drew up from the far wall on its own accord.

'I see, James, you have company tonight,' the friend said.

'That, John,' said the owner of the house, 'is company that I am seldom without.'

Fiona, watching Fintan listening intently, was resentful that he should seem so detached from her, and when at last the guests took themselves off she attacked him. 'How could you let him insult me all day? You could easily have made him stop. Anyway, I don't know how you could even have liked such an ill-mannered creature.' Fintan shrugged and rubbed his cheek with his hand. Glaring at him, Fiona could feel, as his fingers did, the warm dry skin of his face. She wanted to put her cheek against the broad plane of his forehead. 'You don't love me at all,' she complained, and went into the sitting-room to collect more glasses. Fintan looked, a bit helplessly, at the mess of dirty serving plates on the kitchen table. He was annoyed that Philip hadn't liked Fiona but he hadn't blamed Philip. Fiona was his wife; therefore she should have been in herself pleasing to his friend. It was awkward that they didn't like each other. He supposed they were jealous since they were both attached to him. What, after all, was love? His mother loved him, of course. That was natural. Mothers love their children. And, he assumed, his father loved his mother — all that business of protecting her from worry about him. He didn't feel like protecting Fiona. She was a big girl, clever, rich. It might be the way he felt after making love successfully, but then when she found him inadequate he felt like slitting her throat. She came into the kitchen, clattering glasses. 'We'll have to knock down that wall between those two rooms,' she said. 'I can't bear that little poky room. It gives me claustrophobia.'

Fintan protested. 'We've just painted the whole place white to give you space. We're not going to start knocking down walls. Anyway, it's a supporting wall.'

'Come in and I'll show you what we could do,' she said, putting her two hands on his arm and feeling him tense against her.

'What idiot turned on the television?' she exclaimed when they were at the sitting-room door. The sound had gone wrong. On the screen was an old-fashioned room with a coal fire in a black iron fireplace and an old lady sitting in a rocking chair knitting and talking vigorously, but it was impossible to make out a word she was saying. 'Somebody's been fooling with the buttons,' Fiona said. 'Turn it off.'

'It's not on,' Fintan said exultantly. 'The plug's out.'

She gripped his arm then but he didn't notice; he was

concentrating hard on the picture and on the strange light old voice. She was a fine-looking old lady with white straight hair brushed back into a bun at the nape of her neck. She wore little gold-rimmed glasses and a black skirt and blouse with a jet rectangular brooch at the throat. She put down her knitting and took up a hank of wool, spreading it round her knees to wind it into a ball. She had a black shiny apron with a black frill all the way round. The rocking chair moved as she wound the wool. Above the rockers the wooden frame was composed of little carved pillars and the seat was like a deckchair seat, only made from some kind of carpet material. Gaslight came from two globes on curved arms from the wall above the fireplace. The fire itself was only slightly red, not blazing, not reflected in the brass fire irons on the black iron fender. Opposite the rocking chair was a wing chair and a figure in it practically hidden and silent, perhaps sleeping.

They stood watching, transfixed, until the picture faded. Fiona whispered, 'The two old ladies knitting,' and then they both corrected that, 'But it was a man. In the big chair it was a man.' They were quite sure, although when the picture was there it had been impossible to see. Fiona was trembling. Fintan was nervous but exuberant, wanting to telephone their friends and tell them, unable to stay still. Fiona suggested that they continue clearing up, that maybe it hadn't happened, she didn't really believe it had happened. It was the wine they had drunk during the day. It was late when they went to bed, Fiona reluctantly, as if there was thunder in the air. They lay stiffly on their backs, not touching.

For several nights after that they stayed out of the house until late and hurried to bed without looking into the sitting-room, but everything seemed quiet and gradually, without mentioning it to each other or to anyone else, they pushed it to the back of their minds. Fiona even brought up the idea again of knocking down the wall between the two rooms. Fintan said no. Fiona thought her father could be consulted before they scotched the idea out of hand. Fintan said no, it was his house and nothing at all to do with her father. He had bought a haunted house so as to owe nothing to her father and he wasn't going to backtrack now over a silly notion of hers. 'That wall stays up,' he shouted, thumping against it.

The television screen flickered and bright horizontal lines ran from the bottom to the top. The unintelligible commentary began before the picture settled. This time the woman was on her knees at the rocking chair which had come unstuck and had lurched to the side away from the fire. The little pillars that held the top part of the chair to the rockers were out of their sockets and she was trying to fix them in. When she got one in another hopped out. The man still sat silent in his big solid chair. After a time she began to cry, a childish cry which increased in volume until it was a terrible wail, on and on. 'God,' Fiona breathed, but Fintan gripped her arm and she put her hands over her mouth. Eventually it all faded, the crying persisting for some seconds after the picture went.

'I can't stand this,' Fiona said. 'I can't live here.'

Fintan was too shaken to hear what she said. During the next month they saw the quiet scene several times, so that Fintan said he was growing quite fond of the old lady. Fiona didn't answer him. Then one night the kneeling woman appeared again, and the broken chair and the same crying. Fiona said, 'Do something, can't you. Don't just stand there.' Fintan spread his hands helplessly and she rushed into the kitchen and came back carrying a stool. He grabbed at her arm

and said, 'Don't, you can't,' but she whirled the stool at the
television set, smashing it through the screen and dealing it
blow after blow. Fintan felt outrage at the ugly look on Fiona's
face and at the wrong use of the sturdy little pine stool with
'Made in Poland' printed in black under the seat. When she
turned triumphantly to him, still brandishing the stool, he felt
frightened for a moment that she meant to attack him. Instead
she said, 'There! That's settled it. How long would you have
stood there before you realised some action was called for?
The active sex! God Almighty!'

'The set was rented. How are we going to pay the company?' Fintan said.

'Money again. I'll pay if you're so upset.'

'You just may. You broke it.' He put the broken set out with
the dustbin the following Friday and they had no more
television and no more ghostly films.

Fiona was careful to be gentle, having frightened herself
with her demonstration of violence. She acquiesced in whatever Fintan wanted, even when he suggested that it would be
better if they went out separately now and again to avoid
feeling suffocated. They didn't talk about their experiences,
but as the weeks went by they relaxed and settled amicably
enough together. Then they were invited to a party given by
Fintan's friend Philip. Fiona said she wouldn't go; Fintan
could make what excuse he liked but she would spend the
evening in comfort at home in her parents' house. They
wanted her to stay the night in her own old room, all aired
and beautiful with its white carpet and mirrored wardrobes
and old mahogany bed. They didn't like her driving home to
an empty house, probably cold. Fiona laughed, said she did it
quite often, and drove off before they persuaded her other-

wise. The house *was* cold. It looked cramped and ordinary, just cheap. The bed hadn't softened yet into any degree of cosiness, and she lay reading for an hour before trying to sleep. A full moon shone in on her face when she turned to the window, so she curled up with her back to it. She was restless, missing Fintan, and she told herself resentfully that she'd probably be just asleep when he would come in and waken her. Then she heard the childish crying downstairs and listened in horror until it reached a crescendo of that frightful wailing. She started to cry herself, 'God, God,' huddling under the quilt. As soon as the noise downstairs died away she got up and dressed, gabbling to herself, grabbed her bag and car keys and drove back to her parents' house. Fintan, coming back at four o'clock and seeing the empty tossed bed, felt only relief that he wouldn't have to justify the lateness of the hour or the fact that he was not sober.

Fiona insisted that the house be sold and every stick of furniture in it. She had no wish to break up their marriage. She would live with him in a flat or wherever he liked, but not with anything out of that house. In the meantime she stayed with her parents and Fintan was lucky enough to get the loan of a flat from a friend who was in America on a training course. Selling the furniture they had got from her family gave him no trouble and he forced himself to part with the pieces he had bought, but not with the walnut desk. He told Fiona it was hers, but she exclaimed in horror that she couldn't even look at its little carved pillars and knobs without seeing the rocking chair, that she'd never live in any house it stood in. He brought it to the flat and polished it lovingly.

They met for lunch or parties or concerts. They were still married, just temporarily without living quarters, only celibate for the moment. When a possibility came up of a job in Saudi Arabia he asked her would she come if he got it and she, tired of the ambiguity of her position, agreed, providing he brought nothing pertaining to the house. He called to explain his plans to his parents and found his father alone.

'There aren't any ghosts in the desert,' Fintan laughed.

'What?' his father said. 'With all those mutilations and executions? You amaze me.'

Fintan mentioned his attachment to the desk.

'Give it to your mother,' he was told.

Fintan laughed. 'What on earth would she want with it?'

'She is not illiterate, you know,' his father retorted, and Fintan hurried to apologise that he had not meant to imply that.

'She will care for it because you gave it to her. God knows none of you have given her much, with all your fine jobs.'

'You didn't give her much yourself,' Fintan said, rattled. 'Nothing but the daily paper when you have done with it.'

His father tapped him on the shoulder. 'Your mother and I understand each other. Don't take it on yourself to worry about us.'

'Such arrogance,' Fintan thought, but he took his father's advice about the desk and was rewarded by his mother's obvious delight. He even managed to sell the house at a small profit to an American who was interested in ghosts.

'You don't realise how very lucky you are,' his mother-in-law told him one day when he called for Fiona before she was ready. She was an elegant woman, partly due to expensive clothes and hair, partly to her very slim figure. He found himself hoping that Fiona would fine down eventually and look like her.

'You have both been given a new chance,' she went on. 'One fright does nobody any harm and you have lost nothing at all. You must have had somebody's prayers,' she finished with an ironic lift to one eyebrow.

'You don't like me,' he said. 'You never thought me good enough for Fiona. Just because I'm not rich.'

'My dear Fintan, there are none of us as rich as people think. Fiona has had a good salary up to now – she didn't need a rich husband. But you are not a kind person. I always wished for my daughters that they would marry kind men. Kindness lasts even if the couple are no longer in love.' Fintan smiled that she should use such a term, and she accused him, 'You are not kind to Fiona.'

'She is not always kind to me,' Fintan answered back childishly. 'Her voice has a very unkind edge to it at times.' His mother-in-law shrugged, and when Fiona came into the room he glared at her so that the happy look on her face slid away. Later on in the evening she asked if it was worthwhile her going out to Saudi Arabia with him at all if he didn't really want her. He said, 'Oh please do, Fiona. I couldn't bear it if you didn't.'

One evening before they left he paid a visit to the house. He had already given up the keys but the American had said it wasn't sensible to move in before the fall. The house didn't look a bit sinister, just slightly pathetic, even though all their curtains had been sold in the deal and still hung at the windows but a little stiffly because no one had touched them for weeks. Fintan regretted the loss of the house, the loss of his status as a citizen and resident with responsibilities in the community. He would even have tackled the garden, he thought, standing and looking at the stony soil with starving ragwort and a couple of frail poppies as its crop. The limestone rock was only two feet down, a neighbour had said, but on this patch it seemed to be breaking through. At least in the desert the sand would cover the bones. He didn't really mind the poor old ghosts. He could have lived with them, even though the crying was hard to take. But then all crying was hard to take. He thought of Fiona and the brightness gone so rapidly from their life. The sadness shook him so that his legs trembled and wouldn't move out of the garden. Sweat broke out on his neck and head even though it was a cool evening for early September with a bank of mist along the foot of the mountains. He reached out to steady himself and held on to the iron railing he'd painted black after they moved in. The spasm passed and he let go, but when he saw a black stain on the palm of his hand he scrubbed at it in panic. Once he had shut himself into the security of his car he wondered had Fiona felt like this during previous emanations while he didn't, and if so was she in this way and, who knows, perhaps in other ways a protection to him. He could manage to be kind, he was sure, if he practised, if that would please her and keep her with him, especially in a strange country with no friends and no position other than as his wife. The street lamp glowed red, suggesting dusk, and he switched on his own lights and drove away from the house, only very slightly shaken now, to meet Fiona in town.

ERIC CROSS

Saint Bakeoven

I don't pretend to be musical, apart, of course, from knowing a good tune when I hear it – the sort of thing that a fellow can whistle in his bath. It does so happen however, that I was almost responsible for what might have been one of the musical sensations of the century, and, before I forget it, I'd better make some record of it for future generations.

I used to spend a part of each year fishing in Kerry in those days. On one occasion, while I was returning from a mountain lake, I ran into a terrific thunderstorm. Below me in the valley I spotted an isolated farmhouse and I worked my way down to it as quickly as possible. I had barely knocked at the door when it was opened by an old man who ushered me in as though I were the prodigal son returning home. He helped me off with my coat, drew up a chair to the fire for me, and, in general, treated me with even more eager hospitality than you usually meet in Kerry.

'You must find it a bit lonely tucked away back here,' I suggested, once the preambles of hospitality were settled.

'Yerra – lonely, is it?' replied the old man, whose name, by the way, was Johnny Quill. 'The divil a bit lonely am I ever,' he went on. 'To tell God's truth, 'tis just the other way about.'

'How come?' I quite naturally asked, considering the situation of the place.

' 'Tis the fairies,' he replied, in a matter of fact way. 'Them divils do be at me, pestering and worrying and annoying and bothering me all hours of the day and night. 'Tis only when a Christian, such as yourself, comes along that the sight of him drives them out and I have a bit of peace and ease for myself as it is now. But the moment you'll be gone them divils will be back again with their whispering and their rustling like mice round a corn bin. They have me patience worn out. There should be a law passed against them by those useless people up in Dublin and then put the police onto them. But, oh, no – they're much too busy passing laws to make hens lay eggs by Act of Parliament to have the time to do anything useful. I tell you that the fairies are the plaguiest, most pestering and bewildering form of creation that man was ever burdened with.'

'Yes,' I agreed, for, after all an old man's fancies break no bones. 'I am sure that you must find them a bit of a nuisance.'

'Nuisance! Nuisance!' bellowed Johnny. 'Why, the divils have me near driven mad. I lambaste them with the handle of a broom. I give them a histe of my boot and a skelp of my tongue, but it's all a waste of energy. A few minutes later and they will be back at their old comether again: whispering hocus pocus; mislaying things and upsetting things on me. There's all classes of them,' he continued, 'but there is one of them – the plaguiest one of me whole pick of divils, who comes mainly by night. A sort of a foreigner I'd say he would be and a damned bad-tempered one at that. There's some of them all mischief but with this one the game is all music. Whenever he puts his face inside the kitchen the whole house does be filled with the sound of music as though it was the air of the place. Then he tries to be telling me something but I can't make head or tail of the queer language he speaks and that only seems to make him madder and he shakes the great head of him and holds the great fists of him in the air, with the fingers spread out like a dealer trying to buy a beast in a fair for ten pounds from a slow-witted man.

' "Saint! Saint! Saint!" he yells. Then "Bakeoven! Bakeoven! Bakeoven!" and I can't make sense of that at all for the divil a bit does he look like a saint and the divil a bit do I know what he means by his "Bakeoven" unless it be one of these new-fangled fakes that they have in the towns for the lazy women to bake in.'

'To hell with you and your "bakeoven",' I yell at him, 'if it's a "bakeoven" that you are trying to sell me or persuade me to buy. It was on the cake from the bastable pot that I was reared and on the same I'll finish my days. Then the music starts all over again till my head is like a hive of bees ready to swarm with the sound of it.'

'All very interesting,' I agreed. 'It looks as though the worst of the storm is over. I think that I'll be pushing on.' I said goodbye to Johnny and thanked him, and, as far as I was concerned, that would have been the end of the business, for fairies aren't particularly in my line.

It so happened however, that there was a professor of music johnny, from Oxford, staying in the hotel, collecting 'folk music', whatever that may be. Naturally he was a difficult subject for conversation and that night I happened to mention the rigmarole Johnny had told me that day, by way of being sociable.

The professor johnny, whose name was Peterson, pricked up his ears almost immediately and showed more signs of life than I had seen so far in him when I told him the yarn. I went away to bed and naturally had forgotten all about it by the following morning but it seemed that this fellow Peterson had, overnight, made a mountain of the story. He had worked out some crazy notion from it about a German composer called Beethoven, who had composed nine symphonies and died before he had finished his tenth; and he had come back in ghost form to worry poor old Johnny Quill about it.

Peterson had worked out that Johnny's 'Saint' was the German for 'tenth' and his 'Bakeoven' was really 'Beethoven' – the composer's name, and the music Johnny heard, was, of course, the music of the tenth symphony, now finished. It didn't seem to be dripping with sense to me.

I happened to go into the bar before lunch for an appetiser and who should be there but Johnny Quill himself, celebrating a deal in sheep. We had a drink together and I left him to it and went off in search of food. But in the dining room I ran into Peterson, bubbling over with some new brainwave on Johnny's story. In the hope of finishing the matter off, as far as I was concerned, I led him out and introduced him to Johnny himself, the fount of inspiration. But it wasn't my lucky day, for in spite of his knowledge of music he could not make anything of Johnny's accent, no more than Johnny could make of his, so I had to stand in as interpreter.

I opened the ball with the first round of drinks, Peterson

having lemonade and going straight into action, instructing me to ask Johnny to describe the appearance of the ghost or fairy or whatever it was, in detail.

'Tell him,' said Johnny, 'that he is a stout block of a bucko with a great stook of hair on his head as though he is in dispute with the barber – and that might well be, for he has a fierce, bad-tempered jowl on him. His clothes? . . . Yerra, he does mostly wear some sort of an ould swally tail coat with an ould choker round his neck and the knee breeches they used to wear in the time of the caroline hats.'

'Hm!' snorted Peterson, like the man who had found the piece of kidney in the pie, when I translated this for him. 'Ask him now what language his fairy or whatever it is speaks.'

'The divil be from me but how would I know that,' replied Johnny. 'Tell the man of the lemonade that 'tis neither English nor Irish but some gibberish makeup of his own and that the only words that I can make out at all are his "Saint" and his "Bakeoven", and to hell with him and his "bakeovens". I'll stick to me bastable pot.'

Peterson was studying Johnny intently as he put him through the third degree. 'Ask him now,' ordered Peterson, 'if anyone else sees this apparition or hears the music.'

'Only the divil himself could answer that,' snorted Johnny, 'but 'tis not likely for ould Bakeoven wouldn't have the time left to be annoying anyone else after all the time that he spends annoying me. He'd scarcely have the time left to wash himself . . . and will you add to that,' Johnny continued, 'that I will answer no more questions till the gentleman puts away the lemonade and has a glass of whiskey with me like a Christian.'

Peterson, in spite of protests, had to yield. Johnny, as the oracle, could call the tune and he called it quickly.

'Would it be possible for me to hear the music and see this ghost if I went along to the house?' was Peterson's next query.

'It might and it might not,' was Johnny's answer to this. 'But mostly I'd be saying against it for I do notice that when anyone comes into the house to me the music stops and ould Bakeoven goes up the chimney or out of the window. But tell the gentleman that he's welcome anytime and if he can salt the ould divil and take him away with him to foreign parts there will be no man was ever so welcome.'

The party spirit was getting into its stride by now. Peterson disappeared for a few minutes and I was hoping that we could adjourn *sine die* but it wasn't to be. He had only been up to his room and he returned with an illustrated history of music. He instructed me to hand it to Johnny and to tell him to look through it and to see if there was a picture in it at all like his 'fairy'.

Johnny licked his thumb and started to turn the pages one by one. I did not translate all his remarks and comments on the pictures of famous composers he saw, though they were amusing. I had doubts if this Peterson fellow had any sense of humour at all.

After thumbing about half way through the book Johnny let out a yell, putting his finger down on a picture of Beethoven.

'The pesky ould divil himself,' he whooped. 'The living split image of him! Saint Bakeoven and the great ugly puss of him!' At this Peterson went up in the air. He ordered another round of drinks immediately. Even I began to wonder if there might be something in it after all.

'Ask him now,' said Peterson, as pleased as Punch, 'if he could describe or remember the music he hears.'

'Could I remember the music!' exclaimed Johnny. 'Indeed, but it would be the day of the greatest aise to me when the day dawns that I disremember every screech of it. As for describing of it,' he continued, after some head-scratching, 'will you tell him that it would be beyond the powers of the worst poet yet born to put words to it. 'Tis such a roaring and a buzzing and a banging and a beating: such a twirling of trumpets and a tweaking of flutes and a scattering of the scraping of fiddles that the like of it was never heard before in the history of the world. 'Tis like the bellowings of dumb animals in pain and the howling of infants in divilment and the scolding of women in crossness and in the midst of it all there is this ould divil of a queer one, waving his hands up and down and about in the air as though the sound was all running out of the ends of his fingers, like porter out of a tap.

'Only once did I hear the match of it in my life and that was in the days of the ould militia in the town of Kenmare when someone had treated the band with decency and the band had treated themselves with equal decency and they marched through the town stocious and every man of them doing his best to outblow the other fellow.'

Johnny now ordered a round and Peterson replied with another question, asking if Johnny could hum or whistle the music or give some actual idea of it. Johnny was now most ready to oblige.

'I'd give you more than an idea of it, with a heart and a half and good riddance to it,' said he, 'but that it is a class of music that has no sense at all to it at all at all. 'Tis what you might call a porridge of a music – not like the "Blackbird" or "The Coolin" or "The Wind that Shakes the Barley" or any of the decent civilised tunes that wake a man's heart and set his feet tapping. But I will do the best I can to accommodate the gentleman for he is turning out to be a better class of a man than my first judgment of him. 'Tis something like this that it goes.'

With that Johnny drained his glass, threw back his head, fixed his eye on a spot on the ceiling and started to screech and to bawl and to roar and to groan until, after a couple of minutes, even Peterson, with all his interest in music, had had enough of Johnny Quill's version of Beethoven's Tenth Symphony. It was a thirst-provoking effort and Peterson thought the game worth while but demanded a quid for his quo.

'Ask him if there is any musical instrument that he can play with which he might be able to reproduce some of the music he hears.'

After probing into the nature of Johnny's polite accomplishments, the only thing that I could discover was that when he was young – and that was a long time ago – he had been able to play the bagpipes – but not very well. About here the party broke up.

The following morning, when Peterson had recovered after a good night's sleep, he had worked out a plan of campaign, for there wasn't any doubt now in his mind, on the circumstantial evidence so far produced. He was on the verge of the most amazing musical discovery of the century. The weather wasn't too good for fishing and as there wasn't much else to do I continued as *aide de camp* and general adviser and interpreter.

The first thing that we did was to visit Johnny's house, and we soon found that the fairies were quite definitely allergic to us. Even Peterson did not hear a note. According to Johnny the moment we entered the house both the fairy and his music faded away. Naturally Peterson was a bit hurt about this but he was quite certain that Johnny was speaking the truth and quite incapable of pulling Peterson's leg on his home ground, as you might say.

This meant that we had to fall back on Johnny himself as medium, interpreter or what you will. And that meant that, by hook or crook, he would have to reproduce what he heard by means of the only musical instrument he knew – the bagpipes. Peterson wasn't at all in favour of my suggestion, my quite practical suggestion, of bringing a band along and letting Johnny conduct it. He even suspected that I was pulling his leg and not treating the matter with sufficient gravity.

So the problem, or rather the practical solution to it, was narrowed down to bagpipes. Somewhere in the district there was reputed to be a pair or set or whatever it is of them but when it came to finding them they were as elusive as the end of a rainbow, flitting ahead of us from valley to valley and house to house. At last we caught up with them. Johnny regarded them carefully, seriously and ruefully. With all his native gift of courtesy he could find little good to say about them. There was a whistle or a tweeter or some such vital part missing. One of the protruding flutes or whatever they were was most obviously cracked. More apparent still was a great rent in the windbag. But, with optimism, a dash of glue, some twine and wire, a splash of tar and a bit of an old tyre, Johnny thought that he might be able to make a job of them.

Eventually, with the help of the 'smith and the carpenter and a man who was a great hand at tying a fly and another man who had an uncle in America who, in his day had been a famous piper, so that he had claims to being an expert, one place removed, we got the contraption fixed up. As Johnny tactfully described it – 'they worked in a kind of a class of a way'. Now all that he needed was a few days' practice to get his wind and fingers into trim.

The appointed night arrived and with it rain in sheets and

floods and torrents. This seemed to me to be a warning to let well alone and sleeping spirits lie. It seemed just any other kind of night rather than one to set off into the darkness and the wetness of a desolate mountain valley to hear the first performance of a symphony played on bagpipes – or played any way at all for that matter. Peterson's mind however was made up and I decided that being in for a penny I might as well be in for a pound.

We borrowed the hotel proprietor's car. I took along a bottle of whiskey and a couple of rugs. As luggage Peterson had a wad of music paper. Long before we arrived at the concert hall it was obvious, even above the storm, that Johnny had entered into the spirit of the occasion and was already having a preliminary canter. It seems that somehow the fairy or ghost had got an inkling of what was in the wind and had readily co-operated with the notion. In fact they had already a dress rehearsal and come to a common understanding of the procedure to be adopted. Beethoven would conduct a few bars and while they still lingered in Johnny's ears he would have a skirl or whatever the musical term is for a dash at it and so they would progress from bar to bar.

Johnny himself was by this time so taken up with the idea and the possible hope of ridding himself of his musical lodger, that he was taking the matter almost as seriously as Peterson himself. He wouldn't even have a drink before we started. 'Only a dart, now and again, of the purest of spring water,' he said, pointing to a bottle at his side, 'just for the wind's sake, until the gentleman is satisfied.'

Still we were not *personae gratae* with fairies and while we were within the kitchen Johnny said there would not be a note of music. When you think of all the trouble that Peterson was giving himself and other people it did really seem a bit inconsiderate on the part of Beethoven, but judging by the picture of him it was about what you might be led to expect from him. So it meant that we – or rather Peterson – would have to eavesdrop through the window.

I, never having been much of an enthusiast for symphonies or bagpipes, retired to the shelter of the car. I wrapped myself up in the rugs and opened the bottle of whiskey. Unfortunately I was still within earshot of the bedlam which was let loose when the performance started, but as the storm increased the howling of the wind and the lashing rain toned it down somewhat. There would be a squealing and a screeching from the kitchen as though a score of pigs were being slaughtered. There was Peterson huddled up against the window ledge, with the rain cascading over him from the roof, while he scribbled down crotchets and quavers. Now and again he would bawl through the window for a repeat. Now and again there would be a lull in the noise, as Johnny took a swig of the purest spring water for his wind's sake.

Mercifully after a short while I fell into a doze. What woke me wasn't a noise. It was the absence of a noise. I came to, conscious that now there was only the howling of the wind and the roar of the swollen mountain torrents around me. There wasn't a sound from Johnny's kitchen. The door was open and Peterson was missing. I made a dash for the house to find Johnny on the flat of his back on the floor, as he would describe it, 'stocious'. The bottle of the 'finest of spring water' lay smashed beside him and from the trickle which was left in it there came a smell which might be mistaken for whiskey. It is not unknown in Kerry where so many improbable things seem to be possible for 'the finest of spring water' to have such a smell. Beside the fragments of the bottle lay the corpse of the bagpipes in a heap.

'Busht! Busht and be damned!' were Johnny's last words as he gave himself up to the soundest sleep that ever fell on any man. The description aptly covered all – Johnny, the bottle and the bagpipes. We made Johnny comfortable for the night in his bed. There was nothing more that we could do. The performance was ended. The carriage awaited at the door.

Peterson was quite happy but very wet. There wasn't a doubt now in his mind. It was the true, authentic Beethoven music alright, recognisable even through the medium of bagpipes. A few score nights such as this and he would have the whole thing down in crotchets and quavers. A few months of work on it and it would be ready to astonish the world.

It seemed unfortunate that Peterson developed a high temperature during the night and had to be rushed off to a nursing home the following morning with pneumonia. But all's well that ends well and a few days later Johnny himself had to be taken to the county hospital. The combination of the finest of spring water, the excitement and the strenuous exercises of bagpipe blowing had not been the best treatment for the heart at his age. So, as it turned out, Peterson would not have been able to do anything more, and anyway the bagpipes were quite beyond any further repair.

I had quite a busy time between the two invalids: writing letters for Peterson, when he turned the corner, and doing a few odd things for Johnny. The doctor had advised Johnny to stay on in the hospital and he wasn't at all unwilling. I arranged the settling of his bit of land to a relative so that Johnny would be able to draw the old age pension and so have no further worry.

As soon as Peterson was well enough I drove him over to see Johnny and, needless to say, Peterson had only one interest in the visit.

'Ould Bakeoven and his music? . . . Yerra, thank God that I have neither sight nor sound of him since the blessed day that I came in here – and good riddance, for at last after all these years I have peace and ease for myself and I'm able to call my soul my own.'

'But, manalive!' almost shrieked Peterson, 'don't you remember the music?'

'The divil a note of it,' answered Johnny, puffing contentedly away at his pipe. 'The divil a note of it have I heard since I came in and the divil a note of it will I hear to the end of my days for I have handed the place and the cow and the sheep to a nephew of mine and I have no mind to budge from here till they carry me out feet foremost. I'll live the rest of my life like a fine civil servant, at the country's expense, taking my aise like a lord, instead of being at the beck and call of a pack of fairies like a boots in an hotel.'

Peterson cajoled, bribed, bullied, pleaded, wheedled and argued but Johnny would listen to no argument and no persuasion. The last thing that he said to Peterson when we came to say goodbye was: 'If you should happen to see Ould Bakeoven at any time during your travels will you tell him from me that I did him a great harm and a great injustice and that I am sorry for it, for after all he was right. 'Tis the new-fangled "bakeovens" that they use in this place for their breadmaking and you never in all your life tasted sweeter or grander or nuttier bread.'

SEAN O'FAOLAIN

The End of the Record

T he news went around the poorhouse that there was a man
with a recording van in the grounds. He was picking up
old stories and songs.

'And they say that he would give you a five-shilling piece
into your hand for two verses of an old song,' said Thomas
Hunter, an old man from Coomacoppal, in West Kerry,
forgetting that five-shilling pieces were no longer in fashion.
'Or for a story, if you have a good one.'

'What sort of stories would them be?' Michael Kivlehan
asked sceptically. He was from the barony of Forth and Bargy,
in County Wexford, and had been in the poorhouse for eleven
years.

'Any story at all only it is to be an old story and a good story.
A story about the fairies, or about ghosts, or about the way
people lived long ago.'

'And what do he do with 'um when he have 'um?'

'Hasn't he a phonograph? And doesn't he give them out

over the wireless? And doesn't everyone in Ireland be listening to them?'

'I wonder now,' said Michael Kivlehan, 'would he give me five shillings for the "Headless Horseman and the Coacha Bowr"?'

Thomas Hunter sighed.

'One time I had a grand story about Finn MacCool and the Scotch giant. But it is gone from me. And I'd be getting my fine five-shilling piece into my fist this minute if I could only announce it to him.'

The two old men sat on the sides of their beds and tried to remember stories. But it was other things they remembered and they forgot all about the man outside who had set them thinking of their childhood.

The doctor had taken the collector into the women's ward to meet Mary Creegan. She was sitting up in bed, alone in the long room; all the other women were out in the warm sun. As the two men walked up the bare floor the collector was trailing a long black cable from a microphone in his hand, and the doctor was telling him that she came from a place called Faill-a-ghleanna in West Cork.

'She should have lots of stories because her husband was famous for them. After he died she went a bit airy so they had to bring her to us. 'Twas a bit tough on her at first. Sixty years in the one cottage – and then to finish up here.' They stood beside her bed. 'I brought a visitor to see you, Mary,' he said in a loud voice.

She did not appear to see them. She was humming happily to herself. Her bony fingers were wound about an ancient rosary beads. Her white hair floated up above a face as tiny and as wrinkled as a forgotten crab apple. All her teeth were gone so that her face was as broad as it was long: it was as if the midwife had pressed the baby's chin and forehead between thumb and forefinger. The doctor gently laid his hand under the tiny chin and turned her face towards him. She smiled.

'Put down the kettle and wet the tay,' she ordered.

The doctor sat on the bed; so did the collector.

''Tis down, Mary, and two eggs in the pot. This poor man here is after coming a long way to talk to you. He's tired out.'

She turned and looked at the stranger. Encouraged by a brightening spark in the depths of her eyes he turned aside and murmured quietly into the microphone, 'Reggy? Recording ten seconds from . . . now.'

'It's a bad road,' she said. 'Ask Jamesy is he keeping that divil of a cow out of the cabbage.'

'She's all right,' the doctor cried into her ear. 'Jamesy is watching her. Be talking to us while we're waiting for the tay. You told me one time you saw a ghost. Is that true?'

She looked out of the window and her eyes opened and narrowed like a fish's gills as if they were sucking something in from the blue sky outside. The collector stealthily approached her chin with the microphone.

'Ghosts? Ayeh! Ha! My ould divil of a tailor is forever and always talkin' about 'um. But, sure, I wouldn't heed him. Bummin' and boashtin' he is from morning to night and never a needle to be shtuck in the shtuff. Where is he? Why don't you ask him to be talking to you about ghoshts?'

The doctor looked across the bed at the collector and raised his eyebrows.

'Maybe you don't believe in them yourself?' he mocked.

'I do not believe in 'um. But they're there. Didn't I hear tell of 'um from them that saw 'um? Aye, and often. And often! Aye'

– still collecting her thoughts from the sky above the bake-house chimney – 'wasn't it that way the night Father Regan died? Huh! They called him Father Regan, but he was not a right priest. He was silenced for some wrong thing he did when he was a young priest, and they sent him to Faill-a-ghleanna to be doing penance for it. When his time came to die it was a bad, shtormy night. And when he sent for the parish priest to hear his confession the priest said he could not come. And that was a hard thing to do, for no man should refuse the dying. And they sent another messenger for the priest, and still the priest could not come. "Oh," said Father Regan, "I'm lost now." So they sent a third messenger. And for the third time the priest could not come. And on his way back wasn't the messenger shtopped on the road by a woman? It was Father Regan's own mother. "Go back," says she, "and if the candles by his bed light up," says she, "of their own accord," says she, "he is saved." And the messenger went back, and Father Regan gave wan look at him and he closed his eyes for the last time. With that all the people went on their knees. And they began to pray. If they did, there were three candles at the head of the dead priest. And didn't the one beside the window light up? And after a little while the candle beside the fire clevy lit up. And they went on praying. And the wind and the shtorm screaming about the house, and they watching the wick of the last candle. And, bit by bit, the way you'd blow up a fire with a bellows, didn't the candle over the priest's head light up until the whole room was like broad daylight.'

The old woman's voice suddenly became bright and hard. 'Isn't that tay ready a-yet? Domn and blosht it, ye'll have them eggs like bullets.' She looked alertly at the two men. 'Where am I? Where's Jamesy? What are ye doing to me?'

The doctor held her wrist. Her eyes faded. She sank back heavily.

'I thought,' she wailed, 'that it was how I saw a great brightness.'

The collector spoke one word into the microphone. The old woman had fainted. Overcome with regrets he began to apologize, but the doctor waved his hand at him.

'Excited. I'll send up the sister to give her an injection. Sometimes she loves to talk about old times. It does her good.'

They went out of the empty ward, the cable trailing softly. They passed the male ward. Michael Kivlehan and Thomas Hunter were sitting on their beds. As the doctor led the way downstairs, he said, 'When that generation goes it will be all over. Wait for me outside. There are a couple more. You might get bits and scraps from them.'

The engineer put his head out of the van and said, in the gloomy voice of all engineers, 'That might come through all right.'

When the doctor came out again they sat with a middle-aged man from Wicklow, named Fenelon. He had been on the roads until arthritis crippled him. When he counted the years he spoke in Urdu. He had scraps of the tinker's language which is called Shelta. He said:

'I often walked from Dublin to Puck, and that's a hundred miles, without ever disturbing anything but a hare or a snipe. I'd make for Ross, and then cross to Callan, and by Slieve-namon west to the Galtees.'

He did not see the microphone; he did not see his visitors; as the needle softly cut the disc he was seeing only the mountainy sheep that looked at him with slitted eyes, a thing as shaggy as themselves.

They moved on to an old woman who sang a love song for them in a cracked voice. She said she had learned it in Chicago. She gave them a poem of twelve verses about a voyage to the South Seas. They were finishing a disc with a very old man from Carlow when the sister came out and hastily beckoned to the doctor. As they folded up the cable he came back. He said, with a slow shake of the head:

'It's old Mary. I must leave ye. But ye have the best of them. The rest is only the shakings of the bag.'

When they had thanked him and were driving away, the collector said, eagerly:

'Pull up when we're out of the town. I want to play back those discs.'

They circled up and out of the town until its murmur was so faint that they could hear only the loudest cries of the playing children. There they played back the discs, and as they leaned towards the loud-speaker and the black record circled smoothly they could see, sideways through the window, the smoke of the hollow town. The last voice was Mary Creegan's.

'. . . and after a little while the candle beside the fire clevy lit up. And they went on praying. And the wind and the shtorm screaming about the house, and they watching the wick of the last candle. And, bit by bit, the way you'd blow up a fire with a bellows, didn't the candle over the priest's head light up until the whole room was like broad daylight . . . Isn't that tay ready a-yet? Domn and blosht it, ye'll have them eggs like bullets . . . Where am I? Where's Jamesy? What are ye doing to me? . . . I thought that it was how I saw a great brightness.'

The listeners relaxed. Then from the record came a low, lonely cry. It was the fluting of a bittern over moorland. It fluted sadly once again, farther away; and for a third time, almost too faint to be heard. Many times the two men played back those last few inches of disc. Every time they heard the bittern wailing over the mountains.

It was dusk. They laid the voices in a black box and drove away. Then they topped the hill, and the antennae of their headlamps began to probe the winding descent to the next valley.

Acknowledgements

MARY BECKETT: 'A Ghost Story', reprinted from *A Literary Woman* (Bloomsbury) by permission of the author.

ELIZABETH BOWEN: 'Hand in Glove', © 1952 by Elizabeth Bowen, reproduced by permission of Curtis Brown, London, on behalf of the Estate of Elizabeth Bowen.

PATRICK BOYLE: 'Rise Up, My Love, and Come Away', reprinted from *All Looks Yellow to the Jaundiced Eye* by permission of David Hodgins & Company on behalf of the Literary Estate of Patrick Boyle.

JOYCE CARY: 'A Private Ghost', reprinted from *Spring Song and other stories* by permission of the Andrew Lownie Literary Agency.

ERIC CROSS: 'Saint Bakeoven', reprinted from *Silence is Golden* (Poolbeg) by permission of Mrs Sheila Longhurst.

ACKNOWLEDGEMENTS

AODH de BLÁCAM: ' "Top of the Morning" ', reprinted from *The Ship That Sailed Too Soon* by permission of Carol de Blácam.

DESMOND HOGAN: 'The Birth of Laughter'. Copyright © 1979, 1981, 1987, 1988, by Desmond Hogan. Reproduced by permission of the author c/o Rogers, Coleridge & White Ltd., 20 Powis Mews, London W11 1JN.

JOSEPH HONE: 'The Captain in the Pipes', reprinted by permission of the author.

JENNIFER JOHNSTON: 'The Theft', reprinted by permission of the author and Sinclair-Stevenson.

JOHN B. KEANE: ' "You're on Next Sunday" ', reprinted from *Death Be Not Proud* (Mercier Press) by permission of the author.

MARY LAVIN: 'The Dead Soldier', reprinted from *Collected Stories of Mary Lavin* (Vol. 1, Constable) by permission of the executors of the author's Literary Estate.

BRYAN MacMAHON: 'The Revenants', reprinted from *The Tallystick* (Poolbeg) by permission of Maurice McMahon on behalf of the Estate of Bryan MacMahon.

SEAN O'FAOLAIN: 'The End of the Record', reprinted from *Stories of Sean O'Faolain*. Copyright © Sean O'Faolain 1958. Reproduced by permission of the Estate of Sean O'Faolain c/o Rogers, Coleridge & White Ltd., 20 Powis Mews, London W11 1JN.

ACKNOWLEDGEMENTS

LENNOX ROBINSON: 'A Pair of Muddy Shoes', reprinted from *Eight Short Stories* by permission of the Abbey Theatre.

PETER SOMERVILLE-LARGE: 'Rich and Strange', reprinted by permission of the author and of Curtis Brown, London.

WILLIAM TREVOR: 'The Death of Peggy Meehan', reprinted by permission of the author.

Biographical Notes

MARY BECKETT: Born Belfast, 1926. Her early stories appeared in The Bell, Threshold and Irish Writing. Having married and moved to Dublin in 1956, she did not write again until the late seventies, when her story, 'A Belfast Woman', was published in New Irish Writing and became the title story of her first collection. This was followed by her award-winning novel, Give Them Stones, and a second story collection, A Literary Woman.

ELIZABETH BOWEN: Born Dublin, 1899, she was educated in England where most of her life was spent. In 1928 she inherited the family estate, Bowen's Court, in Co. Cork, and lived there from 1952 to 1960. The Last September, acknowledged as one of her best novels, and A World of Love were set in Ireland, as were ten of her ninety stories. One of the leading writers of her time, she died in London in 1973.

PATRICK BOYLE: Born in Ballymoney, Co. Antrim, in 1905, he was an official in the Ulster Bank for forty-five years before his first short story won *The Irish Times* competition in the early sixties. It was later revealed that had there been five further prizes, he would have won these too with his other entries. He went on to publish three story collections and a best-selling novel, *Like Any Other Man*. He died in 1982.

JOYCE CARY: Born Derry, 1888, he was educated in England, though most of his boyhood summers were spent in Inishowen, Co. Donegal. He studied art for a few years and then read Law at Oxford, graduating in 1912. He served in the Red Cross in the Balkan Wars and subsequently joined the Nigerian political service, fighting with the Nigerian regiment in the Cameroons in World War I. He was invalided home in 1920, when he settled in Oxford and devoted the rest of his life to writing. He produced sixteen novels and many short stories, much of his work being based on his experiences in Africa. He died in Oxford in 1957.

CONALL CEARNACH: Born in Connemara in 1876 – real name Frederick O'Connell – he was educated at Trinity College, Dublin, and ordained for the Church of Ireland in 1902. He was appointed Rector of Achrony in 1907, later lectured in Celtic at Queen's University, Belfast, and became Assistant Director of Radio Eireann when it was formed. He died in 1925 as the result of a street accident.

ERIC CROSS: Born Newry, Co. Down, in 1903, he was a scientist, chemist and inventor as well as a writer. He was the author of only two books, *The Tailor and Ansty*, the celebrated classic about the Tailor of Gougane Barra, and *Silence is Golden*, a collection of short stories. He died in 1980.

AODH de BLÁCAM: Born London, 1890, of Ulster parents, he worked in Ireland as a Sinn Féin activist, and as a journalist for the *Enniscorty Echo*, *The Irish Times* and *The Standard*, before reaching a national audience as 'Roddy the Rover' of *The Irish Press*. He also wrote biographies of Wolfe Tone and St Columcille, and studies of Gaelic Literature and of Ulster. He died in Dublin in 1951.

DESMOND HOGAN: Born Ballinasloe, Co. Galway, 1951, his first story was published in *New Irish Writing* when he was seventeen. In 1971 he won a Hennessy Literary Award, in 1977 the Rooney Prize for Irish Literature, and in 1980 his first short-story collection won the John Llewellyn Rhys Memorial Prize. A prolific writer of stories and novels, he has also had plays produced in Dublin and London.

JOSEPH HONE: Born London, 1937, he was educated at Kilkenny College and St Columba's, Dublin. He was a producer with BBC Radio before joining the UN Secretariat in New York. Returning to England in 1968, he became a frequent commentator on current affairs. He has published three novels and a volume of autobiography.

JENNIFER JOHNSTON: Born Dublin, 1930, the daughter of playwright Denis Johnston and actress Shelagh Richards, she was educated at Park House School and Trinity College, Dublin. Her early novels, *The Captains and the Kings* and *How Many Miles to Babylon?*, brought her instant acclaim, and six further novels as well as her work for the stage have established her as one of Ireland's most distinguished writers.

JOHN B. KEANE: Born Listowel, Co. Kerry, 1928, he is one of Ireland's most popular and respected writers. Novelist, short-story writer, and producer of many epistolary fictions, his standing as one of the country's most powerful dramatists is unchallenged, his plays being in constant production not only in the Abbey Theatre but also by countrywide amateur drama groups.

MARY LAVIN: Born Walpole, Massachusetts, 1912, he lived in Ireland from the age of ten and was educated at Loreto College, Dublin, and UCD. Her first collection, *Tales from Bective Bridge*, was widely acclaimed, and thirteen further collections established her reputation as one of the world's leading short-story writers. She died in 1996.

BRYAN MacMAHON: Born Listowel, Co. Kerry, 1908, he was educated locally and at St Patrick's College, Dublin. A teacher, and eventually headmaster in his home town, he wrote about his long career in teaching in his first volume of autobiography, *The Master*. Apart from his novels, poems and plays, he was one of Ireland's most brilliant, inventive short-story writers. In 1972 he was awarded an LL.D. by the National University of Ireland for his services to Irish literature. He died in 1998.

SEAN O'FAOLAIN: Born Cork, 1900, he was one of Ireland's most distinguished men-of-letters of the 20th century. Novelist, playwright, biographer, autobiographer, translator, travel writer, critic, he was an acknowledged world master on the short story, and also editor of the mould-breaking monthly, *The Bell*. He died in 1991.

LENNOX ROBINSON: Born Cork, 1886, he became a popular and prolific playwright who was also for two separate periods involved in the Abbey Theatre, as its manager in 1910 and as a director in 1923. In 1916 he published a semi-autobiographical novel, *A Young Man from the South*. He died in 1958.

PETER SOMERVILLE-LARGE: Born 1928, he has written almost twenty books of travel, social history and fiction. They include *Cappaghlass*, which was shortlisted for the Ewart Biggs prize, a social history of the Irish Country House, and four thrillers. His travel books include *A Shaggy Yak Story*, an account of travel in Afghanistan and Turkey, and *To the Navel of the World*, describing a journey to western Tibet, which has been translated into many languages.

WILLIAM TREVOR: Born Mitchelstown, Co. Cork, 1928, he studied History at Trinity College, Dublin. Before turning to writing he had a growing reputation as a sculptor. His novel, *The Old Boys*, won the Hawthornden Prize in 1964 and since then he has gained many awards, including the Whitbread. A prolific author of novels, short stories and TV plays, he was made an honorary CBE in 1978. He now divides his time between Italy and his home in Devon.

A NOTE ON THE TYPE

The text of this book is set in Joanna, which was designed by Eric Gill in 1930. The roman type is light. Its distinguishing features include small horizontal serifs, unusually small capitals and the large bowl of the g. The italic type is simply the roman slightly inclined, with the exception of a and g which remain upright. Gill also chose not to incline the capitals but left them as roman after the practice of Aldus, the first printer to use italic. Gill's *Essay on Typography*, 1931 was printed in Joanna.